Emanuel's

Heat

A special thank you to Melissa Ringsted at There For You Editing (thereforyou.melissa@gmail.com) for editing.

Prologue

Emanuel

There is a rhythm to fire.

A heartbeat.

A pace.

I match my breathing to the cadence of the fire. One deep pull through my nose from the flowing air of my mask. Hold it for five seconds. Then slowly let it out. Repeat. All the while forcing my eyes to remain open, circling the darkened room, pushing my ears to listen for the most minute sounds. Feeling the wooden floors underneath my boots for any slight tremors. A tremble could be an indication of a trapped person banging on a door or floor calling for help, or worse, a signal that the fire has finally burned through the floor's foundation and collapse is inevitable.

I push the latter thought aside and continue my rhythmic breathing. In through my nose, hold for a count of five, and out slowly.

"Allende, get the hell out of there!" booms through the radio that's clipped to my jacket. It would've been jarring if I hadn't expected the command from my captain. Yet again, I ignore it.

There's a fucking kid in here! My mind reels, reminding me why I opted to run back into this apartment fire after pulling out a mother with her newborn baby. Her five-year-old son was in bed with her according to the mother. But I didn't see any indication of him in the master bedroom the first time around. He's still in here.

Breathe, I tell myself. I can't save anyone if I allow the panic from being surrounded by the nearly nine-foot high flames as they roll across the ceiling, and the dark black smoke billowing ahead of the flames, to take over.

I don't think about the chances of my air tank running low or empty before I can make it out of here. All that matters is that a five-year-old boy is stuck in the center of hell. A helpless child. I can't leave him.

"Allende, that's an order from your captain!" Captain Rogers continues as if I didn't fucking hear him the last dozen times.

Reaching my gloved hand for my radio, I turn the volume down.

"Fire department!" I yell out, hoping to get a response. The second floor of the apartment is dark and hot.

So fucking hot.

Bullets of sweat are running down my face, neck, and back, soaking the cotton Williamsport Fire Department polo shirt all firefighters are assigned. But none of that matters. These are the moments I train for. The layers of protective gear I have on will protect me from the flames—for a while—and my tank allows me to breathe unpolluted air. But not five-year-old Jackson.

"Jackson!" I shout, using the name his mother screamed as she frantically searched for her boy once she was safely deposited on the street outside of her burning home.

"Jackson! Are you in here?" Opting to get down on my hands and knees, I decide to re-enter the boy's bedroom, which is all of the way down the hall. I already checked his room and was certain no one had been in here. But I searched everywhere else in the home. Everywhere. This is the last place he could be.

"Jackson!" I crawl on all fours into the room, barely able to see more than a few inches in front of me, due to the thick smoke blanketing everything.

"Shit!" I yell when my hand lands on something wooden to my right side. A door. I hadn't registered it earlier. I feel up the length of the door and it's hot. *No! No! No!* my mind starts calling out.

I find the small finger circle used to pull what I assume is the closet door open. Immediately, I reach inside and feel something hot. I can't quite make out what it is due to the thick gloves covering my hands. But running my hands along the side and inching my body closer I make out strands of dark brown hair. My heart sinks at the sight of the charred skin.

"Jackson!"

A moan.

It's faint but I hear it. He's still alive.

Without much thought, I scoop the limp, nearly lifeless body of the boy into my arms and stand, crouching low to barrel my way through the flames. I push through the door I just entered and am met by a wall of flames. Through the fire is my only way out. There is no escape route behind me. The windows in Jackson's bedroom have been barricaded with steel bars to prevent him from falling out.

"Okay, Jackson," I begin talking to him, not knowing if he can hear me or not, "we have to go through the fire." I start unbuttoning my flame-retardant jacket to wrap around his fragile body. The jacket stretches just enough to enfold most of his body. I look up at the flames and take a deep breath, deeper than any breath I'd taken in the last two hours. When my lungs feel as if they are about to explode from holding on too long, I exhale and without thinking, run and jump through the flame.

"Ugh!" I grunt as I come crashing down onto my backside but having successfully made it to the other side of the wall of fire. However, I don't have time to rest. Flames are everywhere. My captain is still yelling into my radio along with my other teammates. I can hear the panic in their voices. They're fearing the worst. And they should be. I've been incommunicado for some time now.

"Fuck!" I curse as something explodes behind the wall I'm running past, causing a huge hole to open up and flames to come shooting out. It's really time to go. Just as I prepare to pick up my pace, there's another explosion from the far end of the second floor hallway. This explosion is so loud and rumbling it sends me to my knees, but I don't stop. I pick myself and Jackson up and stumble to the staircase only to find that it's gone. Completely engulfed in flames and collapsed.

I look around before making an instant decision. I have to jump. I don't have a choice. *We don't have a choice*, I think as I glance down at the young, moaning boy in my grasp. Another deep inhale and a leap of faith later, I am landing ass first on the first floor. Thank god it hadn't collapsed yet. But the fact that the stairs are gone tells me, the first floor is likely to go out soon. I reorient myself to figure out where the closest exit is to where I am. The front door is just around the wall behind me, but the back door is directly ahead, if I remember correctly. My team had set up a perimeter in the backyard of the apartment building.

Stumbling to my feet, ignoring the pain shooting down my hips and legs, I make my way to the back door, stepping on or over large beams of charred wood and debris. I encounter more flames in the kitchen, which is where the backdoor is located, but I don't stop to think. The door is our only way out, and it's aflame. The explosions I heard earlier were the glass from the windows breaking around the apartment; the inflow of oxygen has spurred the fire even more. The flames are getting hotter by the moment as they reach outside of the backdoor's now busted out window.

But stopping would mean sure death for the both of us.

So, with every ounce of strength I can muster in my body, I heave myself into the flames once again, pushing against the door. Thankfully, the flames have weakened the wood enough that it easily gives way to the force of my bodyweight.

Another leap over the concrete stairs of the back porch, and I quickly distance myself and Jackson from the sudden onslaught of more flames that will be caused by completely opening the door.

I land hard somewhere on the backyard grassy area, directly on my iron oxygen tank. Pain shoots through my entire body. I'm heaving heavily, gasping for my next breath. The edges of my vision begin to blur and I'm certain passing out is inevitable. But just before I do, I feel hands reaching for me. One pair removes Jackson from under my jacket.

"He's breathing but barely!" a deep voice calls out. Arnold. One of the best in our squad.

"Allende!" a different voice calls. Larry. Another good firefighter. "You stupid son of a bitch! We thought we lost you!" He's angry, pissed off.

If I could, I would laugh and tell him that nothing can get to me. But I don't have the energy. And just before I pass out I feel my brothers lifting me up to carry me to what I presume is the paramedic on the other side of the building.

****

"You could've gotten yourself killed!" Captain Rogers seethes a couple of hours later, in my hospital room. "Keep that fucking mask on!" he hollers just as I begin to pull the oxygen mask from my face.

It's a different mask from the type we wear. *This mask could never hold up in a fire*, I think as I let my gaze peruse the plastic, rubbery material of this hospital mask.

"I hope you're fucking happy, Allende. Real fucking happy! The head of the department is likely to be up my ass about this shit! Demanding to know why one of my men can't take orders."

I don't even hide the roll of my eyes. Captain Rogers has always been more concerned with what the higher-ups think than actually doing his fucking job. At least, that's been my experience.

"There was a boy inside," I weakly retort, in spite of the burning in my lungs.

"And I told you to stand down. We had no confirmation of the boy inside. We got the mother and baby out, but you just had to go back in and save the day."

"That's what you—" I can't even finish my comeback

before I start violently coughing.

"Don't talk. You've got smoke inhalation, second degree burns, and a bruised fucking pelvis. You're in fucked up shape."

It was all worth it if Jackson lives.

I can't say that out loud because I'm in too much pain. It hurts to talk.

Captain Rogers merely looks at me, shaking his head, before he turns to exit the room.

A second later, Rich, Larry, and Arnold walk in. The concern in their eyes is evident but they won't say as much.

"For fuck's sake, Allende, we thought you were toasted and roasted in there." Arnold is the first to speak, causing the other guys and even me to chuckle. We never claimed to be a classy bunch.

"N-not th-this time," I manage to stammer out.

"Yeah, Arnie was just hoping because he wants your locker space," Larry adds.

Another round of laughs.

It's partly true. Arnold has been angling for my locker for months now. It's in the corner and has the most room.

"Cap says you're not hurt too badly. A few days of rest and you'll be back at the station being the pain in the ass to him you always are," Rich states.

I grunt, slightly disheartened to go back to Squad Two. I love my job and my teammates, but I feel stifled under Captain

Rogers.

"Bullshit," Arnold says. "We know what a save like this means." He turns to me, tilting his head. "You'll probably get the pick of the transfer you've been wanting for over a year now."

I raise my brows.

"We all know you'd rather be where the action is." Larry's voice is heavy, as if it's a foregone conclusion that I'd be leaving. After five years of working together, I understand.

But they're right. Squad Two is great but we rarely get calls like the one we were on tonight. Ever since the district did some realigning, our calls have become the more docile, run of the mill, saving people from downed power lines and retrieving frightened kittens from trees types of calls. Not a bad gig for family men like Larry and Rich, who want to make it home to their wives and kids at the end of the day, but boring as shit for a guy like me.

"Not only will you likely get the Tom Webster for this, but I'm betting as soon as there's an open spot over at Rescue Four it'll have your name written all over it."

My heartbeat quickens at the thought of getting transferred to Rescue Four. Known around the department unofficially as the elite squad. That's exactly where I want to be. I couldn't give a shit about the Tom Webster or any other medals. No one runs into fires, risking life and limb for a fucking medal.

"We'll let you get some rest," Arnold says after a few moments of silence.

I nod in their direction. However, right before they get to the door, I pull the mask from my face and call out, "The kid?" My voice is weak, but they hear me.

It's evident by the way all three of their backs stiffen.

There's a pause.

The quiet speaks for itself.

Larry slowly pivots to face me again, his head hanging low, and there's a glossy sheen in his dark brown eyes. He'd be the most emotional seeing as how his son is the same age as Jackson.

"He didn't make it, man."

His words become the heavy, solid weight that settles onto my chest, stealing my next breath. Even with the oxygen mask it becomes difficult to breathe, and it's not due to the smoke inhalation.

"Emanuel," Arnold begins, moving closer to my hospital bed, "you busted your ass out there. You saved that woman and her newborn baby. And ..." He hesitates, looking back. "That woman got to hold her boy's hand as he took his last breath because of you. You did your job better than anyone out there tonight, man. Don't forget that."

I can't process Arnold's words at the moment. All I

know is that a five-year-old little boy is dead. A boy that I missed on my first sweep through of the apartment. If that shit isn't my fault, whose is it?

****

Janine

Meanwhile, on the other side of town ...

Jealousy is such an ugly emotion, I remind myself yet again as my hands tighten around the stem of the rose and hydrangea bouquet I hold in my hand. I lift my head to glance up to the center of the pulpit where my close friend, Angela Moore, is pledging to love, honor, and obey, her husband, Eric Kim. Angela looks beautiful in the creme, satin gown she's wearing. The color stands out against her pecan-brown skin. I smile at the curly ringlets in her hair and the purple streak that remains evident. I've always admired Angela's ability to be whoever she wants to be. In spite of my own childish jealousy, I am happy for my friend. I remember just a few years ago how devastated she was when both of her parents were killed in a plane crash. They truly were her best friends. Yet another thing I admire about her. The bond she has with her family, who now includes not only her brother and nephew, but Eric. She'll surely make a great wife and mother someday.

Sighing, I shove my own thoughts aside to focus on the nuptials taking place right in front of me. I will be happy for

Angela—she deserves the wedding and the man of her dreams, and she's getting both. I smile wide and clap along with the rest of the bridal party and guests when Angela and Eric seal their vows with a kiss. I proceed toward the center aisle of the church, and wrap my hand around the arm of one of the groomsmen. I look up to see his dark eyes sparkling down at me as he grins followed by a wink right before we start to follow the rest of the wedding party.

"Weddings make you emotional?" he questions.

I scrunch my eyebrows in confusion, and he tilts his head toward my face. Touching my cheek with my free hand, I realize a lone tear has escaped.

"Don't worry, beautiful. I have just the cure for whatever ails you," he states smoothly.

I roll my eyes, but a smirk plays at my full lips. "No thanks, Don." He's one of Eric's teammates at the fire station. Angela warned me that he was a serious flirt. However, she failed to mention how damn fine he is. Hell, from what I've seen, *all* of the men at Rescue Four are drop dead gorgeous. Almost as if it's a prerequisite to work at the fire station. *Number one, be able to put out fires. Number two, can pull people from a burning building. And last but certainly not least, be over six-feet tall, muscular, jaw chiseled to perfection, and look good enough to set women's hearts on fire wherever you go.* Or perhaps, that's just how the requirements go in my head.

At the exit, all of the guests throw rice at the bride and groom, who then leave to take pictures at a local park. Don moves to step in front of me.

"So what do you say we ditch this reception and go make some memories of our own?" His dark eyes narrow mischievously.

I lift my hand to smooth back the chignon I'd put my permed hair into for the wedding. "I don't think that'd be such a good idea."

Don's lips form into a pout, and for a split second he actually achieves the innocent look he's going for. But too soon, his eyes fill with that mirth I'd begun to realize was natural for him. "Oh yeah? Why not?" He lifts a dark eyebrow.

I raise mine as well. "I don't think my boyfriend would appreciate that very much," I retort, saucily, placing a hand on my hip.

"Boyfriend?" he quips and looks around as if searching for someone. "Where is he? I'll have a talk with him."

I burst out laughing, before throwing my hand over my mouth. I shake my head. "You probably would try, too."

"For you?" He eyes me up and down, his gaze growing heated. "Absolutely."

I don't even try to come back with a response. To be honest, it feels good to have a man openly express his attraction to me. I can't say even if Matt weren't in the picture

I'd take Don up on his offer, but it is a confidence booster to have this handsome man flirt with me.

"Donnie, leave the woman alone. Can't you see she's not interested? Besides, we all know Janine's been waiting on me."

I turn to see yet another drop dead gorgeous Rescue Four member approach us. *It really must be something in the water over there*, I muse. Where Don's skin is an olive complexion, Corey's is only a few shades lighter than my own dark brown coloring. He appears to be about an inch or so taller than Don's just over six-foot height. Both men wear identical tuxedos that hang in a way that you know they were specifically tailored for their individual bodies.

"What's going on here?"

Oh Lord. Yet another one. His name is Carter. Blond hair, blue-eyes, and damned perfect. Just like the rest of them. However, despite Carter's appeal, he reminds me too much of my own boyfriend, which oddly makes him less appealing.

"Janine, are these two fools bothering you?" Carter's crystal blue gaze turns to me.

I don't even have time to respond before Corey answers.

"For your information, I was rescuing Ms. Janine, here, from Donnie. Now if you'll excuse us, we have some pictures to take and a reception to get to," Corey states, smoothly, wrapping his hand around my waist.

I don't argue as I go along with Corey's hold. Don and

Carter follow us, continuing to bicker. I'd bet money these guys are a riot down at the station.

****

"This peach color looks beautiful on you."

Smiling, I turn to the woman of the hour. Angela is beaming. Her smile is so wide, I'm pretty sure all thirty-two of her pearly whites are on display.

"Congratulations on choosing bridesmaids' dresses that *actually* flatter your bridesmaids," I retort, grinning. I smooth down the sides of the satin dress that stops just above my knees. The off-the-shoulder top of the dress does accentuate my collarbones, which are one of my best features.

"You're welcome." Angela smirks as we stand at the center of the bar she owns named Charlie's. She named it after her father. Around us, the wedding guests dance, eat, and sip champagne in celebration of the happy couple.

"Eric still hasn't told you where you're honeymooning, has he?"

Pouting, Angela shakes her head. "No, and I wish he would."

I give her a one shoulder shrug. "Why? Wherever you end up, it's not like you'll make it out of the hotel room."

"You're probably right." Angela and I both giggle.

"Now, there's a sight to behold. The two most gorgeous

women in the room, laughing. Be still my heart."

I roll my eyes, laughing again as Don emerges from behind me.

"Hey, Don," Angela greets.

"Mrs. Kim," he nods, using Angela's married name. "I'm trying to get your friend here to dance with me, but she keeps brushing me off. My feelings are hurt." He tilts his head to the side and tries for the puppy dog look. If I didn't know any better ...

"That's not *all* he's trying to get me to do," I comment, giving Don a mock, stern expression.

"A dance is a great start to the rest." He winks.

Laughing, I shake my head. "Angela, will you please tell this man I have a boyfriend?"

Angela raises an eyebrow at me and gives me an "are you serious" look.

Here we go.

"He's not here," Don speaks before Angela can.

The pit in my stomach grows at his reminder. That envious feeling from earlier begins to emerge once again. Sighing, I use my hand to smooth down my hair. I hate that Angela had all of her bridesmaids wear these chignons. She knows I prefer having my hair down, to hide my ears. I swear they poke out too far.

"He's got a point."

I gape at Angela for her comment, essentially backing up Don.

"Matt couldn't make it," I state, but it comes out more like a mumble.

"Hm," Angela tuts. "One of your best friend's wedding and he couldn't accompany you."

I narrow my eyes but remain silent, not wanting to have this conversation in front of Don. When I go to speak again, a buzzing sounds from the black clutch I carry.

"That's Matt now," I state, pridefully, as I pull my cell phone from the clutch to see I have a text message. I step away from Angela and Don to answer Matt, even though it is just a text. Needing some fresh air, I wind my way around the guests and the tables of food that are set up around the bar, to step out onto the sidewalk at the front of Charlie's. It is mid-spring and the weather is perfect.

I open my message to read Matt's text.

Matt: **When are you coming home?**

Frowning, I bite my lower lip. I haven't heard from Matt in the two days I've been in Williamsport for Angela's wedding, despite my numerous calls, and this is his first message to me.

I'll be back tomorrow evening.

I wait a minute or two for his response.

Matt: **Tomorrow evening? I specifically asked you to be present to attend the art gala with me tomorrow night.**

I knit my brows, trying to remember what he's talking about. I have a memory like a steel trap. I would remember if he asked me to attend an art gala the day after Angela's wedding. It also pisses me off that he's making demands of me to attend yet another one of his high society events while he couldn't be bothered to come to Williamsport with me to make it to Angela's wedding.

So, I'm supposed to change my plans because of an event that you didn't tell me about? But when I practically begged you to come to Angela's wedding with me, you flat out declined.

I wait for his response.

And wait.

I get close enough to the point in which I don't think Matt is going to respond to my last text, since he's been known to do that, that I start to turn to go back inside to the reception again. Just then, my phone vibrates in my hand, with Matt's response.

Matt: **You know I had a work obligation. Otherwise, I would've been there. Are you able to attend the gala with me or not? If not, I will have to make other arrangements.**

My grip tightens on the phone as I read that last sentence. It's his not-so-subtle way of letting me know just how replaceable I am. Besides, he's lying. I know he is. He works at a hedge fund that was founded and run by his father. He takes days off when he wants to all of the time. I'd let him know months in advance when the wedding was, but he still chose not to come. He's being an ass, and for some reason I can't bring myself to call him on it.

I'll change my flight to get in tomorrow morning.

Matt: **Good. See you tomorrow.**

I stomp my foot, hating myself for being so weak, but after nine years, off-and-on, with Matt I just can't let go. We met my sophomore year of college after I'd done the riskiest thing I'd ever done before or since. I used a fake ID to get into a bar, along with Angela and a few other friends. Matt is two years older and I was hooked since the first time I saw him. Nine years later, here I am, at my best friend's wedding, dateless because my boyfriend couldn't be so bothered to accompany me.

Pushing out a heavy breath, I turn for the door. As soon as I step over the threshold of the bar and glance up, my eyes land on a smiling Angela as she looks up at Eric. Even from halfway across the room I can feel the electricity between those two. A lump in my throat begins to form as I watch Eric's tall figure lean down to say something that only his wife can hear. Angela tosses her head back and laughs as Eric tightens his hold around her waist.

I don't know for how long I watch them, absorbed in their own little world. Just the two of them, even in a room full of people. I notice as Eric takes the lead, Angela's hand firmly clasped in his, directing her toward the back of the bar, where I know there are stairs that lead to an upstairs apartment. The lump in my throat grows bigger as I realize that no one has ever looked at me the way Eric looks at Angela. After nearly a decade with my so-called boyfriend, I still long for that. Whatever the *that* is that Eric and Angela share.

If a man wants you, he'll take you off the market. Period. Point blank.

My mother's words ring in my ears as I watch Eric and Angela disappear behind the door that led upstairs. My mother is correct. A fact I'm loathe to admit considering the source. But men don't waffle about what they want. For the last five years, Matt and I have gone back and forth about marriage. He'd say the proposal was coming, even giving me more than one promise ring, but there's never been an actual engagement. He'd take me ring shopping and then a month or two later, the conversation was off the table. There is always something more important coming up. It is never the right time to discuss it. But as I stand in that room full of happy celebrants of the bride and groom, I realize that ring is never coming. Not from Matt, at least. The dream I had of being married by twenty-five and a mother by twenty-seven is long gone.

It's time to move on from Matt. I know that in my head. Now if I can just get my heart to cooperate.

Chapter One

Six months later

Janine

I did it.

My full lips slowly morph into a smile as I inhale the saltwater scent drifting into my hotel room from the open balcony door. I sit in my room, happily eating the fruit that'd come with a stack of pancakes and eggs I'd had delivered to my room. A feeling of peace comes over me, that even the fear and self-doubt that'd gripped me for weeks now can't touch.

I finally ended things with Matthew. Packed up my belongings, moved to a new city, and am now taking a much needed vacation.

A second smile touches my lips when I glance down at my dark-chocolate brown skin and notice the glow. I've been in Cabo for less than twenty-four hours now. However, and after hours of traveling, complete with flight delays the day before, I talked myself into wearing one of the five bathing suits I brought with me, down to the resort's main pool. I laid out for two hours yesterday, just soaking up the sun rays. My skin is at least a shade darker than my usual color, and the moisturizer I'd just put on enhanced it's glow even more. I sit up in my chair a little straighter and turn toward the sounds of the ocean, again, patting myself on the back for booking a hotel right on the beach. The view alone is worth the arm and leg I'd spent on this resort, but after finally leaving Matt, a career change, and deciding to relocate from Boston to Williamsport, I deserve this.

Dragging my gaze from the ocean back to my planner on the table before me, I remind myself that I have a full day and need to get going. Luckily, I met some really cool women the previous night and they invited me to spend the day with them on the tour they booked. I'd already made plans, but decided to go against my usual, by-the-book ways and postponed the glass bottom boat tour for the following day, to hang out with these women. Truth be told, while I was all gung-ho about going on this trip alone, I'm excited to connect with some other women while in Mexico.

After quickly finishing my breakfast, I layer a pair of cutoff jean shorts and a sleeveless, pink T-shirt over the one-piece bathing suit I chose to wear. Though the suit is one piece, the sides are cut out, exposing much of my mid-section. The bathing suits I'd bought for this trip go completely against the more conservative and covered look I typically wear. But, much like the rest of my life, I'm looking for a change in my wardrobe, at least while I on vacation.

Standing, I take one last look in the mirror. I run my hand over the cornrow braids I'd gotten for the trip. I haven't worn my hair in cornrows since I was ten years old, but now at twenty-eight, I'm wondering why. The braids look great. I'd opted for extensions so they stopped halfway down my back. I'm sure the style will hold up great against all of the sightseeing, swimming, and genuine relaxing I plan on doing during the trip. Smearing some clear lip gloss over my lips and placing my square-rimmed sunglasses at the top of my head, I grab my bag, slide my feet into my strappy sandals, and head out the door ... only to run into a damn brick wall.

"Oof!" I grumble, almost panicking when I feel myself falling backwards. Just before I can make a total fool of myself, two strong hands wrap around my arms, preventing my fall. I can't decide which hold is tighter—the arms or the scent that wrap around my entire body, filling my nostrils with the most delicious smell. He smells like patchouli, with a hint of oranges and something unique. I know it is a *he* because of the goosebumps on my arms that stand.

"Whoa there, beauty. Are you all right?"

Holy hell.

No man's voice should be that deep. Or that sexy.

"I—" I start to reply but the words fizzle on my lips when I peer up into the most alluring eyes. They were a honey-brown color with flecks of gold in them. And to top it off, they're framed by the longest lashes I've ever seen on a man. I suck in a deep breath when he stands to his full height, and the edges of those eyes wrinkle as a smile creases his plump lips. This man's entire face was put together perfectly. Da Vinci himself couldn't have done a better job.

"I-I'm okay. I'm sorry. I should've been paying attention." I take a step back and swallow when his smile spreads even farther. A twinkle in his eyes shoots off alarm bells in my ears.

"Don't worry about it," he replies, rising up to his full height. He has to be at least six-four. "You've got a great room."

I blink, shaking my head. "What?"

He nods his head toward my door but all I notice is his smooth, tanned skin. It makes me wonder about his background. From his looks, I surmise that his heritage has to come from somewhere in the Mediterranean.

"Your room. It's got a great view of the ocean. I'm right next door."

I turn my head, blinking again, realizing that he's talking about our hotel rooms.

"We're neighbors."

Did his voice get deeper when he said that?

"That's nice," I add, not knowing what else to say. I can't remain in this man's presence much longer. His eyes are too alluring and his scent too captivating. He is just too ... everything. "Well, uh, sorry again. Enjoy your stay!" I wave and immediately feel like a fool, as I pivot on my heels and proceed down the hall. I take about six steps away when I wonder if he is still there. Daring to take a glance over my shoulder, I turn and almost trip over my own two feet to see him still there, watching me, sporting a grin.

"Nope," I mumble to myself, turning back around and picking up my steps. I am not on vacation to meet men. I just broke up with Matt three months ago. I'm still grieving the loss of that relationship. At least, I should be. But even as I stroll off the elevator toward the lobby of my hotel, pulling my sunglasses down to cover my eyes, the smile that'd played at the man's lips and his scent remain with me.

****

"I had so much fun!" I exclaim. "Thank you for inviting me," I tell the group of women I'd spent the day with. We'd gone on a day-long excursion that included snorkeling, lunch in a lagoon, and cave sightseeing. It was one of the best days I've had in a really long time.

"Oh, the day's not over yet, my friend," Rose, the blonde-haired vixen of the group, states as she wraps her arm around my shoulders. Rose always seems to have a little mischief in her hazel eyes.

"Not by a long shot." This was said by Tracey, who is the polar opposite of Rose physically with her chestnut coloring and shortly cropped haircut, but I can tell the two are akin to soulmates by the twin mischief in her eyes. Tracey intertwines her arm with mine and tugs me along toward our hotel lobby. "We're going dancing tonight after dinner on the beach. I hope you brought going out attire." She laughs.

"I may have a little something," I respond, feeling comfortable around these women. Their two other friends, Shawna and Jackie, who are staying at a different hotel, were dropped off there by the shuttle. We're going to meet up with them on the beach at six o'clock for dinner and drinks. And now, apparently, going out somewhere after that.

"Excellent!" Rose claps. "We'll meet you down here at ten of six."

I nod in agreement. That gives me plenty of time to rest a little and then shower and change before meeting up with the ladies again. This is the first vacation I've ever taken alone. At first, I feared I'd spend most of my time solo and in my room, but so far, it's going great. A smile I hadn't even realized I'm wearing, welcomes me as I turn, seeing myself in the mirrored elevator door.

A few hours later, after a shower and a short nap, I glare at the two dresses laid out on my bed. My confidence has waned slightly. I can't decide which one to wear. One dress is an off-the-shoulder, light blue, floral print dress. It's cute and flirty. The second is a rose-colored wrap dress with spaghetti straps, stopping just above the knee, but with a slit that exposes a lot of thigh. Both dresses are out of my wheelhouse, though the floral dress is something I feel safer wearing.

I reach for the floral print dress, but at the last second, I opt for the more revealing of the two. I don't know why but something is driving me to be a little more daring than I usually am. And hell, I *am* in Mexico. My first international trip. Maybe for a little while I can get over playing it safe.

I quickly don the dress before I can change my mind, matching it with a pair of five-inch stiletto, strappy gold sandals, and going a little more dramatic with my makeup than I usually do. I opt for a smoky eye with my new rose gold eyeshadow. It's so new, I actually had to tear the plastic packaging off when I first sit down to do my makeup. Now, standing in front of my floor-length mirror, I'm struck by the same jitters as I was two days prior, when talking myself into wearing a bikini out in public.

Twisting and turning in the mirror, I observe how the dress lays on my body from every angle. It comes up about an inch higher in the back than in the front, thanks to the swell of my butt. While this almost makes me change dresses, or worse, opt for the jean shorts I had originally pulled out, I have to admit the heels I'm wearing make my already toned legs look divine.

I swallow the bite of nervousness in my throat and push out the breath I've been holding. I really need to get a grip. Wearing a dress and some heels for a night out to dinner and drinks is far from risqué.

You look cheap. His voice rings in my head. I'd lost count of the times my ex would make such a disparaging comment whenever I tried to dress sexy early on in our relationship. Eventually, I just stopped trying.

Shrugging, I push his words out of my head. He doesn't get to dictate my attire tonight.

"Let's go," I finally say to myself. I give my hair one last glance to make sure I don't need to gel down the baby hairs at my edges. Everything appears good to go. I strut toward the door, checking the time on my cell phone to make sure I'm not running late. I place my phone inside of the white clutch I carry, make sure my wallet and keycard are inside, and then step over the threshold, feeling strangely confident.

"There she is," Tracey says excitedly as the doors of the elevator open to the lobby.

"Wow! Look at you," Rose exclaims with wide eyes.

"Me? You both look stunning," I compliment back, because they do.

The ladies laugh and do a spin, showing off the entirety of their outfits. They're both wearing dresses that are fun and definitely flirty. Rose's is a lot shorter than mine, and she's paired it with leopard thigh-high boots. In this moment, I'm glad I opted not to wear the jean shorts and floral kimono blouse I'd originally chosen. I'd be way underdressed.

"Your turn. Spin for us!" she insists.

I do, and a smile crests my lips when I hear their cheers

of approval.

"This must be where the party is!" a female voice interrupts. It's the rest of our group. The other two ladies, Shawna and Jackie, chose to walk over from their hotel so we could all catch a taxi to the restaurant where we're having dinner.

We all talk excitedly about the restaurant. It's supposed to be one of the best in the area for fresh seafood. And seeing as how it's located right on the beach, it's no wonder.

"And next door is the salsa club I was telling you all about," Tracey says after we pile into the taxi.

The driver overhears our conversation, and to our surprise, speaks pretty good English. He seconds what Tracey just said, informing us that the nightclub is where he first met his wife, some four years prior.

"Now, she is home pregnant with our second *hijo,* and I drive taxi for extra money," he chuckles.

Recognizing the Spanish word for son, my heart squeezes just a little.

There's that look again, I think as I peer into the rearview mirror glancing at our driver's eyes as he talks about his wife and son. Ever since Angela's wedding, I swear I've been seeing that far off gaze with regularity. Either that or I've just been noticing it more frequently. And again, I'm brought back to the realization that after ten years with Matt, not once could I recall seeing that emotion in his gaze.

"We're here," squeals Rose.

Thank god, because another minute and I'd find myself lost in the trail of ugly memories. A road I refuse to go down while on vacation.

"Oops!" I yelp as I stumble out of the taxi and try to get my footing.

"Careful," one of the women with me warns as she braces my arm to steady me.

I give Rose a smile. "Thanks. It's been a while since I've worn heels this high."

A slight frown adorns her face. "You better get used to it soon because we don't plan on letting you sit down too much once we hit the dance club. Right, ladies?" she yells to the three other women with us, and they all whoop and clap in agreement.

A sliver of nervous tension courses through my belly at the thought of trying to dance in these heels. But I push it aside with thoughts of possibly faking feeling ill after dinner and heading back to my hotel. A coward move, I know, but I've pushed myself enough by coming to Cabo and hanging out with a group of women I just met ... right?

"Mmm, smells delicious in here," Jackie, one of the other women, hums as we enter the restaurant.

Immediately, my stomach begins growling, alerting me

of my own hunger. And she's correct, it does smell amazing in the restaurant. Thanks to the reservations that were made days earlier, we are escorted by the hostess to one of the outside lounge areas that is only a few feet from the white sands of the beach. Less than a hundred feet away are the crashing waves from the beautiful Pacific Ocean. Though it is dark I can still imagine the crystal blue waters.

"Earth to Janine."

Blinking, I turn to find three pairs of eyes staring at me. I flash an embarrassed smile. "Sorry, I tend to drift off into daydreams sometimes."

"What were you daydreaming about?" Jackie asks just before sticking a guacamole-filled tortilla chip into her mouth.

My stomach rumbles again and I reach for a chip of my own, opting to dip it in the pico de gallo salsa instead of guacamole. Before stuffing the chip in my own mouth, I answer, "The beach." I pause to chew and swallow my chip. "It's so beautiful. I was supposed to come here a few years ago with my boy ... my *ex*-boyfriend, Matt."

"What happened?" Shawna questions.

I shrug. "He canceled, said he had work obligations he couldn't leave behind." I leave out the part when just two weeks later he took a four-day trip to Greece with a group of his college friends.

I glance up from my thoughts to see the other two

women are engaged in talking to one another about their own exes, while Tracey continues to stare at me. Something tells me she is the most intuitive of the group.

"And you didn't come by yourself?"

I shake my head. "No, I never even thought of it. Not until now."

"So what changed?" Tracey inquires.

Squirming a little in my seat, I take another chip. This time not because of hunger but to occupy my mouth while I decide how much of my business I want to divulge to this practical stranger.

Once I swallow the chip, I say, "Because I finally broke up with him once and for all, am moving to a new city and changing careers. I thought it was time I did some traveling on my own for once."

"Heyyy!" Tracey and the other women cheer at my response.

"We definitely need to toast to that!" Lisa waves over our waitress and requests a round of margaritas.

I find myself relieved at the women's responses and I happily clank glasses with them once our drinks arrive, even though I usually abstain from alcohol. By the time our food arrives, we are two drinks in, and Rose makes sure to tell the waitress to keep them coming.

I gleefully indulge in the deliciously grilled shrimp and

vegetables with authentic Mexican rice and beans in some kind of sauce. The food is decadent but light at the same time, and the drinks continue. It seems whenever I reach the bottom of my glass one of the women is already filling it up thanks to the pitcher we've ordered. Somewhere in the back of my mind, my more reserved side is screaming at me to remind me of the dangers of possibly being roofied in a foreign country, or falling down somewhere with my dress above my waist, a stranger taking a picture and embarrassingly I end up all over the internet as a meme of "what not to do while in Mexico".

But as I glance around the table and notice the women I'm with indulging and laughing, having a great time, I decide to throw caution to the wind. In all of my twenty-eight years on the planet, I've rarely taken time to indulge, let go, and just have fun.

"Oh, man, I'm stuffed," I say, patting my belly as I sit back in the chair. "I know I've definitely eaten more carbs than are necessary today." I frown as I look down at my plate at the few remnants of the rice and beans.

"Who gives a shit about carbs? We're on vacation! Plus, we're going to work off all of this food dancing," Jackie cheers.

Minutes later we're paying the waitress for our dinner and opting to exit through the restaurant's front entrance to walk down the sidewalk to the nightclub, instead of the beachside since we all have heels on. We pass a number of partygoers, likely most of whom are on spring break. The energy is a little intoxicating, but even so, my nervousness about dancing begins to crest yet again. I'm not a great dancer without heels. Add to that the number of drinks I had at dinner, and I am feeling off kilter already.

"All right, ladies," Tracey begins after we've all paid the entrance fee and gotten our hands stamped. "Let's order another round. This time, tequila!" she shouts. "Jackie, you grab us a table," she insists.

I follow Jackie while Shawna, the fourth and most quiet member in our party, follows Rose and Tracey to help carry the drinks over to the table. Lisa finds us a table a few feet from the dance floor, but quiet enough that conversation is still an option.

"You ever salsa dance before?" Jackie questions.

I shake my head. "You?"

Smiling, she happily nods. "I'm a dance instructor full-time."

"Really? Salsa dancing?"

"I started in ballet, which I still do, along with salsa, tap, jazz. My students range in age from toddler to young adult so I get a pretty good mix at the studio."

"You own your own studio?"

"Yup," she proudly responds.

"Cool." I admire her striking out to own a business. She

continues to share a little bit about her schooling all the way up until she just got burned out with professional dance and decided to leave the big city and return to her hometown to open her studio.

"Here ya go!" Rose says as she bounces over, and places shots of tequila on the table.

Tracey, Rose, Shawna, and Jackie quickly down their drinks and then pin me with their expectant gazes. Hesitantly, I reach for the shot, lifting it to my nose, sniffing it first before putting it to my lips. Then I make the decision to down it as quickly as possible as to not taste it. But no such luck; within seconds the burning in my throat is causing me to cough and gag.

"I'm not much of a drinker," I manage to eek out after a few moments.

There's a collective giggle around the table.

"We've figured that out," someone chimes. I'm too busy trying to swallow down the taste of the tequila to look up and see who.

Thankfully, Jackie has also ordered a round of rum and cokes for everyone. Though the drink is strong, it's not as potent going down as the tequila.

"All right, enough drinking, let's dance!" Jackie shouts. She attempts to grab my hand but I wave her off.

"Next song," I say, hoping to buy more time before I am

forced to embarrass myself.

Thankfully, Jackie leaves me, and she and Rose hit the dancefloor, and are immediately scooped up by two men. It's easy to see the dance instructor in Jackie. Her movements are fluid and confident. She doesn't hesitate or second guess herself at all. Her face is light and laughing as she looks up into the surprised face of her dance partner. Maybe he wasn't expecting such an adept partner but he got one. The two whirl around the floor to some song with words I can't make out.

Tracey and her partner are not as able to keep up with the other two, but that doesn't mean they aren't just as interesting to watch. Tracey is quite the dancer herself. And what she lacks in technical form, she makes up for in enthusiasm. I smile at the pair as she easily moves into the following song.

"You said the next song."

I blink and look across the table at Shawna who is eyeing me.

"Another one," I answer.

Her smile drops a little but she shrugs and turns.

My lips part in surprise when she swiftly grabs one of the men standing at the edge of the dance floor, leads him onto the hardwood, and begins moving in time with the beat, leaving him to follow. He does so easily.

I shake my head, wondering how someone could have

so much confidence. And even though I'm not dancing, I am enjoying myself watching the women I'm with dance the night away.

"Just going to watch from the sidelines?"

Goosebumps shoot down my arms at the sound of the male voice behind me. I don't turn to look but I know I've heard that voice somewhere before, though I can't pinpoint it. *Ignore him and he'll go away,* my reserved side tells me. Any man with a voice that deep and sexy is trouble. And trouble is the last thing I need right now.

However, someone clearly forgot to tell that to all of the alcohol I've consumed over the past three hours, because in spite of my better self, I can't help but turn to look at the man who has now interrupted my solitude.

It's him.

The man from earlier in the day, at the hotel. His eyes are too intense to stare at for too long, so I allow my gaze to drop to his perfectly formed, full, pink lips.

"What did you say?"

Those lips curl upwards on one side.

"Are you just going to watch the entire night or enjoy the fun?"

"Was that an invitation?"

I have no idea where that retort comes from but something releases inside of me when his smile widens, notifying me that it pleases him. I swallow the lump forming in my throat.

"It is," he smoothly responds, holding out his hand.

My eyes dip to stare at it. His hand is large and I don't miss the few dried calluses and blisters. He must work with his hands for a living.

"Don't be scared," he urges.

My gaze connects with his, and I see the challenge in his eyes. He's pushing me, goading me and he wants me to know it.

"I'm not frightened." I lift my chin in defiance.

"Prove it."

I narrow my eyes. What he thinks shouldn't matter. He's a stranger. And yet ...

"It's just a dance."

Decision made.

I place my hand in his, and he swiftly guides me to the dance floor. I try to hide my stumble once we begin but the small smirk on his face shows that he saw it. Still, he's gentleman enough not to point it out.

My movements are jerky. I wish I could blame it on the alcohol but I know that's not the case.

"Easy, butterfly," he coos as his hand moves to my hip, pulling me in closer, but not too close to be inappropriate or uncomfortable.

I glance up into his eyes, mine widening at the new

name he's donned me with.

"Feel that?"

"What?" I ask.

"The rhythm. Salsa timing is on counts of four. Step with me." He takes a step back with his right foot, urging me to step forward with my left. "Now take a step with the back foot in place."

I follow this instruction as well.

"Now reverse it."

I step backwards with my right foot and he follows with his left. Our bodies aren't touching except for our hands but they're moving in sync.

"Don't look at the floor. Look at me," a command, further enforced when he lifts my chin to stare into his eyes.

Why does he do that? Because as soon as he pins me with his gaze, I lose my rhythm and stumble backwards. But his strong arms are there, preventing me from getting too off balance.

Wordlessly, he moves my hands to his shoulders and lowers his to my hips, our gazes still locked on one another.

"That's it. You've got it now."

I almost drop my gaze to look down at the front of my dress, hoping that my nipples aren't poking through because between his hold, his gaze, and his words I am completely turned on. The rest of the people on the dance floor fall away and it's just him and I. Not once does he look away from me, nor I him. We're the only two out here. I hardly notice when the song changes to another, and then another. Only when someone bumps into us on the dance floor, breaking our concentration on one another, do I notice that we're not actually alone.

I spot a flash of anger in his eyes when he narrows his gaze on the man who's just knocked into us.

Withdrawing my hands from his shoulders, I decide to head back to the table to see if I can spot the women I came with.

"Would you like a drink?" he questions before I can turn around.

I hesitate but then shake my head. "I don't take drinks from strangers."

A dark eyebrow raises. "Are we still strangers? I'll have to change that."

My heart rate quickens at the promise in his eyes. He moves closer and parts his lips to say something, but just then Rose appears.

"Hey, we're about to head out. Early morning flight, and I still need to pack up."

"I, uh, what time is it?"

"It's almost two."

I blink.

"I can take you back to your hotel."

I turn to the man in front of me.

"Sure, if you—"

"No!" I insist, cutting Rose off. I am not letting this man take me back to my hotel. He could be a serial killer for all I know. "I'm ready. Let's go."

I rush off, grabbing Rose by the hand and pulling her behind me before anyone can say anything. I don't even slow down when my left ankle tilts and nearly causes me to fall again. I just keep moving. I don't bother to share with Rose the fact that I'm anxious to leave because I was incredibly tempted to say yes to his invitation. We spent nearly an hour on the dance floor and it felt like all of five minutes. I didn't know what was going on but I sure as hell didn't want any part of it. Not from him. He might've been friendly but just under the surface he had danger written all over him.

No thank you.

Chapter Two

Emanuel

"You're not going to chase after her?"

I cut my gaze to my cousin. "Since when the fuck do I chase after pussy?"

The mischievous grin that is constantly at play on Christian's lips grows. "Just asking, you seemed to like that one. You were on the dance floor with her for a while. You looked ready to strip her down and fuck her right on the floor.

I was. But that's none of Christian's business. *Besides* ...

"I know where she's staying," I say as I look ahead toward the exit where she's fleeing. And that's exactly what it was ... fleeing. She was uncomfortable as all hell. It was damn near palpable.

"Whatever. There's plenty of pussy in the sea, right?" Christian adds.

I frown in his direction once again. "You're a sick fuck. You know that?"

Chuckling, he nods. "It's taken you six years to learn that, huh?"

I shake my head and turn to look out over the dance floor. Christian and I have only known one another for six years. He's my cousin, but circumstances of my own birth have kept me from knowing either side of my family until recently, hence the reason I'm in Mexico.

"The rest of the family arriving day after tomorrow as scheduled?"

Christian nods before taking a sip of his drink. "Everything's on schedule," he answers, but there's something in his tone of voice. Absent is the underlying mirth I'd come to associate with him. But Christian, like the rest of the family, only shares something when they're good and ready to. It seems to be a family trait I inherited.

"I'm ready to call it a night," I state.

"Same."

Again, that was another surprise from Christian. I don't think I can ever recall him being ready to leave before a nightclub closes, and definitely not solo. But then again, I've rarely done it either.

"What's up with that promotion? You start when you get back, right?" he questions as we walk toward our hotel, foregoing the taxi.

"It's not a promotion. I was transferred."

"But it's a transfer you've wanted for over a year, right?"

I nod and grunt. "A couple of years."

"To a better station?"

"Rescue Four. More action, more fires, more lives to save."

"Sounds like a promotion to me."

I don't say anything.

"Congratulations on that award, too. What was it? The Webster Medal or something?"

I sigh. "Thomas Webster Medal," is my only response. I don't explain that it's basically the bronze medal of the Williamsport Fire Department. The medal I earned for pulling five-year-old Jackson out of a fire, only for him to die a few hours later. I rub my hand across my chest, something that's become a habit every time I think about that night.

"Sorry I couldn't be there to see you pinned."

Stopping, I tap my hand against Christian's chest. "Not a big fucking deal. Don't bring it up anymore, all right?" I say looking him in his eyes.

"Touchy subject? I know when to back off. Anyway, what are your plans for the rest of your time in Cabo until the wedding?"

An image of the woman I spent half the night with on the dance floor comes to mind.

"I can think of some things." I don't bother to expand on my comment out loud, but in my head, I've already got an array of ideas that will extend over the next three days of my vacation. And I don't plan on spending them alone.

****

Janine

"Ugh!" I groan as I'm thrust awake by the pounding on

my door. For a split second I think it's my imagination, hoping that it's my mind playing tricks on me. But when the pounding comes again I'm confronted with the reality that there *is* somebody at my hotel room door.

Rolling over, I push the satin eye mask I always wear up to my forehead.

"Coming," I say weakly at the continued knocking. "I thought I canceled room service this morning," I grumble. I totally believed I'd canceled my room service order once I got back to the hotel the previous night. Though my memory is a bit fuzzy from the drinks I'd consumed, I distinctly remember saying good-bye to the women I was with, as they were all leaving today, and then heading to the front desk to cancel my breakfast order. I planned to sleep in, knowing I'd have a hangover in the morning. The one time I had indulged in alcohol in my life was my twenty-first birthday and I had, as the Bostonians say, a *wicked* hangover the next day.

My guess turned out to be true, if the roiling happening in my stomach and the headache I could feel coming on was any indication.

"Hi, I—" What I'd intended to be a quick dismissal of the breakfast delivery was quickly aborted when I was confronted with a large bottle of cold water. Confused, I raise my gaze and gasp at the sight of *him* smirking down on me.

"Figured you'd need one of these this morning."

"How did you—"

"Know where you were staying? You literally walked into me yesterday. Remember?"

I do remember. But I had completely forgotten that last night when he offered to walk me back to my hotel room. I move my gaze from his eyes to the bottle of water.

"How do I know that that's not drugged?"

He points to the bottle cap. "Seal's still intact. Besides, drugging isn't my style."

I bet it isn't. This guy looks as if he could charm a snake out of its hiding spot. Which is why I should've shut the door right in his face.

"Whoa, you definitely need this," he asserts when I sway a little, holding onto the door to hold me up.

I am totally hungover.

Right in front of my eyes he opens the bottle of water and holds it out to me. This time I don't hesitate to take it from him and down almost half of the bottle right there. I lick my lips once I've gotten my fill.

Those honey brown eyes of his watch my mouth, and I swear I see them darken but I can't be too sure because in a matter of a nanosecond the look is gone.

"You don't drink much, do you, butterfly?"

I frown. "Am I that easy to read?"

"Yes."

My heart sinks a little at the quickness of his answer. I once read in one of those women's magazines that men like their women to be a little bit of a mystery and alluring. Then I remember I was reading that particular article in yet another attempt to change myself to get my then-boyfriend to put a ring on my finger.

"Stop thinking about him."

The command grabs my attention and my eyes lock with his, the man at my door.

"What?"

"Whoever you were thinking about. Stop thinking about him. He isn't here."

"I wasn't—"

"Lying doesn't look good on you, butterfly."

I squint at him. "You have no idea who I am or what I'm thinking about."

His smile grows. "There she is."

I crumple my face in confusion.

"A glimpse of the woman from the dance floor last night. The one who comes out when you let your guard down just a little bit."

His words anger me. "Look, I don't know who *you* are, and you have no right to stand at my door trying to tell me who or what to think about."

He nods. "There she is again. I'm not trying to shrink

you, but I know a woman who comes down to Cabo by herself is for one of a few reasons."

"How do you know I'm by myself?"

"The women you were with last night left today."

"How do you know—"

"I overheard them."

"Are you some sort of stalker?"

The chuckle he lets out is rich, heavy, and dipped in a little bit of danger. It sends a chill through my body, and I find myself unscrewing the cap of the water bottle and taking another long sip.

"I don't drug women and I don't stalk them. I'm on vacation just as you are. And you can trust me."

I lift an eyebrow. "How am I supposed to know that?"

"Because I'm a firefighter," he responds cockily. "I save lives for a living. Would anyone with that type of job be a threat to you?"

I part my lips but no words come out.

"Exactly. Drink up. I'll give you thirty minutes to change, and then I'm coming back so we can have breakfast before we get our day started."

"*We?*"

He takes a step back. "That's what I said, butterfly."

"I don't even know your name."

"Emanuel. And yours?"

My mouth flaps open. "N-Nadine," I lie.

He pauses and tilts his head. For a second, I think he's going to call me on my lie. As if he somehow knows my name isn't really Nadine. I wrack my brain to recall whether I gave him my name the night before. I don't think so. And he doesn't call me out.

Instead, he tips his head toward the bottle of water still in my hand. "Finish that up, Nadine. I'll be back in thirty minutes."

I watch as he turns, sauntering off. My eyes rove over the hard contours of his bronzed skin. His shoulders are broad, as is his back. The dark, sleeveless T-shirt he wears looks as if it's been sewn just to etch out his muscles perfectly for spectator sport. The navy blue swim trunks he wears are long, leaving only his toned calves exposed.

How can a man's calves be attractive? I question as I stare on for a few more seconds until he turns to his hotel room, looks back at me, and tosses me a wink before entering his own room.

Stepping back inside of my hotel room, I shut the door and chug the last of the water. This time it has nothing to do with my hangover.

I should make this guy go away. One call to the front desk to inform them that I'm being harassed should do it. *Right?* And what would I tell them? That a man kindly brought me a bottle of unopened water because he suspected I wasn't feeling well?

I slap my hand to my forehead, silently reprimanding myself only to remember I still had my eye mask on during the entirety of our exchange. I move my other hand to my hair, and yup, sure enough, the silk scarf I sleep with at night is still there. I roll my eyes at what a pathetic image I must've made.

Matt always hated it when I wore my scarf when I spent the night over his place. No matter how many times I told him I did it to preserve my hairstyle or to keep my hair from drying out against his cotton pillowcases and sheets, he never cared. Eventually, I just took to buying silk pillowcases for when I slept over his place.

"No," I say out loud in the empty room. I am not going to allow myself to think about Matt any longer. He's a part of my past. *A long part of my past, yes, but he won't get my future.*

Those are my final thoughts on my ex as I head into the bathroom to shower and get ready to spend some time with Emanuel. I'm not completely sure about this guy no matter how attractive and delectable he might be. I figure if he's boring or an asshole, I can ditch him after breakfast.

****

Emanuel

"This place serves a great breakfast," I say as I hold the

door open for *Nadine* to pass through. Yeah, I know it's not her real name but I don't press the issue just yet.

"How many?" the hostess asks.

"Two."

Nadine turns to me. "I'm hungrier than I thought I'd be."

"A hangover will do that to you."

She frowns. "How do you know I'm hungover?"

I give her a funny look. "Aren't you?"

"Possibly."

"The fact that you're nearly done with that second bottle of water says it all." I tilt my head to the bottle in her hands. The one I'd brought over to her when I picked her up for our day out.

"I like water."

"And maybe you're full of shit."

Those golden eyes of hers widen in shock, and I smirk. I can already tell I'm going to enjoy keeping her off-kilter.

"Do you kiss your mother with that mouth?"

I grin. "Maybe."

"Your table's ready. Right this way," the hostess interrupts before she can say anything back. After showing us to our seats, the hostess places the menus in front of us. "Your waitress will be right with you."

"You've been here before?"

"The day before yesterday," I answer.

"What do you recommend?"

"I had breakfast tacos with chorizo. They were pretty good."

"Are you getting that again?"

I shake my head.

"Why not?"

"Variety is the spice of life. I'm going to get the veggie omelet with hash browns this morning."

"That sounds good. I'll get the same."

Just as Nadine says that, our waitress arrives, ready to take our orders.

Once she leaves, I fold my arms on the table and lean in. "So, Nadine, this is your first time in Mexico?" I question, staring directly into those golden eyes.

Her head dips slightly. "Yes."

"First time out of the country?"

She nods.

"And you decided to come by yourself. That takes some courage."

She shrugs as if it were no big deal, but a tiny smile crests her rose-colored lips. She's not wearing any makeup like she was the previous night, and yet, the dark brown skin of hers glows.

"I suppose," she states.

I don't miss the shifting she does in her chair. This topic

makes her uncomfortable for some reason. And my first instinct is to wipe away the sadness I see appear in her eyes.

"Lucky for you, you bumped into me."

She raises both eyebrows. "Is that so?"

I nod. "Oh yes, butterfly. I'm a shit ton of fun, and you don't have to worry about getting hurt because, as I said earlier, I'm a—"

"Firefighter," she finishes.

My grin widens. "You're catching on. I like that."

Our drinks of fresh squeezed watermelon and orange juice are brought out and placed in front of us. Sitting back in my seat, I watch as *Nadine* takes a sip of her watermelon juice. Her full, glossed lips look inviting as she swallows. I run my tongue along my own lower lip.

"What did you come to Cabo looking for?" I question, inching closer.

Her eyes narrow as if she doesn't understand the question. "Looking for? Nothing."

"Bullshit."

She blinks.

"No woman goes on vacation by herself unless she's looking for something."

Setting her glass down, her gaze lowers for a heartbeat before she returns it to me. "We've already established that you don't know me."

I nod in concession. "I don't know basic stuff like where you live, where you were born, etc. All of the unimportant things ..." I lean in closer, drawing in even more of her attention. I carefully watch as the small vein in her neck quickens its pace. A result of my nearness, I'm certain. "But I do know that you came searching for something. You got on a plane, flew from wherever you live in the States, all by yourself, to rekindle something you've lost. Or at least, something you *think* you've lost."

She glances away, then toward something over my shoulder. A second later, our waitress is placing our plates of food in front of us. Though I don't say anything, I continue to hold her in my gaze. And though she does her best to look everywhere but directly at me, I know she can feel the heat of my stare.

"How many days do you have left in Cabo, Nadine?" I question as soon as our waitress walks away.

"Three."

"Give them to me."

Those golden pupils of hers bulge at my request ... no, not a request, a command. One I hadn't intended on giving until the words left my mouth.

"Give them to you? What does that even mean?"

"It means, the women you were with have all gone, you didn't come with anyone else, and I'm guessing you're not expecting anyone else to be arriving. You're free to spend your time as you please. Give me your time."

"Why?"

"Because you're wrapped tighter than a spring coil. And with just the right amount of pressure you'll spring loose. You're just waiting for the right man to crawl in between those slick thighs of yours and show you exactly who you are. You're waiting for the right man to set you free, butterfly."

She shifts in her chair, gaze lowered to the table as she reaches for her half empty glass of juice again. Once she swallows, she says, "Do you use this type of pick-up line with all the women you meet in foreign countries?"

"Only when the mood strikes me," I retort, grinning.

My chest warms when her face again registers shock. I sit back and pick up my fork and knife, cutting into my omelet and taking my first bite. I'm confident before she even says anything that she'll be spending the final three days of her vacation with me. And to be totally honest, I don't know who is more surprised by this, her or me. I'm not the committed type, nor am I the type of spend more than a day or two with the same woman while on vacation.

"What do you have planned?" she finally questions.

A smile crests my lips. "That's for me to know and you to find out."

She shakes her head and turns fully to me. "If I'm going

to give my final three days of vacation to a random man, I need to know what's on the agenda."

"Agenda? I bet you're the type to plan out your entire vacation hour by hour."

"What's wrong with that?" The crease in her forehead displays her genuine perplexity.

I shrug and lean in, letting my gaze travel over the smooth skin covering her collarbone and chest. Slowly, I let my gaze rise to meet hers. "Nothing if you want predictability. But if you want adventure you need to be amenable to change."

Her lips part slightly. She's measuring her next words. "I'm new to adventure, Emanuel."

For some reason, my name on her lips pushes my heart against my damn ribcage. Something hot stirs in my lower abdomen.

"I'm the perfect man to do some exploring with."

"Then what's on the agenda?" she questions again.

I let out a chuckle. "What had you had in mind for the next few days?"

I'm not all that surprised when she pulls out a planner from the over the shoulder bag she's carrying. She lists off a glass bottom boat tour, hike of a local canyon to a waterfall, and she even scheduled in "relaxing time" by the pool or at the beach.

"The hike and boat tour can definitely be added to the

agenda. But let me surprise you with a few other additions to this list."

Her eyes narrow on me, contemplating. "You'll have me back home by midnight?" she teases.

I shake my head. "Hell no."

She giggles. "Okay," she finally responds.

Her agreeance settles something in my chest. As if I'd needed it to be able to fully enjoy the rest of my time here in Cabo before my cousin's wedding.

Chapter Three

Janine

I don't do things on a whim. I like my life neat and orderly. I like my vacations planned down to the hour, to the minute sometimes. And that's on the rare occasion that I do take a vacation. I'm saying all of this because the fact that I now find myself glancing around the small, glass bottom boat I'm in, all alone, looking for the man I came out here with, is beyond me.

And that's the reason I said yes to Emanuel's proposal. Why I agreed to giving him the next three days of my vacation. Because just looking into those honey brown eyes of his, I felt an excitement and anticipation that I hadn't felt in years. No. Truth be told, I'd never felt it. I came to Mexico searching for an adventure, but didn't even know it until I stared into those eyes. It feels as if I've reached a turning point in my life. Maybe that's a bit dramatic but saying yes to Emanuel felt like taking a leap of faith.

"Boo!"

"Ah!" I yell and flail so damn dramatically that I nearly tip the boat over.

All I can hear behind me is his deep laughter. A sound that shouldn't reach so deeply inside of my body that it feels as if it's taking me over, but it does.

"That wasn't funny!" I swat at him as he reaches the side of the boat. "You could've drowned."

"But I didn't. Were you frightened?"

I swallow and tighten my lips, not wanting to admit that when he jumped off the side of the boat and pretended as if something bit his leg, causing him to go under, that yes, I was scared shitless.

"You're an asshole."

He shrugs just before hoisting himself back onto the boat.

I watch as rivulets of saltwater run down his bronze, muscular chest and washboard abs. Not for the first time I notice a few scars along his abdomen and arms. They look like burn marks but I don't ask, out of politeness.

"You can ask me," he says as if reading my mind.

Briefly, I wonder how he knew what I was thinking, but when my gaze catches his again, I realize it's because he's watching me just as intently as I've been watching him. I still find I can't look into his eyes for too long because I begin to feel way too off balance.

"Are they from your job?" My voice is low, as if talking quietly will lessen the impact of the question.

"Yes." He nods.

"I'm sorry."

He looks at me quizzically, cocking his head to the side. "Do you even know what you're apologizing for?"

I blink before frowning. I start to say I'm apologizing for asking about the scars, but then remember he invited me to ask. Maybe the apology was for ... "I'm sorry you were injured doing your job."

"Injury is part of the job. No one becomes a firefighter and doesn't expect to get burned by a fire at least once or twice." He leans closer, so close our faces are only a few inches apart.

I find myself leaning closer as well. He smells like a mixture of saltwater and man. I catch the sight of a droplet of water just above his collarbone. It would only take another few inches for me to lean down and lick the water from his body. My mouth waters at the thought.

"Wanna know the secret?" he whispers, close to my ear.

"What's that?"

"Learn to live with the burn," he says before capturing my lips for our first kiss.

To say the kiss is potent would be an understatement. *Hot* doesn't even begin to describe it. More like searing. When I part my lips, allowing our tongues to touch for the first time, a feeling I've never felt before wells up in my body, starting from the soles of my feet. A feeling of excitement entangled with a deep yearning for more.

And Emanuel provides, pulling me in to deepen the kiss. He draws me closer, parting his legs so that my knees slide in between his, allowing us more proximity. His large, calloused hands brace the sides of my face, and his lips pull at mine, demanding more.

I'd kissed my ex-boyfriend for ten years, and not one time could I ever remember a kiss feeling like this.

Abruptly, Emanuel pulls back. His beautiful eyes hold a shimmer that hadn't been there before the kiss. He searches my own eyes for something. Maybe trying to figure out what the hell just happened, as I was. But before either one of us can speak, he pulls back, stands, and jumps fully in the water once again, splashing me.

"You got my hair wet!" I yell.

He just chuckles. "Get your ass in then."

A shiver runs through me as I stand.

"Hell no. Remove those shorts and T-shirt first. I want to see that sexy ass bikini you're wearing underneath."

Feeling desirable, and more importantly, safe, I lift the T-shirt and reveal the purple, green, and black African-print bikini top that comfortably holds my small breasts. Despite my less than *stacked* nature up top, Emanuel's eyes light up like a Christmas tree. This boosts my confidence even more as I unzip the denim shorts I wear and push them down over my hips, revealing the high waist bottoms of the swimsuit. I am almost taken aback by Emanuel's reaction as he continues to wade in the clear blue water. Hunger is the only way I can describe the look in his eyes.

Self-consciously, I look down at my bottoms, making

sure they are adjusted correctly. I run my hand alongside the gold strips of elastic that connect the front of the bottoms with the back, showing glimpses of the skin covering my hips.

"Get your ass in the water," Emanuel growls, beckoning me to do just that.

I take a step forward and then leap headfirst into the water. I barely swim a few feet before I'm splashed by water.

"Emanuel!" I yell only to be met with his laughter. A sound I find myself wanting to hear more of.

We spend the rest of the afternoon laughing, splashing each other, racing one another, and pointing out brightly colored tropical fish with the snorkeling masks we rented along with the boat. I don't remember a time ever having so much fun with a man.

****

Emanuel

"You cook like you dance," I state, glancing over at the sad looking concoction Nadine is making.

She peers up at me, lips turned downward. It is the cutest fucking thing ever.

"What is that supposed to mean?"

"Señorita Nadine," the head chef, and host of tonight's cooking class, interrupts before I can answer.

I frown not appreciating his closeness.

"Like this," he begins in accented English.

"I got it." Holding up my arm, I brace him from moving in any closer. And just to make sure we're clear, I glare at him. "I'll help her," I state firmly.

The chef holds up his arms, stepping away.

I turn back to Nadine who is none the wiser to what just happened as she stares down into her sad looking guacamole, biting her lower lip. I have to stifle a moan at the sight of her moistened bottom lip.

"I don't know how I messed this up," she mumbles.

I take a second to admire the above-the-knee black dress she wore to tonight's cooking class. The dress shows off her smooth, toned legs, and shapely hips and backside. The top of the dress has a sexy little cutout that shows just enough of the tops of her breasts to have left me hungering to lick them ever since she opened the door and I saw her in it, over an hour ago. I'd booked a cooking class for us to attend. There were four other couples in the class with us. We are preparing an authentic Mexican dinner: pico de gallo, guacamole, and handmade tortilla chips for the starters. Pork filled chiles rellenos, and chicken enchiladas with a mole sauce as the main course, and flan for dessert. We started the flan first since it took the longest to prepare between baking and letting it cool down afterwards. I'd had to takeover finishing our flan and getting it in the oven.

"You're overthinking it," I state, moving in behind her, letting my front press up against her backside. I smile to myself when her breath hitches. "It's not complicated. It's just food," I say in her ear.

I push one of the long braids over her shoulder, giving myself a better view of the dark brown, smooth skin of her long neck.

"What are you doing?" she questions, her voice low.

"Showing you how to cook." I press into her closer, essentially trapping her body between the counter and myself.

"Feel this," I say, placing the fresh avocado I just picked up in her hand. "How's it feel?"

"Kind of soft but firm."

I nod. "That means it's ready. Take the knife." I place the handle of the knife in her right hand and wrap my left hand around her left hand. "The best way to cut an avocado open is like this ..." I begin demonstrating, using her hands still in mine, cutting along the outside of an avocado and then splitting it open. Wordlessly, I continue using her hands to tap the sharp edge of the blade into seed, turning it and ultimately removing the seed, leaving the avocado meat behind. Together we scoop the fruit out into the granite mortar and pestle.

"Wait," I command when Nadine tries to get ahead of me to begin mashing the avocado. "Seasonings first."

"Why?"

"Because otherwise you'll have to add them at the end and then have to continue mashing out all of the chunks. The best guacamole is the chunky kind."

"Salt, right?" She reaches for the pink Himalayan salt that's in front of us.

"Just a pinch."

I release her hand to allow her to take just a pinch of salt and sprinkle it over the top of the guacamole.

"What else?"

"Do you like your food spicy or not so much?"

"Um, not too much spice."

"Great." I take the spicy pico de gallo that I just finished making and add a spoonful of it in.

She looks back over her shoulder, frowning.

"Trust me, you'll enjoy the spice." And without thought, I lean down and press a kiss to her pouting lips. In spite of the urge I have to deepen the kiss, I lift my head. I reach for the half of lime and squeeze it over the avocado, before gesturing toward the mortar and pestle and taking her hands into mine again.

"Now, we mash."

I move her hands, slowly, using the pestle to break the halves of the green fruit into smaller and smaller pieces until it forms a thick dip. Just as that happens, the timer we were given goes off, signaling that our tortillas are ready to come out of the oven. I grab the oven mitt and stand to the side slightly as I pull the oven open, reaching in for the tray holding our tortillas. Before closing, I check on our flan on the bottom rack. It's looking good.

"How's the flan?" Nadine asks as I arrive back to our counter with the tortillas, sliding them into the wooden basket that's been lined with paper.

"Should be done in about ten minutes."

She nods. "I'm starving," she comments, eyeing the chips but holding back to let them cool off.

I pick one of the chips up and blow on it to make sure it's cooled down enough. Dipping it into the guacamole we'd just made, I then lift it to those perfect lips of hers. "Taste."

She hesitates before doing so. But when her eyes catch mine, her lips part, allowing me to slide the chip inside of her mouth. A small amount of guacamole gets caught at the corner of her lips. I use my thumb to wipe it away, and raise it to my own mouth, sucking it off my finger.

"Perfect."

Her eyelids flutter. "Yes," she says, a sexy ass note in her tone.

We spend the rest of the night in the cooking class, me helping Nadine to cook, relying less on the instructions and more on her gut. She's reluctant. I surmise it's how she's lived her life up until this point. Follow the rules, if you want to get ahead. Her entire demeanor screams it. I look forward to seeing her break out of that more and more as we spend time together over the next few days.

****

Janine

"I'm stuffed," I hum as we arrive at the door of my hotel room.

Emanuel looks down at me, those sizzling eyes of his dissecting my every move. At least, that's how it feels.

"Thank you for planning such a great day." He'd had the day all planned out since we left for breakfast in the morning. A glass bottom boat and snorkeling excursion followed by a light lunch on the beach, a walking tour of the city and an opportunity to pick up some souvenirs before heading back to our rooms to shower and change before our three-hour long cooking class. It was a great class; the food was delicious as well as the drinks.

"We've still got two more days, butterfly."

I wrinkle my forehead. "What's with the butterfly thing?"

A slow smile materializes on that handsome face of his, and it's far from innocent. "It's how I see you."

I don't get the chance to inquire what he means by that because he dips his head and captures my lips with his own. I don't know if it's the three mojitos I had with dinner, but this time, I'm much less caught off guard by the kiss. I don't hesitate in parting my lips for him and giving in to the moment. I've wanted him to kiss me all day since that first time.

When his hands encircle my waist, pulling me into his hard body, I allow myself to be pulled. I gasp into his mouth at the feeling of his erection as it pokes my belly. He chuckles against my mouth before biting my lower lip, eliciting a moan from me. I should be embarrassed at how turned on I am. But I'm not. I want more.

Lifting my arms, I wrap them around his broad shoulders, pulling his body to mine as much as he's pulling me into his. Our tongues, explore, taste, and retreat, repeating over and over again the deep inspection of one another's bodies. Emanuel lets out a tight groan and my nipples instantly pebble.

I feel one of his large hands moving down the side of my body, reaching my thigh and moving around to the front, reaching upwards to my inner thigh. I gasp when his strong hand reaches the sensitive skin in between my legs. A place only one man ever had the privilege of touching. Shame isn't what I feel, however. It's excitement. And anticipation.

Emanuel knows this because he draws out every second as he trails his hand up, closer and closer to my hidden treasure. When he reaches the apex of my thighs, bumping against the cotton thong I wear, his thumb begins searching for my clit. He makes tiny circles, rubbing against my sensitive flesh.

I moan into his mouth.

His other hand wraps around the back of my head, taking the ends of my braids and pulling my head back, giving him a better angle to continue stealing the air from my lungs with his kiss, while his lower hand sends my entire body spinning.

I cling onto his shoulders when his prodding below intensifies. His thumb flicks my clit once, twice, three times, and before I know what is happening, my eyes squeeze shut, and I pull back from his mouth, burying my head into his chest, instinctively clamping my mouth shut as an orgasm takes hold.

I continue to pant against his body for a long while.

I don't even know how long it is until he leans down and whispers in my ear, "We still have two more days, butterfly. Go inside and get some rest. I'll pick you up for breakfast in the morning."

He takes a step backwards, releasing me.

I'm too hungover from the orgasm to be embarrassed. Emanuel watches me carefully as I dig into my clutch and pull out my hotel room key. On shaky legs I turn and step inside, pausing to give him one last look. He's watching me with a hooded gaze and dark look in his eyes. I shake my head, thinking I'm just imagining things before turning and shutting the door behind me.

Leaning back against the door, I listen to his footsteps as they retreat down the hall to his own room.

I sigh in relief. Had he asked me to come inside, I probably would've let him, given the state I was in. And I know I'd wake up tomorrow regretting it. Somehow, I sensed he knew that. Closing my eyes, I let out a breath, before smiling at the anticipation of seeing him the following morning.

Chapter Four

Emanuel

She would've regretted it, I remind myself as I lay in my bed the following morning, staring up at the sky.

The cresting waves and saltwater breeze entering my room through my opened balcony door isn't enough to wipe away the memory of the night before. She was primed and ready. If not before, then definitely after the orgasm I gave her with just my fucking hand. And never in my life, had the idea of how a woman's feelings for me would change afterwards, stopped me from getting my dick wet.

I wasn't the longterm kind of guy and I had no qualms about letting it be known. But Nadine ...

She had me thinking differently.

And I knew that wasn't even her real fucking name.

I grunt in anger when the phone on the nightstand by my bed rings. I can tell by the ring that it's not a call from inside of the hotel. And there's only one person who has my room's direct number.

"What?"

"What the hell crawled up your ass?"

"You. What the hell do you want, Christian? It's barely seven o'clock."

"Oh, am I interrupting quality time with the next lady in your life?" He snickers.

"Fuck off." Sometimes my cousin is just as bad as the guys at the fire station.

He laughs again before clearing his throat. "There's been a change of plans."

I sit up in the bed. "Everything all right?"

"Yeah, yeah. But there's been a delay on the family's arrival. Something about the brother of the groom and his cakes or whatever the fuck," he mumbles. "Anyway, I need to fly back to the States, to help figure out how to get all of his shit down here before Emilio and his bride arrive."

I frown. Emilio is Christian's older brother. And there's something he isn't telling me. I don't prod. While we may be related by blood, I didn't come up with these family members, nor do I work in the family business. While Christian and I are relatively close, Emilio and I have only met a handful of times because he lives full time in Palermo.

"Anything you need me to do while you're gone?"

"No. It's all being taken care of. If there are any problems with your room just let the front desk know. I'll see you in a couple of days."

I nod even though he can't see me. He tells me a few more details before we hang up.

Emilio is getting married here in Cabo in a few days. While his soon-to-be wife is from the U.S. and he is from Italy, she wanted to get married in what she called a *neutral* location, so they chose Mexico. The truth is, however, that there is no neutral location where Emilio and the family are concerned.

Even in Mexico, people bend to the Genovese family name. It's a sight I'm still getting used to after six years, especially given the way I grew up.

I blink, turning my head to focus on the ceiling again, pushing old memories out of my mind. Folding my arms under my head and staring upwards, my thoughts once more float back to the night before.

Nadine.

Not her real name. I could easily find out her real name but I tell myself for the hundredth time that I don't want it. This isn't anything that will extend past the next two days. I don't want it to.

Again, I have to continuously remind myself of that declaration as I climb out of bed, shower, and get dressed in a pair of swim trunks, sleeveless T-shirt, and pool shoes. By eight-thirty I am exiting my room heading for her.

She answers after the second knock.

"Good morning," she greets with a smile, causing something funny to happen inside of my chest.

I don't try to decipher why seeing her already dressed in a floral dress, which covers the bathing suit top's black straps that reach up to tie around her neck, has me so excited, but it does.

"You're wearing a different suit from yesterday," I say out loud.

She glances over her shoulder back into her room. "The one from yesterday is still drying."

"I bet it is."

Her gaze narrows, trying to figure out the meaning behind my words. I don't give any further explanation. Instead, I reach out my arm for her to wrap her around. She does, and I wait for her to shut and make sure the door is locked behind us. The doors lock immediately here at the hotel but she always double checks, I've noticed.

"Breakfast is at the pool this morning," I tell her before pressing the down button for the elevator.

"I didn't know they served breakfast poolside."

"They're making an exception for us," I reply easily. The family name comes in handy, even if it's not my actual last name.

"Oh," she says with raised eyebrows. "So you're still not going to tell me what's on the agenda for today?"

I give her a sideways grin. "You don't like just going with the flow, huh?" I pivot and step aside as the elevator doors open, stepping off first to hold them open for her exit.

"I can." Her voice is defensive. "I just like knowing what I'm doing on my vacation."

"Butterfly, this has become *our* vacation."

Shit.

Where the hell had that come from?

Nadine seems just as surprised by my comment as I am, but I won't take it back. "You agreed to give me your final three remaining days. That makes this our vacation."

She looks at me for a moment and then shrugs. "You're right."

We make it out to the bar by the pool where there is a sign reading *Emanuel y Nadine.* The hostess welcomes us, and shows us to the bar. There's no one else in here at this hour. I made sure of that.

"What would you like to drink?"

"Mango juice, please," Nadine says.

"Make it two," I add.

"They're bringing us the chorizo sausage and egg breakfast burritos," I mention once the hostess leaves us.

"Sounds good. How did you sleep?"

"Well." I move my hand to her right knee, letting it linger there. Again I'm paid off for my touch with an increase in the beats of the small vein on her neck. "How about you?" My voice has deepened on its own.

"N-not bad."

"After that orgasm I bet." I grin when a tiny gasp escapes her lips. She probably thought I was gentleman enough not to mention our little nightcap. Silly woman. I've never been a gentleman a day in my life.

"Are you always like this? Or is this just the vacation you?"

I lift an eyebrow. "Always like what?"

"Saying whatever's on your mind. Fly by the seat of your pants ... I don't know ... like this?" she finishes, gesturing toward my body with her hands.

I shrug. "My nickname in the military was Chaos."

"Seriously?" There's a grin on her face. "I should've figured. Wait ..." She pauses as our breakfast is brought out and placed in front of us.

We remain seated on the bar's stool, our bodies turned toward one another instead of facing the bar directly.

"Let me know if you need anything," our waitress says before departing.

"You were in the military?"

I nod.

"For how long?"

"Eight years."

"What branch?"

"Army."

"And then you became a firefighter?"

"Right."

"It ... suits you."

"How so?" I inquire, suddenly interested in hearing her

take on me, as I take a bite of my burrito. I don't miss how her eyes fall to my lips as I chew. I swallow and learn forward. "I really wouldn't do that if I were you," I growl.

"Do what?"

"Look at me like you're prepared for me to bend you over this fucking bar."

"Oh my god!" she screeches.

"Those are the exact words you'd be screaming."

"Emanuel!" Her voice is scolding and her cheeks inflamed.

I shrug. "I'm just warning you."

"Finish your breakfast."

I chuckle but do take another bite of my burrito.

Breakfast finishes without much fanfare, and before we know it, we're interrupted by a spry, older Mexican man dressed in a white-collared, short-sleeved shirt and khaki shorts.

"Listo, Sr. Allende?" He turns to me, smiling, holding up his clasped hands as if he can't contain his own excitement.

"I am, Sr. Gonzalez." I look to Nadine making sure she's finished her breakfast.

Her eyes are curious her gaze bounces between myself and the new man that's just entered. "So ...?" she drags out the question.

My smile widens. "We're going parasailing."

And just as I knew they would, her eyes enlarge, nearly bugging out of her head. Her head immediately begins shaking from side to side. I don't pay that any mind, stepping beside her and practically lifting her off the barstool, pushing her toward the door. We follow behind Sr. Gonzalez.

"Emanuel, I cannot go parasailing!" she insists even as we continue down the concrete walkway to where Sr. Gonzalez has parked his small, four door vehicle.

"You can and you will," I order as I hold the door open for her.

In spite of her protests, Nadine easily gets in the car, telling me all I need to know. She wants to go parasailing, there's just some fear. Which is fine, we can work past that.

"I'm not doing this. I'll just watch you do it and take pictures or something," she says, folding her arms.

"Why?"

Turning, she gives me an incredulous look. "Because I don't want to."

I reach up, tugging at her chin for her to release the pout on her lips. Not because I don't like the look but because if she keeps that shit up I might decide to take her ass in the back of this car. And I highly doubt Sr. Gonzalez included seeing *that* as part of his hourly rate.

She swats my hand away.

"Why?" I question again.

She remains silent.

"You're afraid of heights, aren't you?" It wasn't that she couldn't swim. We'd spent half of the afternoon out in the water the day before and she had no problem keeping up.

"So what if I am?"

My hand goes to her knee again. "It's not a problem, butterfly. I'll be right there with you."

She glances my way again, and her face softens.

In less than ten minutes we arrive at the beach where Sr. Gonzalez keeps his speedboat.

"Ah! Put me down!" Nadine insists after I catch up behind her, lifting her into the air, to hold her in the cradle position.

"Afraid I'll drop you?"

"Yes! Put me down," she insists, squirming.

"I won't let you fall," I assert, my voice deepening.

She stops squirming and looks me in the eyes.

I stare back directly into hers. "You have nothing to be afraid of ... okay?" I tell her with a seriousness in my tone that surprises even me.

She doesn't say anything. Instead, she wraps her arms tightly around my neck, silently conveying her trust. Warmth blossoms in my chest as I carry her toward the boat. I loathe that I have to separate our bodies so we can actually climb onto the boat.

"Thank you," she says lightly once I climb aboard after helping her on.

Sr. Gonzalez, in his broken English, begins to explain the waters we're about to parasail on. He directs the boat far offshore, as to decrease the risk of running into any swimmers while moving. One of Sr. Gonzalez' employees came with us to assist him while we were parasailing.

Once we come to a stop, he begins giving us instructions on how to properly wear our life jackets and strap ourselves into the harness. However, when I see him struggling to explain everything in English, I tell him it's okay to switch to his native tongue. I simply translate the instructions to Nadine.

"You're fluent in Spanish?"

"Appears so," I respond, while tugging on the snaps of her life jacket to make sure they're secure. "How's that feel?"

"Pretty good. How long have you spoken Spanish?"

"Long time." Pulling the harness up around her legs, I allow my fingers to graze the smooth skin as I go. I don't miss the shiver that courses through her body. As I kneel down in front of her, I allow my fingers to rove over the sensitive skin in between her legs. Peering up, I see her eyelids are hooded. She's remembering the previous night, just as I am.

"Okay ..." begins Sr. Gonzalez.

I stand and snap my life jacket closed, securing it and then stepping into my own harness. We already agreed that I would go up first, to give Nadine a sense of security, to see how it's done. She'll go up alone after me, and then we'll do some parasailing together.

I watch Nadine holding her breath as I'm slowly raised higher and higher. Sr. Gonzalez heads to the steering wheel, taking the boat out of its parked position and hitting the gas to get us all moving again. I am smacked in the face by the wind mixed with the smell of the saltwater. It feels invigorating. It's a beautiful, clear day in Cabo, granting me the ability to see for miles. Not only can I see the entire beach we're on, but two and three beaches down shore. I don't bother pulling out my phone to take pictures. I'd rather take it all in and store these images in my memory bank. All too soon, the ride ends, and I'm being lowered to the boat, but I'm even more excited for Nadine to try it.

"Are you sure these straps are secure?"

"He's sure," I answer, using my hands to double check all of the equipment and make sure it's fastened correctly. "Are you ready?"

She nods her head in the affirmative, a nervous smile on her lips.

"You'll be fine." Lowering, I press a quick kiss to her lips. The tension in her shoulders lets up slightly.

I step back and she starts moving backwards from me, the natural propulsion of the sail beginning to carry her higher and higher. She raises up even higher when the boat picks up speed. I resist the urge to yell at Sr. Gonzalez to slow the boat down for some reason. Not having her in my grasp begins to cause me nervousness for some reason.

I move closer to the edge of the boat to get a better look at her face. Squinting, I work to see if I can pinpoint any signs of distress. I tell myself it's just because I promised her that she would be okay with me. I never break a fucking promise.

Relief courses through my body when I hear her giggling. "This is beautiful!" she calls down, her voice full of a lightness I haven't heard before.

"Are you holding on tight enough?" I cup my mouth to shout to her.

She glances down at her hands, then back to me. She nods. "Yeah, I think so. Whoah" she yelps when the boat hits a small wave.

"Watch the fuck out!" I angrily growl at the man steering the boat.

He looks at me in confusion. "Sorry," he hurriedly responds.

I turn back to Nadine, whose legs are happily swinging as she looks around at the same views I was privy to not too long ago.

"Bring her down," I turn and insist.

Sr. Gonzalez and his employee seem confused.

I repeat myself in Spanish.

"Is something wrong?"

"I want to go up there with her."

Nodding, Sr. Gonzalez begins slowing the boat down, causing Nadine's parachute to fall lower and lower, until she reaches the water. I help the employee bring her back onto the boat. Minutes later, we're both strapped into the harnesses and slowly rising off the back of the boat, moving higher and higher.

"This is fun. Thank you for convincing me to do this," she says cheerily once we reach the maximum height. "I doubt I would've done this on my own."

"Glad I could pop that cherry for you." My entire body feels more alive when she throws her head back, laughing at my words.

"C'mere," I nearly groan.

She leans toward me, and I reward her by grazing my lips against hers. A small sigh escapes her lips.

Something over Nadine's shoulder catches my eye, causing me to pull back. "Look." I point in the direction.

She turns and gasps. "No way!" she exclaims at the sight that continues to hold my attention as well. "Another one!" she yells, pointing as the fin of what I presume to be a humpback whale rises in the distance. "I read whale sightings were common in this area."

The scene is breathtaking. I can't tell which view holds my attention more—the whales or the enthusiastic smile plastered on Nadine's face. Both are sights to behold.

The rest of the afternoon is spent on the boat, inching closer and closer to the whales so Nadine can take at least a hundred pictures of them. I had to pay Sr. Gonzalez extra for that, but to see her excitement is well worth it.

Chapter Five

Janine

"Where are we going tonight?" I question as Emanuel leads me off the elevators and into the lobby of our hotel. Once again, he refuses to tell me what his plans are until the last minute. The only thing he told me was to wear something sexy with high heels.

Knowing him in the span of the few days that I have, sexy could mean a lot of different things. The man could be unpredictable at times. Jumping off boats, going parasailing and hang gliding in the same day. Yes, that was the second part of our adventure yesterday after we got off the boat. There was another guide just waiting to drive us about thirty minutes away where we could hang glide. I put up more of a fight about that than I had over parasailing, but in the end, Emanuel won, assuring me that it was safe and he wouldn't let anything happen to me. Earlier today we hiked the canyon I'd had on my list, and of course once we reached the waterfall, Emanuel was one of the first to take the leap over. After something like a hundred assurances from him and the tour guide that it was safe, I jumped as well. Most exhilarating thing I'd ever done. And worth it when Emanuel wrapped his arms around me, once I broke the surface of the water, telling me he was proud of me.

In spite of his seemingly unpredictable nature, I trusted

him when he promised to keep me safe. So far, I haven't been let down.

"First, we need to get some food in you so you can keep up the rest of the night," he replies, as we pass through the double doors of the front lobby, stepping out into the warm night air. "Your dress is perfect by the way," he says in a low voice behind me, his warm breath caressing the back of my neck.

Swallowing, I turn my head to look up at him over my shoulder. My knees weaken a little when I find his eyes searching the length of my body.

The sleeveless, long, red dress is classy enough to make me feel comfortable in it, but with the high split that shows off a huge portion of my thigh, along with the deep, plunging neckline and backless nature, it's my definition of sexy. Particularly when paired with the same gold, strappy heels I donned that first night I went out with the women and danced with Emanuel.

"Thank you."

He moves to my side and pulls open the door of the awaiting taxi, allowing me to get in first. Once he's inside, he gives the driver the name of the restaurant we're headed to, in perfect Spanish ... or at least it sounds perfect to my untrained ears.

The driver, noting Emanuel's Spanish, kicks up a conversation with him. I pick up some of the words in the exchange thanks to the few classes I took back in college.

Emanuel suddenly turns to me, asking, "Did you have fun today?"

"I don't know. It depends on how hard it's going to be getting the sand and dirt out of my hair," I tease.

He grins. "Won't be too bad."

I shake my head. "I can't believe you took me hang gliding. I would've never thought to do something like that here."

"It's a good thing I was here to save you."

I cover my mouth, giggling only because I don't want to admit out loud that I'm glad he's here as well. I'm certain my vacation would've turned out much differently if he hadn't. I likely would've had fun but not nearly as much fun without him. It's been a long time since I let my hair down, so to speak.

"What are you thinking?" Though his voice is low, the deep richness of his tone pulls me back to the present.

Biting the inside of my cheek, I hesitate. "Tomorrow," I eventually respond. I hate to even bring it up, but my flight back home is scheduled for the next morning. We haven't even mentioned seeing one another beyond this night. Hell, I hadn't even given him my real name, a decision I regretted more and more as the hours passed. The first day it would've been fine to clear it up, telling him I had given him a fake name because I didn't trust him. But as the day wore on, I felt more and more silly about it, and then the next day, and then the next. Now, we are three days in, I'm leaving in the morning and he doesn't even know my real name.

"Don't think about tomorrow. We still have a full night ahead of us."

I find his words comforting. The questions of tomorrow remain but fall to the background as I realize what is in front of me right now. A smile grows across my face.

"And you better feed me something delicious on my final night," I tease.

"I've definitely got that covered," he says smoothly, and I get the distinct impression he's not just talking about food.

Thankfully, I'd opted to wear the new adhesive bra I purchased on a whim prior to my trip. Otherwise, I'm certain my nipples would be poking through the thin material of this dress.

Minutes later, we pull up to a seafood restaurant. As soon as I exit the car, with Emanuel's assistance I am hit by the smells of the food cooking inside. My stomach begins doing tumbles of excitement. When Emanuel slides his hand down the bare skin of my back to reach my covered lower back, my belly begins vibrating with a very different type of excitement. Both hungers, but for disparate things.

We are immediately shown to a table by the window, thanks to Emanuel making a reservation. Throughout the night

I can't help but feel cared for by the big and little things. The fact that he showed so much care by planning ahead, requesting a window table because he knows I like looking outside as I eat, the fact that he remembered how much I enjoy seafood. To someone else those things may not matter much, but getting this kind of attention from a man that I've only known a few days feels almost like a dream. I'd been with someone for years who never put this much thought behind taking me out. Not often, anyway.

"Caught you thinking again," he says as he escorts us out of the restaurant and into the night air.

I sigh. "You did." I pause, waiting for him to respond or ask what I was thinking about as he'd done earlier, but he remains silently watching me, as we continue down the street. His silence strangely makes me want to tell him exactly what's on my mind.

"You can be with someone for years and never really know them. Or they, you." I sigh.

Emanuel stops and comes to stand directly in front of me, not seeming to care that we are in the middle of a busy sidewalk. Passersby are forced to walk around us but his sole focus remains on me. His hands raise to cup my face.

"If someone had you and never got to know the real you, then they didn't deserve you to begin with."

I try to ingest his words, to decipher their meaning.

However, when his head dips, allowing his lips to clash with mine, my brain short circuits. There is no room left for thinking, just feeling. And what a great feeling it is. His lips are soft yet demanding. When the tip of his tongue scrapes along the roof of my mouth, it feels as if he's trying to pull my very soul from out of my body. I moan into his mouth before pulling back.

In my peripheral, I see people walking past us, and even notice a few stares. "Emanuel?" I whisper.

"Yes, butterfly?"

My eyelids suddenly feel heavy and I close my eyes for a second, gathering my next words. "Take me back to your hotel room."

He'd made plans for us to go out dancing after dinner—that's where we are headed, right down the street from the restaurant we'd just left—but I was in the mood for a different kind of dancing. And by the look in those honey eyes that had darkened with lust, I could tell that he was ready for another kind of dancing as well.

Before I can speak my next words, his hand goes up, flagging down a passing cab. As soon as it pulls over, Emanuel opens the door open and helps me inside. He quickly tells the driver the name and address of our hotel, and we are off in a matter of minutes.

A silence grows between the two of us. The comfort of

my hand in his as he firmly holds onto it is almost enough to keep the doubts from creeping in. Unfortunately, years of overthinking and analyzing begin to resurface. Am I making too rash a decision? Will he look at me differently if I go through with this? Does it even matter? Will it be worth it? Will I satisfy him?

That final question is the one that has me holding my breath and biting my lower lip.

"Look at me," he commands firmly, pulling me out of the musings of my imagination and back to those sexy as sin eyes of his.

I stare up at him as he cups my face.

"Stop thinking so damn much. Just feel."

I swallow and nod.

But my thinking is really put to a halt when he kisses me again.

I don't know how long we remain in that particular lip lock, and any thoughts I might have about what the driver must think of us full-on making out in the backseat of his cab don't even come to mind. All that matters is that Emanuel doesn't stop kissing me.

Chapter Six

Emanuel

A better man than I would probably ask if she is certain she wants to do this. A more admirable man would see the nervousness in her eyes and opt to take her back to her hotel room. Hell, an exceptional man would even choose to stay with her in her hotel room, talking all night until she or they both fall asleep, to ease her worry.

But I am not that man.

As I stand in front of Nadine in my hotel room, with all of the lights turned on so I can see the entirety of her body, I know I am weaker than the man I just described. Because as I allow my eyes to rove over the dark brown hue of her skin as it shines against the red fabric of her dress, and the way her legs look extra sleek and toned due to the high heels and revealing split, I know there is no way this woman is leaving this hotel room without my having tasted, touched, and viewed every inch of her frame.

But she is nervous.

I can see that in the way she keeps shifting from one foot to the other. And by the way she keeps chewing on her lower lip. I glance toward the hotel's bar. There's an array of drinks I could offer her but I won't. We're going to do this sober, in our right minds, so that when we both leave this country, the memory of this night will remain forever with the both of us.

Stepping closer, I take her face into my hands. Her hands immediately go up, encircling my wrists. I pull her face to me and she acquiesces in a way that has me wondering what it would be like if I made her mine. Permanently.

I push that thought right out the window. She's leaving tomorrow. I'm leaving a few days later. No need to complicate this thing.

"I'm going to strip you naked ... except for the heels. Those are staying on for a little while longer," I say.

Her breath hitches in surprise. She wasn't expecting those words.

"Turn around," I order, releasing her face.

"Why?"

"Turn around," I repeat more sternly, moving her body with my hands.

"Oh," she says as she takes in the vision in front of her in the full-length mirror.

I place a kiss to her shoulder, and she shivers. I begin to lower the straps of her dress, letting the tips of my fingers trail down her arms as the top of her dress lowers. I swallow and more and more of her smooth skin is revealed. When the dress reaches her hips, I don't stop there. I push the dress over her hips and let it flow freely to the floor.

"You're fucking gorgeous," I growl just before wrapping my arm around her waist and burying my face into the crook of her neck.

"That feels nice," she whispers, leaning her body and head against my chest.

Letting my free hand snake around her waist, I run my fingers along the top edge of the cotton bikini cut panties she's wearing. Her breath increases and she raises her hand to run her fingers through my hair. Growling, I nip the soft skin of her shoulder with my teeth, and my cock jumps in my pants.

I should've warned her that a woman running their fingers through my hair is one of my main turn ons. I allow my hand to move farther down inside of her panties to graze the neatly trimmed pubic hair that's there. I reach lower until I can feel the hot, sticky wetness that has already begun to pool.

Another short moan is pulled from her lips when my first finger enters the source of her wetness.

"Shit," I groan from how tight she is. I add a second finger while adjusting my hand to use my thumb to massage her already swollen button. The feeling of my working both her pussy and her clit excites her because her hips begin moving at an awkward pace, trying to keep up with my ministrations. She continues to nibble at her lower lip, eyes tightly closed. Her orgasm is building. I pull my eyes from her to the mirror in front of us, granting me a better view of the entire scene before us. My eyes dip to her covered breasts and I frown. I want to see all of her. With my free hand I maneuver the adhesive bra away from her body, allowing the fullness of both her breasts to be seen. I take one into my hand. They are smaller than a handful considering my large hands, but they're fucking perfect.

I tease and prod a hardened nipple while my other hand continues to work her core. Eventually, I pull my two fingers free from her body and concentrate on working her clitoris. Within minutes her body begins tightening and shivering as I wring the orgasm out of her body.

I don't give her time to recuperate before spinning her around and fusing our mouths together. I can still feel the shivers as they course through her body. Stooping low, I pick her up by both legs to wrap around my waist and walk us to the huge bed at the center of the room.

As I place Nadine down on the bed her eyes pop open. Her eyes dart around the room a little as she attempts to reorient herself. It's a look I've seen plenty of times from women. When her eyes land on me, satisfied expression appears. It also seems like she wants to say something but holds back.

My eyes narrow. I don't like that. I don't want her to hold anything back from me, not tonight.

"Now, it's my turn to taste you," I assert while pushing her back against the bed by her shoulders.

"Taste?" I hear her say as I begin pulling her panties free

from her body.

"Spread your legs, butterfly." I don't wait for her to begin moving, instead helping her to separate her legs with my own hands. I place her legs over my shoulders, and glance up to see the view of her heels resting on my shoulders in the mirror. The sight alone has my cock bumping against the zipper of my pants, demanding to be set free. *In due time,* I silently tell my body. For now, we have work to do. *I plan on wringing out at least one more orgasm from her body before I get my dick wet.*

That is my final thought before I lower my face and use my thumb and forefinger to spread her pussy lips, granting me a beautiful view of her pink, wet core. I move my tongue to first lick and taste the lips surrounding her core. Another hitch of her breath followed by her back bowing slightly. But that response isn't nearly enough for me. I fully encircle her distended button with my mouth and start suckling at it.

The heels of her shoes begin digging into my shoulders and upper back. If I were naked they would likely cause scratches but that certainly wouldn't deter me from pulling this next orgasm from her body with my mouth alone. I continue tasting and priming her body, cupping and squeezing the skin surrounding her hips with my large hands. I pull her closer to my mouth as she attempts to wiggle away. She's not going anywhere.

I hear a deep sigh, followed by an arching of her back and her hands tightly gripping the bed sheets. I can feel the tension from her body releasing as the orgasm rolls throughout her body. Her breathing is harsh but other than that, very few sounds emanate from her mouth.

Moving back, I sit up on my knees to give myself a clear view of her face.

Her eyes are shut, and her lips are twisted in ecstasy, savoring the last vestiges of her climax. Slowly, her eyes peel open, pinning me. They are now filled with a light I haven't seen in them before.

I begin undressing, unbuttoning the shirt I wore and undoing the buckle of my belt and jeans. Then I push myself off the bed so I can strip out of my clothing completely. Opening the top drawer of the nightstand, I pull out a box of condoms.

"Have you ever put one of these on a man before?" I question, knowing the answer before I even ask it.

She shakes her head.

"Good," I climb back onto the bed, "I'll pop that cherry, too."

After helping her to sit up, I hand her the condom. She tears it open and pulls out the lubricated, latex protection. Taking the wrapper from her, I toss it over onto the floor somewhere.

"Pinch the tip," I instruct.

She does so.

"Now ..." I guide her free hand to my erect cock.

Her fingers curl around me and she looks up at me in shock. I'm sure it's due to her realizing she can't actually fit her fingers all of the way around it. That nervousness enters those golden pupils but I don't allow her to go down that road of thinking. Pulling the hand with the condom to my erection, I show her how to cover the tip. Slowly, she guides the condom down my shaft. It may have only been a handful of seconds, but the ache that develops in my body tells me that it's a few seconds too long.

I reach around the back of her head, pulling her to me, kissing her with a deepness that both of our bodies demand. She keeps up with the kiss, giving as well as she is getting. Pressing her backwards onto the bed, I cover her with my body. Her arms move around to my back, pulling me even more into her body. There is not enough space between our bodies for even air to get through. I don't want there to be any separation between us. Neither one of us does.

While remaining with my lips on hers, I adjust my hands so they are reaching underneath her thighs, bringing her legs to once again wrap around my waist. Positioning myself at her apex, I begin to guide my cock inside of her body. Her breathing increases as I fuse our bodies together.

I grunt. "You're so fucking tight."

Adjusting, I hike her right leg even higher up my body, giving myself just a quarter inch more room. A little farther and I am fully seated inside of her body. She wraps her arms tighter around me, silently begging me to give her more. Her words aren't there but her body tells me what she needs.

I pull out and push fully back into her, again and again, starting a rhythm that comes naturally. Her breathing moves in spurts, but her kiss-swollen lips remain quiet. Needing more from her, I lower my head, kissing her and using one of my hands to again play with her nipples. This causes her back to arch farther off the bed and a small moan to escape, before she cuts it off. Wondering what that was about, I pull back to look down at her, but her head lifts and she captures my lips with her own.

The kiss increases the urgency of the moment. I have to pull another orgasm from her. That need drives me to increase the speed of my hips and angle my body so that I penetrate every inch of her insides. Shortly, I feel her inner thighs begin to tremble. A suffocated moan breaks through the kiss as she comes for the third time.

Not until I feel her release do I let my own body go, surrendering to my climax. The tingling that started in the soles of my feet, works its way up my legs, through the rest of my body, completely engulfing me. I pull Nadine to me tightly, using her body as a comfort to release my own pleasure.

Before I allow my body to completely give out from the pleasure-induced exhaustion, I turn us so that she is now laying on top of me, with my back to the bed. It takes both of us a long time to recapture a steady breathing rhythm.

****

Janine

That. Was. Insane.

Is sex supposed to be like that? I question in my head, as my eyes continue to wander around the now darkened room. After that incredible, mind-altering third orgasm, Emanuel got up from the bed, turned off the lights, and went to the bathroom. He came back with a warm cloth to clean me up before climbing back into bed, pulling me to him.

Now, I'm laying in his strong arms, wondering what the hell is going on because I'm certain sex with someone for the first time isn't supposed to go like that. *Is it?*

Though the room is silent, he's not asleep either. The movement of his fingers trailing up and down my arm as I lay on his chest makes that clear. I suddenly find myself wanting to ask him all types of questions. I want to know more about him—like what are his hobbies, why did he become a firefighter, where did he grow up, and what do his parents do for a living? However, those very questions terrify me because what if he asks me the same? I can't answer them. I haven't even given the man my real name.

But I still want to talk. I need to hear his voice so that I can believe that the last few hours haven't all been a figment of my imagination.

"What brought you to Cabo San Lucas?" I ask, hoping that's a safe question. Besides, he pretty much guessed accurately why I came to Cabo on my own, the least he could do was tell me his reasoning.

"A wedding."

My head snaps up and my eyes bulge. "Emanuel, if you tell me you're in Cabo for your own wedding, I'm going to—" I don't get the chance to finish my threat when he begins chuckling. The deep sound of his laughter pulls an errant smile from my own lips.

"No, butterfly. I wouldn't deceive you like that. My cousin. He's getting married in a few days. I came down early to vacation and hang out with my other cousin before the wedding."

Suddenly, I feel a sense of guilt. "You came down to spend time with your family but you've been with me the last three days?"

Shaking his head, he wraps his thumb and forefinger around my chin, pulling me to him for a kiss. "I spent time with who I wanted to. Christian had to go out of town for a few days anyway. He arrives back in Cabo tomorrow with the rest of the family."

I frown. "So, I was your back-up plan?"

Why did I ask such a silly question? Because as soon as I do I find myself flat on my back, staring up into the glinting eyes of Emanuel's. He eases his body in between my legs.

"Does that feel like a back-up plan to you?" his deep voice questions as he grinds his cock against my core.

I can't speak so I shake my head no.

"Good. I ditched Christian for you long before he had to go out of town." He lowers and grants me a kiss before pulling back.

A wash of sadness suddenly overcomes me. The realization that in a few short hours I will be on a plane to Williamsport and am likely to never see him again hits me. I won't ask for more than the last three days, or this night. I've learned the hard way that if a man really wants more with you, he'll pursue it. He'll make his feelings clear.

"Stop thinking."

I look back up at Emanuel.

He lowers, kissing me and pushing all thoughts of the next day away. Right now is all that matters.

Chapter Seven

Emanuel

Today is a good fucking day. I'm excited and ready to get out of my place and head to work. However, when I lower the navy blue shirt that reads 'Williamsport Fire Department' on the top left, over my head and stare into the mirror in front of me, the ache of emptiness that's been with me for the past week doesn't subside.

Before this day, nothing felt better than putting on my uniform. Nothing. Couple this with the fact that it is my first day starting with my new squad, a squad I'd been angling to be on for over a year and I am fucking confused. No, that's a lie. I'm not confused at all. I know exactly why I'm feeling the way I am.

It began the morning I woke up with Nadine still in my arms. The feeling expanded and grew tenfold once I dropped her off at the airport and we said our final good-byes. As I watched her walk farther and farther away from me, I couldn't help but notice the feeling of loneliness grow. It's an emotion I hadn't felt in a very long time. Not since I was a young boy wishing for a family of my own. But I gave that shit up a long time ago.

Now here I am, on one of the greatest days of my career, pining after a woman that I'd only known a few days.

"Let it go," I chide myself as I tuck my shirt into my

black, department-issued pants, before buttoning them. Giving myself one last look over to make sure my uniform is impeccable, I head out of my bedroom, cross my spacious living room, and pluck my keys off the wall mount where they hang. After I grab my bomber jacket, I head out the door, locking it behind me.

"Hey, Emanuel."

Turning, I see the real estate agent that I'd worked with to find my condo greeting me. "Jack, how's it going?"

He steps over the threshold, closing the door of the condo directly across from me.

"Same ol' same. Got a new tenant for this place."

I lift my brows. "That's good news." The condo had been empty for about a month after the owner's previous tenants abruptly picked up and moved out.

"Yeah, she'll be moving in this weekend."

I nod. "It'll be nice to have a new face around here," I say absentmindedly. "I'll see you later, Jack." I don't wait for his good-bye as I turn on my heels and head toward the staircase. I rarely take the elevator at home since I only live on the third floor and waiting takes longer than taking the stairs.

I reach the enclosed garage where I pay extra to park my maroon 2018 Ford Mustang. Hopping in my car, I rev up the engine because it's been a few days since I've had the pleasure of doing so. Backing out of my parking space, I turn to pull out of the parking garage and make the twenty minute drive to my new station. My commute to work is longer at Rescue Four but it's worth it.

A short while later, I am pulling into the fire station with the words Station Rescue Four emblazoned at the top of the brick building. The welling of pride that I was searching for earlier begins to emerge and I breathe a little easier. Thoughts of my time in Mexico still dance around in the background of my mind, but for right now I'm ready to take on a new adventure.

Parking alongside the other vehicles, which presumably belong to my new squad members, I turn my car off and exit, taking a moment to look around at my new home. Rescue Four is larger than my previous assignment, Station Two. To my left there are two fire trucks parked halfway out of the garage. The trail of soap and water from the garage tells me the trucks are being washed.

I walk toward the garage and enter that way instead of the front door. I've already memorized the layout of the station. And having been a firefighter for over seven years now, I know that the kitchen is the most likely place to find the guys hanging out.

"You're shitting me?" are the first words I hear as I enter the kitchen.

I turn to see Don who is talking to Carter about

something. Carter looks over and catches sight of me. A lift of his eyebrows is partnered with a sideways grin.

"You finally made it, huh?" he greets, walking over to me. He raises his hand.

I slap fives with him and pull him into an embrace. Carter and I go back to our time spent in the military. We weren't in the same squad but there was some overlap from time to time. We got along well.

"Captain put you on for the evening on your first shift?" he asks.

I nod. "Seems to be the case."

He whistles low. "He's throwing you into the lion's den head first ... literally."

I chuckle. He's right. Everyone knows that evenings shifts at the fire station are busier with often larger and more chaotic fires. And since more people tend to be home during the evening hours, it also means more lives need to be saved in those fires.

"Just how I like it."

"Damn straight," Carter agrees, his blue eyes glinting at me. "You've met everyone?"

I open my mouth to respond but am interrupted.

"Allende!" a deep, gruff voice calls.

I look toward the swinging door of the kitchen to find my new captain standing at it. I'm not surprised to see the deep frown and wrinkle in his forehead that he's known for. Captain Waverly has a reputation around the department for being one of the toughest but most efficient captains in the city.

"Captain." I nod.

"This way." That's all he says before he turns and exits, leaving the kitchen door swinging and me to follow along.

When I pass through the door to the living room space of the station, a couple guys are on the couch watching an early season football scrimmage. I nod at a few who look up at me and keep walking. Though I haven't spotted him since he left the kitchen, I assume the captain went upstairs to his office, which is the direction I head.

After taking the steps two at a time, I hook a right at the top, and go down the hall a few feet where I am met with a closed door. I knock.

"Open."

I turn the knob and enter Captain Waverly's office to find him parked at the edge of his desk reading over some forms in his hands.

"Close the door," he instructs, not even lifting his eyes from the papers.

Once I do is when he finally lowers the papers and looks up at me. His gaze could be intimidating to someone else. But the man does have my respect.

"Do you know why you're here?"

I lift an eyebrow. "To be a firefighter." The tone in my voice comes out snarkier than I'd intended but the answer should be obvious.

Captain Waverly must not think so because his frown deepens.

"You want to be a firefighter, sign up with a department in some podunk town in the backwoods of no-fucking-where. You don't show up in Williamsport, and not in my goddamned squad, just to be a firefighter. You're here to be a damned soldier," he states adamantly.

I like this guy already.

"Now, do you know why you're here?"

"I'm here because one of your soldiers lost their leg on a rescue."

His lips pinch. The distress on his face becomes apparent.

"Corey."

I nod. "Corey."

"Some of my guys aren't going to like you right off the back. You're here to replace one of their brothers. A guy they pulled out of the fire. They saved his life but he hasn't been to this station in over two months. His presence is missed every day."

There's a long pause. I don't have anything to say to that, nor does the captain actually want me to respond. The purpose of this conversation isn't to feel me out. It's to inform me of what I'm walking into.

"I'm not here to replace anyone," I finally reply. "I'm here to do my job. To be a soldier as a member of the best squad in the Williamsport Fire Department."

His lower jaw works as he stares at me, digesting what I'd just said. "Words are meaningless."

"Don't I fucking know it."

He pauses again. "Captain Rogers warned me about you. He didn't like you very much."

I clamp down on the urge to tell him Captain Rogers was a fucking joke for a captain.

"He said you were loose cannon."

"I'll take that as a compliment," I casually remark.

"Don't." He eyes me. "He didn't mean it as one," he adds.

I nod. "All due respect, Captain Waverly, but my former captain and I didn't see eye to eye on a lot of things."

"I can tell."

"And that may have had an impact on how he and I viewed my performance, but I'm a damned good—"

"Firefighter," he finishes for me. "I'm well aware of that. I've checked your file." He holds up the papers in his hands. "I know what you're about. Congratulations on earning the Thomas Webster."

My chest tightens. I hate being reminded of that damn

award.

"That was a hell of a save."

I shake my head. "I didn't save him." My voice is heavy, filled with the guilt and remorse of that fucking night.

"Bullshit."

I look at my new captain.

"You pulled a mother and her two children out of a fire that night at great risk to yourself. As far as I'm concerned, that partially qualifies you to be assigned to my station."

"Partially?"

"You still have to prove yourself. To me and to your new squad. Take these."

He tosses me a set of locker keys.

"Your new uniform is waiting for you inside." With that, he turns and walks around his desk, sitting in his chair and looking down at a new stack of papers. Apparently, I've been dismissed.

Taking the keys, I head back down the hall, past the stairs, and around the corner to the row of lined metal lockers with made up cots in front of them. I match the number on the set of keys with one of the lockers, and use them to open it. Hanging inside is a brand new navy polo but this one has the name Rescue Four emblazoned across the back. I remove the shirt from the hanger and hold it up, looking it over.

"It's our new shirt."

I turn to find Carter leaning against the wall behind me, eating an apple.

"Nice, right?"

"Not a bad look but fuck off." I ball the shirt up and toss it at him.

He begins chuckling.

"You guys are going to have to try harder to get over on me," I insist, laughing at the goofy prank they tried to pull. "Rescue Four is supposed to be the best of the best, and that's all you can do?" I shake my head, disappointed.

"Oh, trust me, we're just getting started." Carter wiggles his blond eyebrows and saunters off, chuckling to himself.

After putting my bag inside of my locker with my car keys and wallet, I close my locker, locking it with the keys before placing them in my pocket.

I take on final look around before heading down to the main floor of the station.

"Roll call!" I hear as soon as my foot hits the first floor.

"Townsend?"

"Yup!" Carter replies as he moves past me, retrieving a form from the guy doing the roll call.

"Donnie?"

"Fuck off," Don yells, moving closer.

A few laughs are heard around the room.

"Tighten up, Donnie. You're on inspection duty."

Don grumbles and heads in the direction of the garage where the fire trucks are parked.

"McClellan?"

"Present!"

A louder round of laughter ensues.

"Who the fuck says *present?* This ain't the third fucking grade, McClellan!" Don tosses over his shoulder as he walks toward the garage.

"Leave 'em alone, Don, he's still wet behind the ears," Carter responds. "I'm pretty sure his mama even made him lunch today. Did she cut the crust off your PB&J, too?" he inquires in a mocking voice.

"Enough, enough!" the guy taking roll call says while still chuckling.

"I think that's it. Car—"

"You missed one." I finally emerge from behind the man.

He turns to me, eyes widening in surprise. "Shit! Allende, forgot you were starting tonight."

"That doesn't bode well for me, does it, Sean?" Sean is one of the lieutenants at Rescue Four.

"Nah, you're fine. Why don't you help Don with inspection?"

I nod and head in the same direction as I saw Don walking earlier. I'd already been introduced to most of the Rescue Four squad a few days earlier while at the fire department's annual firefighter competition. I was fresh off the plane from Mexico and wanted to swing by the Williamsport Park to meet my new squad. It might've also had something to do with the fact that I didn't want to face going directly home to an empty place.

"Hey," I say to Don as I enter, "Sean sent me out to help with inspection."

Don's dark eyes narrow. "I don't need help."

I frown at his tone. "I'm here whether you need it or not."

Grunting, he turns back to rifling through one of the compartments of the truck with the clipboard and pen in his hand.

I know what the cold shoulder feels like, and something tells me this isn't a part of one of the squad's practical jokes.

"Did you get this side?" I question.

"I just came out here a minute ago. It look like I did a full side already?"

"What the fuck is your problem?" I retort, my temper getting the better of me.

Again, he's unresponsive, grunting and going back to counting.

I give him a dismissive glare and head to the side table, picking up another clipboard and pencil. Rounding to the opposite side of the truck, I press open the side compartment door that holds a lot of the equipment that's taken out on runs.

"Shit!" I yelp when I'm sprayed by freezing cold water, soaking my face and entire front side.

All I hear in the background is bellows of laughter.

I step from around the truck to find nearly all of the squad at the door, bent over in hysterics.

"Hey, Allende, you're supposed to point the water at the fire. Not yourself!" Sean yells, causing more goofy ass laughing.

I toss them all a middle finger but that only results in more laughter.

"Holy shit!"

"Welcome to Rescue Four," three of them say in tandem.

"You can believe there's more where that came from." Carter winks at me and they all enter back into the station, still falling all over themselves.

I roll my eyes but laugh to myself. *I might like it here*, I think as I turn and catch Don's eye.

He's frowning as he goes back to counting and checking the equipment on his side of the truck. He doesn't say a word.

****

Janine

"I don't know why I agreed to help you with all of this. I hate moving. Why don't you just throw everything away and buy new tuff?" my best friend, Angela, complains as she helps me drag in my rolled-up area rug.

"Most of this stuff *is* new," I remind her. I stand from the bent over position I was in to survey the space around us. My new home is covered in boxes and wrapped-up furniture that all needs to be put together and arranged.

"Why'd you buy so much?" Angela huffs as she slams the door behind her.

"Hey, easy with the door! I don't want my new neighbors to think I'm inconsiderate by making too much noise."

"But you *are* inconsiderate, making me lug all of this stuff up here."

I glare at her. "You're being dramatic. We've brought up one rug and a couple of bar stools. The movers did the rest."

Heading over to the bar area, she retrieves her bottle of water and sighs. "You're right. I was just teasing."

I smirk, but when I continue to look around the smile fades. I start to feel intimidated, not knowing where to even begin with everything. "Why did I get so much?" I ask out loud.

"Because this place is double the size of your apartment in Boston," Angela helpfully answers.

"More than double, actually." My place in Boston had been around four-hundred square feet. It was tiny, but on a teacher's salary in one of the most expensive cities in the country, it was what I could afford. Thankfully, my new job meant a doubling of my salary, which meant a larger, more comfortable living space.

"Yeah, and you spent years waiting for your ex to propose so you kept putting off getting new furniture or a new place, hoping to one day share it with him."

Cocking my head to the side, I place my hands on my hips and stare at my friend. "Really?"

She merely shrugs as she continues drinking her water.

I shake my head. Angela has been with me through all of the ups and downs of my previous relationship. I knew she disliked Matthew, but she's a good enough friend not to voice those opinions directly to me, even when I knew she really wanted to. All that's gone out the window since I broke up with him.

"If Eric wasn't working today, I would've asked him to help us put all of this furniture together."

I wave her off. "It's fine if you need to take off. I can put this stuff together myself. You both have done enough for me as it is." Angela and Eric allowed me to keep my furniture at their home while I went to Mexico, and let me stay with them for the past week and a half until my new home was ready to move into.

"Oh no, you definitely owe me some pizza for helping move this in and put this stuff together. Let's go. The sooner we get started, the sooner you feed me."

"You don't have to work tonight?" Angela owns and

operates her own bar. Considering it's a Saturday, I figured it'd be one of the busiest times of the week and she would want to be there.

She shakes her head. "I can go in later. My new manager has it covered. She's been great."

I nod. "Good. I really didn't want to have to do this on my own," I confess, causing Angela to laugh.

We spend the next three hours putting together my bed frame, couch, bar stools, and dining room table. By the time we come up for air, not everything is completed but it is starting to look more and more like a place I could get used to living in. The undercurrent of anxiety that's been with me for the last few days begins to ebb just a little bit as I can feel myself getting more settled.

Now, only if this deep sadness I've felt ever since I got on that damn plane in Mexico to fly home would go away, too. *He's gone, Janine,* I tell myself. Again.

I know he's gone. And wherever Emanuel is, he's probably not thinking about me.

"Hey, don't forget the extra cheese," Angela says as she hands me my cell phone. "Oh, and garlic knots. Definitely don't forget the garlic knots."

I give her a funny look. "Hungry much?"

She laughs. "I'm starting to eat like my husband. Don't let that muscular build on him fool you. That man can eat. Just like the rest of those guys. You should see them when they come into the bar and order food. My poor kitchen staff falls all over themselves to get their huge orders out." She shakes her head.

I give her a suspicious look as she continues to peruse the menu.

"Oh, and make sure they add the sausage, onions, and peppers to the pizza. Do you want pepperoni, too?"

I giggle. "Yeah, blame that appetite on Eric if you want to." I suspect her husband is responsible for her increased hunger for one reason or another, but I keep those thoughts to myself. "I'll get half with all of your toppings and half plain."

She shrugs.

I make the call to order the food, and since it will be another twenty to thirty minutes before it arrives, I convince Angela to help me continue setting up my bedroom. That way, I'll at least have a comfortable setting to sleep in tonight amidst all of the chaos of my living room, dining area, and kitchen.

"Why do you still have this?" Angela questions, holding up a framed photo of Matthew and I. The picture is about five years old but it was one of my favorites of he and I.

"I forgot I still had that." I reach for the frame, but Angela moves it just out of my reach.

"Uh uh," she tuts, shaking her head. "You better not be posting this photo up in your bedroom."

I roll my eyes. "That's the last thing on my mind." Snatching the frame from her, I turn it over to undo the snaps holding the picture in place. I remove the photo, flipping it over to look at it for a few seconds. I stare into my brown eyes that were so smitten as they stared at the man next to me. Matthew had his arm draped around my shoulders, staring straight ahead, winking at the camera.

I snort and shake my head, tearing the photo in half and tossing the remnants into the large trash bag we've been using to dispose of useless items and garbage.

"Oh thank god!"

I give Angela a teasing look.

"I was nervous that photo actually still meant something to you."

"The past is the past." Besides, I haven't thought about Matt one time since I arrived in Williamsport. There is still another man that is heavy on my mind, however. But I haven't told Angela about Emanuel.

"You know, there are a lot of single guys down at the station."

I jut my head back in surprise. "Station?"

"Yeah, Rescue Four. Let's see, there's Don, you met him at the wedding. If it were a few months ago I would've totally tried to hook you up with Carter but he's engaged now." She frowns as she taps her chin with her finger, thinking. "Oh!" She snaps her fingers. "There's—"

"Saved by the bell!" I declare as the buzzer to my apartment rings. I quickly exit my bedroom, running to the intercom by the front door. "Yes?"

"DeMaggio's Pizza delivery for Janine."

"Thank you." I buzz the delivery guy up, and then head to grab my wallet out of my purse in the kitchen, pulling out the money for our late lunch. My stomach growls as soon as the knock sounds at my door as if it just knows food is on the other side.

"Janine?" the delivery guy questions.

"That's me." I hand him the money for the food plus tip. "No change needed," I tell him as he begins rooting around in his pocket for money.

"Thanks." He nods, tips the red hat with the Demaggio logo of a pizza on it, and heads back down the hallway.

Just as I start to turn back into my apartment, I hear the door across the hall opening. I paste a smile on my face, hoping to meet my new neighbor for the first time. I look up as a tall figure emerges and an electrified feeling begins in the very tips of my toes.

His back is to me as he pulls his door shut.

I swallow as I take in his muscular frame, but it's the tribal tattoo that traces along the thick tricep and bicep muscles that has me nearly swallowing my tongue. I'm frozen in place, as I'm thrown back in time, to a week ago as I watched Emanuel shut the door of his hotel room.

"Impossible," I whisper, suddenly catching his attention.

He glances over his shoulder and then does a double take, his honey eyes doubling in size. He turns fully to stare at me, taking me in from head to toe.

"You're here." His voice is filled with an enthralled enthusiasm that has my belly performing somersaults. "How the hell are you standing here?"

I blink and point at the number on my door. Turning back to Emanuel, I say, "I-I live here."

Again his handsome, perfect face is overcome by shock. His gaze lifts to peer at the number behind me, before his eyes fall back to my face.

"You live here, in Williamsport? In my building?"

I swallow and just stare because I have no idea what to say. I'm just as taken by surprise as he is.

"Janine, is that the food?" Angela's voice sings behind me as she pulls the door wider. "Emanuel?" she greets happily. "Great, food's here!"

I don't even realize she's taken the pizza and bag filled with the garlic knots and salad from my arms.

"Janine?"

"Wait ... Emanuel, you live in this building, too?" Angela questions.

I shake my head to gather myself, and turn to glare at Angela. "How do you know Emanuel?"

She gives me a funny look. "He works with Eric. He's the new guy at Rescue Four. Oh!" She snaps her fingers again. "He's also the guy I was about to tell you to hoo—"

"Pizza's getting cold. Go eat your food," I say, shoving her into the apartment. I turn and am startled when I realize he's moved closer, practically standing over me now.

A long finger reaches out, moving under my chin, pointing my head upwards so that I can only look him in the eye. "*Janine,* is it?" His voice is low.

I swallow and nod.

"I knew Nadine wasn't your real fucking name." He removes his finger and steps back.

"So you really are a firefighter," I mention, not knowing what else to say.

"I never lied to you."

My heart sinks at his words. He never did. And I never even suspected that he lied.

"I'm sorry. I—"

He takes my chin into his. "Don't apologize, butterfly." His eyes lift to the door behind me. "There are much better things you could be doing with those lips to make it up to me."

My mouth parts on a gasp. "Like what?"

His lips widen into a mischievous grin. "You'll find out."

He steps back, releasing me. "I have to go to work now. But I'll be seeing you real soon." He turns and saunters off down the hallway, reaching the entrance to the stairway and giving me a final look before disappearing behind it.

I stumble backwards into my apartment and close the door behind me. Of all of the places to move in this world, in this country, in *this city*, and I wind up directly across from the man who swept me off my feet while on vacation. How does that even happen?

After locking the door, I turn and my head lowers when I see Angela standing there, arms folded, tapping her foot against the hardwood floor.

"Spill it all," she insists.

I don't even bother trying to pretend that I don't know what she's talking about. I simply plop down on one of the put together barstools, open the pizza box, place a slice onto one of the Styrofoam plates, and hand it to her.

"You're going to want to sit down for this."

Chapter Eight

Emanuel

I wake up with her on my mind again this morning. The longing that I was certain would've ended by now hasn't let up. And there doesn't seem to be an end in sight. By the time I got up, dressed, and was ready for my shift, I had already determined that I was going to give Christian a call to get in contact with someone who could find her. Then I step out of my condo and there she is.

Janine. Not Nadine as she's told me. She lied. I should've been pissed at the confirmation that she lied to me but it was a relief to know her real name. And to find out that not only was she here but that we're neighbors.

Now, as I enter the doors of Rescue Four, there's a whistle emanating from my lips and a calmness in my stride that wasn't present just the day before.

"Someone got laid last night," Sean chuckles as he walks past me, clapping me on the back.

"Mind your fucking business."

He just laughs harder. "Hey, you're on kitchen duty today."

I frown. "You fuckers are just lazy and don't want to make your own food."

He turns to me, holding his arms out and shrugging. "Maybe. Either way your ass is in the kitchen. And hurry the hell up we're starving."

Waving him off, I head upstairs to put my stuff in my locker before returning downstairs to properly set up my boots, turnout gear, and mask so they're all in the perfect order when I need to jump into them quickly if we get a call.

I go to the kitchen where I spot one of the rookies. "Hey, you're helping with the dishes," I say.

He frowns but doesn't say shit. Rookies know they're the lowest common denominator in a fire station, even next to the new guy like myself, since I do have seven years in the department.

Opening the refrigerator, I find two large packages of ground beef, peppers, onions, and tomatoes. I pull the ingredients out, placing them on the counter, and then remove the two large cans of beans from the cupboard.

"Looks like we're making chili," I say to the rookie.

"I don't know how to cook chili."

I grunt. "Fucking rookies."

"You were a rookie once." I turn to see Carter entering the kitchen and swiping an orange from the fruit basket at the center of the table.

"That was a long time ago."

He snorts. "You sure you know what you're doing over there?"

I wave him off. "I've got this covered."

"Good. I'm fucking starving. Skipped breakfast this

morning. Diego has a class assignment so I let Michelle sleep in while he and I headed to the library and then dropped him off at the school so he and his classmates could finish their project with the teacher. I picked up breakfast for him but forgot it for myself." He shakes his head chuckling.

Turning my attention away from the cutting board where I'd begun chopping the onion, I stare at Carter for a moment. His expression is content as he chews on the orange he just peeled.

"How is it?"

"How's what?"

"Being a father and husband." Now that is a statement I didn't see myself wondering about even a few short weeks ago.

"Well, I'm not there yet. The wedding's not for two months, and we're still waiting on the adoption to go through for Diego …"

"Yeah, yeah, but you're all in. You're committed and living together. He calls you *dad*. The other stuff is just a matter of time and signing some forms. What's it like?"

Carter's eyes narrow on me.

Shit. I return my attention to the cutting board and continue chopping before looking over at the rookie. "Don't just stand there. Clean something."

He jumps and turns toward the sink, beginning to fill it with water. That's when Carter moves in on my left side.

"Is the Man of Chaos, himself, actually asking these questions?"

Sighing, I shake my head. "I knew a fucker like you would make this into a big deal. I'm just asking a question. Besides, I haven't been called *Chaos* in a long time." I toss the onion into the large stockpot that has been heated with oil, while avoiding Carter's stare.

"I'm just fucking with you. In reality, it's great. My father always told us that finding our other half would be one of the great joys of our lives. I didn't believe him until I met Michelle."

I look from the pot to Carter. He's completely serious. I don't say anything because there is nothing to say. I don't know if what he's talking about is even for a guy like me. Not with my background.

One thing I do know, is that no other woman in my life has even had me asking these types of questions. Not until Janine.

Both my and Carter's eyes rove upward toward the ceiling as the alarm for an incoming call goes off.

"Rescue Four called to respond to a two alarm fire at an elementary school. Reports of children trapped on the roof."

"Shit!"

"Fuck!"

Carter and I both yell at the same time. I immediately turn off the stove and rush through the kitchen doors, behind

Carter to the garage. Running past me are Sean, Don, and Captain Waverly. The five of us pile into the garage, taking less than a minute to step into our boots and turnout gear. We're joined by the rookie who'd just been in the kitchen with me as well.

"Hurry up!" I yell at him as he stumbles to properly put on his turnout gear. "Let's go," I growl, jumping into the back of the fire truck and holding the door open for him. With one hand I pull him inside, as he still struggles to get his gear on correctly.

I bang on the side of the truck, alerting Sean, who's in the front behind the wheel, that we're all ready. The captain is in the passenger seat, communicating with headquarters. I turn up the volume on my intercom to be able to hear the information that's being conveyed to him.

"What's the name of the school?" Carter shouts up to the front, asking the captain.

Captain radios dispatch to get the name. The panicked expression on Carter's face isn't ordinary. I've been on a few calls with him over the past couple of days, not to mention having worked with him in the Army. He doesn't get panicked. But he is now. That, I realize, is the look of a father concerned for his son.

"P.S. Fifty-six," Captain calls back.

A sigh of relief is released. It's not Diego's school.

But that doesn't mean he isn't completely focused on ensuring the safety of the children at this school.

"Why were there even children at the school on a Saturday?" I question.

"Some type of play rehearsal or something. Don and Emanuel, you two are on rescue. Carter, you're assisting the rookie with the hose. Sean, you're going to set up the perimeter. Got it?"

"Got it," everyone responds, just as we pull up to the front of the school.

I hop out of the truck and my heart plummets to see smoke billowing out of one of the top windows.

"We need to get inside," Don yells at the captain.

"Wait!" he urges.

I frown, my gaze bouncing between the captain and Don. I start to have doubts about Captain Waverly. I'm all too familiar with the captain who cares more about preserving his reputation than saving lives.

"There are children in there!" I yell.

Waverly glares at me, pissed. "I said wait!" He turns his back, telling Carter and the rookies where to set up the hose. And Sean begins setting up the perimeter, pushing onlookers back.

I grow anxious, the ax in my hand feeling heavier and heavier as the desire grows to break through something and pull out anyone I can find. I take a step forward, ready to ignore the captain's orders, when a hand clasps my arm. I glance to my right to see Don's angry face.

"Captain said wait so we fucking wait."

"There're fucking kids in there."

"No one knows that better than him."

I glare at Don, snatching my arm away. "Don't fucking touch me."

He moves closer, getting in my face.

We have a stare off. Out of everyone at Rescue Four, Don has been the slowest to warm up to me. Which is fine, I get it, but if he thinks he's going to stand in the way of me doing my damn job ...

"All right, front door's blocked by chairs. Can't get in that way. Don and Emanuel, you'll have to head around to the back and climb in the first story windows, back there," Captain Waverly yells over.

Don and I immediately start running to the back of the school. The first story windows are a few feet off the ground but not too difficult to hoist my bodyweight through. We both work, breaking through the glass of the windows easily with our axes, and then toss them inside. Using our hands and arms to lift our bodies up and over windowsill, we fall into the school.

I land right next to my ax. Picking it up, I also lower my

face mask over my face and glance over to see Don has done the same.

"Fire department!" we both begin calling out, as we wind our way down the hall.

"The auditorium is at the far end of the first floor, closer to the front door," Captain says into the intercom, guiding us to where we believe most of the children and staff are located.

Don and I take either side of the hallway, checking classroom by classroom for any signs of students, putting out small fires along the way with the fire extinguishers we're carrying.

Arriving at the auditorium doors on my right, I wrap my hand around the metal bar to push the doors open ... only to realize there is a chain around it.

"The hell?" Don asks next to me.

"Cut it off," I demand, not waiting to try to figure out why the hell it's there. Without another thought, I lift my ax and hammer at the chain link. Pausing to inspect it, I see that while it made a big cut, the chain is still holding on.

"Again!" Don yells.

By that time, my ax is already in the air, coming down a half a second later, breaking through the chain. Yanking it free, I toss it aside and push through the doors.

"Help!" I hear a male voice yell.

"Fire department," Don calls.

From the sides of the auditorium children and a few adults begin emerging. There are about ten children and two adults, one male and one female.

Grabbing the man, I ask, "Is there anybody else in here?"

"Yes, Linda Walkowski. She went up to the roof with five of her students to practice. They haven't come back down." He begins coughing due to the thick smoke in the auditorium.

"Okay," I respond, and turn my attention to Don.

"We're going to have to take them out the back way."

I nod, knowing the pile of chairs in the front of the door would take too long to move before these kids and adults were taken over by smoke inhalation.

"We'll have to take 'em," Don says. He radios to Captain and Sean outside that we'll need assistance to lower the kids out of the window, the same way we entered. "Where're you going?" he yells to my back.

I've already taken off for the back entrance of the auditorium, which leads to a stairwell with roof access, according to the man we rescued.

"I'm going to get the rest of those kids."

"Like fuck you are," he growls. "Get your ass back here and help me get these people out."

The anger that fills my body at the demand I hear in his voice is enough to have me thinking just for one split second of using the ax I wield on him instead of a locked door.

"I don't fucking take orders from you. Get these people out of here. I'm going up to the roof."

Turning, I run through the rest of the auditorium, reaching the back door. I head up the stairs that I've been told reach the roof of the building. All the while, I'm listening to the walkie clipped to my right shoulder. Don has reached the back set of windows with the children and staff. Sean is helping to pull everyone from the windows.

I arrive at the third floor of the stairwell to find a door that reads "Roof Access." I attempt to push through but find something jammed inside of the keyhole, preventing the knob from turning. Taking a step back, I glance over my shoulder to make sure no one or nothing is behind me as I raise the ax over my head and bring it down hard over the doorknob. It bends and comes partially off but not all of the way. I do it again and again. The third time is the sweet spot, as the doorknob finally falls to the ground.

With my hand, I push the other side of the knob to the floor and am able to open the door.

"Oh, thank god!" a woman on the other side cries.

"Is anybody hurt?"

"No, no. Just scared, I think." She reaches her arms around the children, cradling them to her body.

"How many are up here?"

"Six. Five of them and me."

I peer down into the frightened faces of the children, taking a head count, to make sure all five are accounted for. When I'm satisfied, I radio to my team. "Five children and one adult female on the roof. Unharmed. Coming down now."

I'm just able to get the words out as Don comes barreling up the stairs.

"It's okay," he soothes the startled children. "Come with me."

I have the woman get in front to have the children follow in line behind her.

"I'm scared," a tiny, innocent voice whines.

I glance down into the big, brown eyes of a little girl. She can't be more than eight years old.

"I got you." Picking her up, I turn to follow behind Don and the rest of the children. "Cover your mouth and nose," I instruct, lifting the top of her shirt to show her how to best protect her from breathing more smoke than her little body can handle.

"No, no! Back exit!" Don instructs when the teacher and children start to turn toward the front entrance.

We race down the hall as quickly as possible. The smoke is thick but clearing out. Most of the fires have been put out. Once we reach the window again, Sean is there helping the teacher and children get out. Don is next to hop out, followed by myself.

We guide the children around the front of the school and into the arms of the awaiting paramedics who will check them over.

Lifting my face mask, I head toward our truck.

"Nice job!" Sean yells, clapping me on my back.

I give him a nod and a tight smile. Suddenly, I am thrust backwards, hitting the truck with my back.

"What the hell was that?" an angry looking Don fumes.

I smack his hand away from my chest and push him just as forcefully as he pushed me. "What the fuck is your problem?"

"You're my goddamn problem," he yells, getting in my face.

I'm not sure where his anger is coming from, but at that moment I don't give a fuck either. He's had a bug up his ass about me since I arrived at the station house, and if we need to solve it right here and now so fucking be it.

"Don't ever put your fucking hands on me again!" I seethe.

"Don't ever—"

"Hey, hey, what the hell is going on here?" Captain Waverly intervenes, getting in between the two of us. "We've still got a fucking fire to put out. Let's go!"

I give Don one last glare before snatching my ax off the ground and turning to round the truck and help complete this run.

As I do, I look farther down the street to see a worried, distressed woman running toward one of the ambulances. I can't hear what she says but I see the instant relief that washes over her when she spots her daughter on one of the gurney's sitting up with arms outreaching.

My heart squeezes in my chest and that pang of guilt I've learned to become familiar with seizes me. I avert my eyes, unable to take in the scene anymore.

Chapter Nine

Janine

"The hell?" I groan as the banging on my door seems to grow louder. *Who the hell is knocking on my door at ...* I lift the satin eye mask I wear to bed every night and blink, glancing at the clock on my nightstand. It's almost two in the morning.

I struggle to get out of bed, nearly stumbling over another unpacked box by the door.

"Who is it?" I call out, as I move closer to the door. When I peer through the peephole, I'm not totally surprised by the man standing on the other side. I should've known to expect him to pop up when I least expected it.

I step back, and for one second I think about not opening the door.

"Open the damn door."

My hand, which was already reaching for the knob, moves faster at his demand. "It's nearly two in the morning."

He shrugs. "It's a Saturday." Without more preamble than that, he brushes past me, entering my place.

"Come one in," I say sarcastically.

"Don't mind if I do."

After closing the door, I turn to face him with my arms folded.

He takes his time looking around my undecorated apartment. "This place is shaping up nicely." He nods as if approving.

"I thought you were working."

"I was. Shift ended about an hour ago." He moves closer, his face turning serious.

I don't know what it is but there's an intensity about him as he moves closer to me. I drop my arms from in front of my body at the same time his hand reaches around the back of my head, cupping it and bringing our mouths together.

I let out a moan of both shock and pleasure. His tongue lines my lips, tasting them first before slipping inside of my mouth, forcing my lips to widen so he can take his fill. My core begins weeping as if it's being given exactly what it's been asking for for days. Ever since we left his bed back in Mexico.

"Shit," he mutters as he pulls our lips apart and places his forehead against mine. "I wanted to see if it was just as good as it was in Mexico."

I wrap my hand around his wrist. "Was it?"

"Better."

Sighing, I smile and close my eyes. He was right. That kiss was better than the ones we shared in Mexico.

"You lied to me, butterfly," his voice takes on a dark note.

I open my eyes and look up at him. "You were a stranger."

His free hand moves to my hip, then a little lower, his fingers touching the skin of my thighs due to the short, cotton pajama shorts I wear. He gives my hip a squeeze before I begin feeling his fingers creep beneath my shirt, feeling the skin of my belly.

"Was I a stranger when I was inside of that tight little cunt?" The hand in my hair tightens as he brings our faces closer together.

I clamp my lips shut in surprise. Shaking my head, I push against his chest to move from his embrace.

"We shouldn't do this," I say, crossing my arms over my chest again—mainly so he can't see my hardened nipples through the thin top I'm wearing.

His eyebrows raise and he blinks. "We shouldn't?"

I release a long breath through my mouth. "No. I've been thinking about this since you left for work," I declare, moving farther away from the door and around him, deeper into my apartment, forcing him to turn around to look at me.

"Thinking. Of course you've been thinking about this."

I frown, wanting to ask him what he means by that comment, but I refuse to let myself get sidetracked.

"What we shared in Mexico was great, fantastic even, but it was short-lived. A fantasy. And this ..." I wave my hand between our two bodies, "us being neighbors is real life. It's not sustainable."

"Sustainable?"

"Yes." I nod. "You're ... you. And I'm ..."

"You?"

I nod again and step back as he prowls closer. "Yes, I'm me. You like jumping off boats and I don't know, parasailing—"

"You enjoyed all of those things, too."

"Yes, but not every day. You run into fires and save lives. I was watching the local news earlier." I gesture to my newly mounted television screen, the cable to which was set up earlier that evening. "I saw you carrying that little girl across the street from the school. It got me thinking that perhaps you and I just aren't compatible. Maybe outside of a few great days in a foreign country we don't have anything in common. And it'd be terrible to find that out and then we're still living across from one another. Then I'd have to see you with—" I pause, breaking off before I admit to being hurt at seeing him date other women.

I shake my head. "No, it's way too complicated now. Mexico was easy. We didn't have to think about anything. Here, it's different."

Finally, I stop talking, and look up to find Emanuel's eyes transfixed on me. He steps closer. "You don't even believe the words that are coming out of your own mouth."

My gaze narrows on him defiantly. "I do, too!" I insist, sounding like I did when I got into a fight on the schoolyard as a child.

He shakes his head.

Before I know what's happening, he lunges toward me,

pulling my face to his and kissing the life out of me. I moan into his mouth but don't get the opportunity to fully give in because the kiss ends as abruptly as it began.

"*That* is what's between us. You're scared shitless. I know fear like I know the back of my hand. I'll forgive you this time because that's the fear talking, but this shit," he waves his hand between us as I'd done a few moments ago, "isn't going away anytime soon, and neither am I." Releasing me, he steps back and gives me one last glare before leaving my apartment.

I startle when the door slams behind him. I'm left standing there, wondering if he'll make good on his promise, and if what I said was true, why did I want him to?

****

I wake up with a nervous pit in my stomach. It's Monday morning and I haven't heard or seen Emanuel since late Saturday night. Aside from that, it's my first day at my new job. A whole new career change.

I should be used to so much change happening in my life at once. I lost count of the number of different cities and towns I lived in growing up. A change in location meant a change in schools, teachers, and friends. We never settled in any place for too long, so I learned to adapt quickly. But after the relative peace of living in one city for the last ten years, being with the same man, and holding the same job for seven of those previous ten, this sort of upheaval is challenging.

I push myself out of my low sitting, queen-sized bed, over the wooden frame, and onto the carpet. I head to the bathroom to brush my teeth and wash my face. Staring into the mirror, I frown at the reflection looking back at me. It might do me some good to do an eye mask before getting my day started, since the bags under my eyes from lack of sleep the last two nights are so evident.

As I go about my morning routine, I keep looking toward my front door, possibly hoping that he'll come knocking. Shaking those thoughts loose, I finish making my coffee and pouring it into my insulated cup to carry with me to the office. An hour later, I'm looking into my full-length mirror, examining the black trousers and white, button-up blouse I chose to wear for my first day. I paired the outfit with a pair of flat black loafers. Smoothing my shirt out one final time, I feel ready. I head to the kitchen, grab my purse, lunch bag, and coffee, and head out.

I retrieve my silver Kia from the parking garage and turn my GPS on to connect to the bluetooth in my car. Keying in the address of my office, I note it will take approximately twenty-five minutes to get to work, leaving me with fifteen minutes to spare before nine a.m.

"Let's hope it's right," I mumble.

Exactly twenty-four minutes later, I arrive at the office.

Taking my work badge out of my pocket, I place it over the machine, and within a half a second the glass panes part, allowing me to pass through from the lobby to the elevator banks of the office building. I nod at the front desk security attendant. He tilts his head acknowledging me.

Luckily, I make it onto the elevator just before it closes. Hearing a sigh behind me, I look over my shoulder to see a tall, slender man who appears to be in his late twenties staring down his nose at me.

"Sorry," I apologize, thinking I must've cut him off or something. I reach out to hit the tenth floor. Once we arrive, I step off the elevator and square my shoulders to ready myself for my new career, but I am almost knocked over by the guy behind me as he rushes past, and of course, into the double doors of the same office I'm preparing to enter. However, I don't let his rudeness deter me. After opening one of the doors that reads Lux Advertising, I head to the receptionist's desk on the left hand side.

"Hi, I'm Janine Thompson, it's my first day," I say to the smiling receptionist. I briefly admire the high afro puff she's put her hair into, and the purple, gold, and white silk scarf that adorns the sides of her head.

"Hi! Danny told me you were coming in today. Said you'd probably be early. He's not in yet but he did give me some of the HR paperwork you need to fill out." She places a clipboard onto her desk, and I immediately recognize the usual W-4 form, and the form for my banking information for direct deposits. "You can have a seat over there while you fill those out. Here's a pen." She places the pen on top of the forms. "Can I get you some water, coffee, or tea while you wait?"

Holding up my cup of coffee, still warm despite my commute, I shake my head. "Got that covered. Thanks."

I move to the other side of the room, placing my belongings in an empty chair. Sitting in the one next to it, I begin filling out my paperwork. I get to the last page when I hear a deep voice speaking. Lifting my gaze, I smile as my new boss enters the office.

"Janine," he greets, warmly.

I stand. "Mr. Wilson." I extend my hand to shake his.

"Please, Danny. You're an employee now."

I release a breath. One of the reasons I was so happy to get this job was because of Danny's enthusiastic and professional nature. He has a reputation in the advertising world for being one of the best, and hiring only the best. Which is why I was almost certain I wasn't going to get this job when I applied for it. I was floored when I did.

"You finished your paperwork?"

"I did."

"Good. I'll take you around to HR in a little bit to show you who those forms go to. Follow me."

I quicken my pace to keep up with his long strides as we turn down a short hallway to an open floor plan. There are desks on either side, along the wall, separated into cubicles. The desks are separated into pairs where two employees sit on either side facing one another.

"As I explained in your initial interview, each associate is partnered with another associate. You'll work as a team on your projects and present your ideas to a higher ranking partner or to myself. If we deem your idea quality, you'll have an opportunity to present it to the client. If the client likes it, you'll have the opportunity to take lead on the project. If not ..." Pausing, he gives me a *so much for you* look and pushes the door to his office open.

The lights immediately turn on as we enter. "I've decided to partner you with Zeke. He's been with the company since he graduated from Williamsport University. Very sharp, knows what he's doing, and a hard worker. I think you two will get along well." He lifts his phone, pressing a button.

"Yeah, Danny?" a voice says from the speaker of the phone.

"Can you come in here? I want to introduce you to Janine."

"Sure thing."

Danny hangs up. "Do you have any questions for me?"

I circle the room with my eyes. "No, not at the moment."

He nodes. "I run an open door policy. I try to make myself as available as possible, but I'm often in client meetings, on the phone, or out of the office for travel. When I'm occupied, anyone else in the office would be more than happy to answer anything for you. You've already met Shelah, our receptionist. She's great and can answer any questions you have about where to locate files, forms, office supplies, and things like that." Danny looks to his door at the same time I do when there's a knock.

"Zeke, come in." He waves the man in.

My stomach tightens to see the tall, slender man who sighed in the elevator.

"Zeke, this is Janine, she's the new associate I was telling you about."

I extend my hand. "Hi, nice to meet you."

A brief look of hesitation passes over his face before a fake smile is plastered on and he gives my hand a limp handshake. "Pleasure."

I've taken pizza out of the freezer that was warmer than that handshake.

"Zeke, I just remembered I have a call with our West Coast clients for their new soda line. This is going to be a long call. Can you take Janine over to HR and show her who to give her paperwork to? Oh, and have Rob create her a new login and password so she can log into our servers. Once that's handled, you can start showing her how to access our servers and files, then show her what you're working on."

Danny immediately gives his attention to another task in front of him. From the interviews I had with him, I could tell he was the type to talk fast, give instructions once, and move on to the next thing. Not rudely, but he just expected his employees to be as efficient as he was.

"Let's go."

I look to the man who is now halfway out the door. My eyes narrow at the rudeness of his tone but I don't say anything. Following behind him, I doing my best to keep up with his long strides. Unlike Danny who was walking fast just because he's always on the go, I get the feeling that Zeke is walking fast to lose me, actually wanting me to fall behind. Or maybe I'm making that up in my head.

"Thank you for taking me over to HR," I say when we reach the doors to try and break the ice. "Danny said he would but it seems he has a busy day."

"Danny's schedule is always packed, but that doesn't mean he doesn't know what he's doing." His dull hazel eyes narrow down at me.

My eyebrows lift in surprise. "Oh no, that's not what I was implying at all. Of course he knows what he's doing. He's one of the best in the business, and Lux Advertising is very successful because of him, I'm sure. I was just saying—"

"This is HR," Zeke interrupts in a bored tone, as he pushes through another set of glass doors on the other side of the elevator bank.

I follow him through the doors.

"This is Connie. She can take your paperwork. Once you're done with her, go on over to Rob in the back. He'll get you your login information. Come find me when you're done." Zeke doesn't wait for any questions I might have as he skirts around me and exits the door we just entered.

"Don't be perturbed, hun. He's like that with almost everyone."

I smile at the woman at the desk in front of me. "Hi, I'm Janine, the new associate at Lux."

She nods, and I notice the black string that attaches to her red-framed glasses. I can't tell which is brighter, the red of her glasses or her red hair, and from the looks of it, it's natural, or just a really good dye job.

"I know, hun. I've got your file right here in front of me. Just give me a sec to finish settling in for the morning and I'll be right with you. Have a seat." She extends her hand to the empty chair in the corner of her enclosed desk space.

I move passed her and take a seat, glancing around the walls that she has lined with pictures of herself in different locations and with family. I smile to myself, my heart squeezing in my chest as the thought of a family comes to mind.

"Are those your children?" I question, pointing at one of the pictures of her posing with Mickey Mouse ears in front of a Disney castle, with two teenage children.

"You're sweet, hun." Smiling, she pats my knee. "Those are my grandkids. We all took a family vacation in Disney World last summer."

"That must've been fun."

"It was, but I had more fun when my husband and I went by ourselves," she chuckles. "We didn't have to worry about not being able to get on the rides for being too short." We both laugh. Connie goes on to explain that she has three adult children and five grandchildren with another one on the way.

Once she has retrieved a fresh cup of coffee from the staff kitchen, she takes my W-4 from me and begins entering my information into the system. When that's complete, she walks me over to the guy who will give me a new login and password so I can get onto Lux's network as an employee.

About twenty minutes later, I'm walking back across the hall into the main offices of Lux Advertising, searching for Zeke. When I spot him, I notice he's on the phone. I head to the kitchen to stowaway my lunch in the refrigerator, and then to my new desk that is facing Zeke. I hold up the folded sheet with my login information on it to let him know that I can log in. Rolling his eyes, he continues on with his call. Taken aback but still ready to work, I sit and turn my computer on, waiting for it to boot up so I can log in. When it does, I take the time to look through the Lux database which was front and center on the desktop.

Reviewing the database, I discover I am privy to the different clients Lux is currently working with, or have worked with in the past. The information is good to know to determine how the company operates. I'm unaware of how long I spend perusing some of the files, but when I look up I see Zeke is off the phone and working on something on his own desk.

"Good, you're off the phone. I was just taking the last few minutes while you were on your call to look through the database, and I see—"

"Who gave you permission to do that?" His tone is sharp.

My head juts backwards. "Well, I assumed since I now have my own login and—"

"Don't assume." Another roll of the eyes.

"Ooookaay, no need to get so defensive..." I pause, waiting for him to say something more about what it is we'll be working on today but he doesn't. So I do. "Would you be able to explain to me the current project you're working on so I can get caught up?"

"You won't be able to get caught up." He shakes his head as if he's already deemed me incompetent.

"Then maybe—"

"Look," he sighs, standing up. He pulls a thick binder off the windowsill and brings it around to my side of the desk, nearly slamming it down in front of me. "This is a comprehensive cataloguing of all of the business systems we use here at Lux. It includes how to use the phone system and all other modes of communication, procedures for developing product and service brands, how to pitch a client, and what to do once a pitch is accepted. That should be more than enough to keep you occupied for the rest of the day." And without another word he circles back around his desk, sits, and begins typing on his computer.

"This is a lot of material to absorb. Will there be a quiz at the end of the day?" I quip. The joke, of course, is lost on Zeke who sighs heavily again and picks up his phone to place another call. All without granting me even a passing glance.

Realizing Zeke is obviously not the friendly type, I opt to make the best out of an awkward situation. I try to remind myself that I have no idea what is going on in Zeke's world. He could be going through a rough time personally, and is one of those people who brings his problems from home into the office with him. With that thought, I open the binder, pull out the brand new hardcover notepad that's in the top drawer of my desk, and begin jotting down notes I believe will be helpful to know from the binder.

As much as I wish I could say things got better

throughout the day, I can't.

Chapter Ten

Janine

My day goes from bad to worse once I step off the elevator on the ground level of my office building and begin rifling through my purse to find my cellphone which is ringing. Just as I exit the main door, I pull my phone out, and my heart sinks as the name of the caller which appears.

"Watch it," a male voice behind me grunts as its owner nearly knocks me over to get out the door.

I look up and of course it's Zeke. He glares at me before turning and moving past me, as he continues down the sidewalk.

I don't have time to give his attitude with me too much thought because the sound of my still ringing phone continues. Without thinking, I answer.

"What took you so long to answer?" his voice demands through the line.

I pull the phone from my ear to look at it.

"*Hello!*" I hear as I stare.

I consider hanging up. It's been months since Matt and I talked. I can't imagine what he's calling me for. And this isn't the type of greeting that makes me want to continue the conversation. But, being the pushover that I am, I don't hang up.

"Hi, Matt," I respond. "How are you doing?"

"I'm fine. When are you coming back to Boston?"

Taken completely off guard by his question, I ask "What?" as I climb behind the wheel of my Kia Sorento.

"Is the connection bad where you are? I asked when are you coming back?"

"Going back to Boston for what?" I tied up all of my loose ends before I left. My employer was notified, of course, and my landlord was given a forwarding PO Box for any mail or packages that may be delivered. My savings account with my local bank closed. Medical and dental offices notified of my moving.

"For what? For me!" he says in a raised tone.

"Why on Earth would I—"

"Look, I get it. You're having one of your bratty tantrums. I may have misled you here and there about a wedding date. But if it's something you *really* want we'll talk about it. Now, when are you coming back? I'll even buy your ticket back. Who knows how much money you've wasted with this fake move."

"Matthew, are you delirious right now?"

I turn my key in the ignition of my car, and a second later, I see on the screen that the bluetooth has kicked on, connecting the call so that it comes through the car's speakers.

"I'm not *going* back to Boston. There is nothing left for me there. I have a new apartment, a new job, and a new m—" I stop myself when I almost say a new man but Emanuel isn't my man. I made that clear the past Saturday night. "A new life. Here. In Williamsport."

"You're being ridiculous."

"And you are sounding like you should be on meds, or get some sleep, or something because you're not making any sense whatsoever. We broke up, remember?"

"We *always* break up. And get back together. That's our thing."

"That *was* our thing. It's not anymore."

"Janine, you're really starting to piss me off."

I begin shaking my head. This was the last thing I needed at the end of a trying first day of work. And as much as Matthew was starting to sound like the child he was accusing me of being, something in me felt tempted to acquiesce. A small part of me wanted that safety of my past relationship and living situation. No matter how dysfunctional it was, or how unhappy I'd grown living in my tiny apartment, at a job I'd come to loathe going into each morning. Yeah, I became miserable but it was *familiar.*

I really was starting to recognize what my college counselor meant when he said many people will remain in a bad situation for the comfort. The discomfort of change is often scarier than continuing to live a life you don't really want.

"Matt, I've got to go." I don't wait for his reply as I press the end call button. Because even while his words were harsh and chastising, simply hearing his voice was easily tricking my mind into believing something that just wasn't real.

When my phone begins ringing again, I'm ready to press the dismiss button, thinking it's Matt. Luckily, I look before I do, and a small smile touches my lips.

"You must know I needed to hear your voice."

"Rough first day?" Angela questions in a soothing voice.

"You could say that." I won't bother to tell her about the call with Matt.

"That's okay because I'm calling to invite you to the bar. Food and drinks are on me, and since I'm the owner that means they're free." Her giggle is infectious, causing me to join in.

"I'm never one to turn down free food. I just need to go home and change—"

"No!" she insists, taking me aback.

"Whoa."

"I just know that if you go home, the chances of you coming back out are slim to none. You were like that in college, too."

I frown at the accuracy.

"Come straight to the bar. I'm already here and it's filling up for happy hour."

It takes me less than five seconds to make a decision. "I'm on my way."

"Good."

****

Emanuel

I watch Angela expectantly once she hangs up the phone, but lift my eyebrows when she doesn't say anything at first, just a tiny smirk playing at her lips. I narrow my gaze on her, growing more pissed off by the second. She obviously has intentions of drawing this shit out.

"Well?" I demand.

"You boys are so impatient," she giggles.

My annoyance grows.

"She's on her way."

I push out a relieved breath. "That's all you had to say."

"I know, but I wanted you to sweat it out just a little."

"I don't sweat."

She rolls her eyes. "I know, I know. You're a *firefighter*, used to the heat."

"Damn straight."

"Leave my wife the hell alone," Eric interrupts, coming up behind Angela and wrapping an arm around her shoulders.

"Lieutenant." I nod mockingly. "Don't worry, it's not your wife I'm after." I toss him a wink as he growls angrily.

Chuckling, I walk off in the direction of the wooden booth toward the back of the bar where a number of other Rescue

Four guys have gathered after our latest twenty-four hour shift.

"That school fire was brutal the other day. Lucky everyone got out all right." Sean glances my way. "Fucking dumbass teens," he grunts, shaking his head.

After an investigation, the police discovered some neighborhood teens had wanted to play a trick on the elementary school with smoke bombs. They waited until the weekend custodial staff was doing a deep clean to place chains around the doors to keep them from getting out. What the teens didn't know was that there was a play rehearsal going on that day. And that their smoke bombs would misfire, the sparks causing actual fires, and the chains trapping children inside. The police were looking to charge the teens with some serious crimes.

"You might be a real firefighter yet, Allende," Sean says, clapping me on the back.

The table laughs boisterously when I toss Sean a middle finger.

"Play nice you two." Carter takes a sip of his beer. "Shit," he says, hopping up and heading off somewhere without another word.

I follow his long strides, and am unsurprised to see him pull open the door, allowing his fiancée, Michelle, to enter. I watch for a second longer than I should, noting the look they share.

Blinking, I let my gaze travel past the couple at the door, to see if another woman is on her way in, only to be disappointed when I don't see Janine. I glance down at my watch and realize it's only been five minutes since Angela hung up the phone.

"Waiting on someone?"

Shifting my attention to Sean, I see his gaze intently fixed on me. Any other time, I would've tossed him a *yeah, your mother's running late* joke, but knowing his parents died tragically a few years prior, I forego the dark humor. Instead, I tell him, "Mind your damn business."

There truly was no one nosier than a firefighter. You think your workplace is a destination for the rumor mill? It's got nothing on a firehouse.

A couple of the other guys get up to head to the bar for another round of beers, leaving Sean and I the only two at the table. He slides closer.

"You're waiting on Janine."

My brows pinching in confusion. "How the fuck—"

He begins chuckling. "Angela is my sister."

"She told you—"

He shakes his head before I can even finish the question. "Nah, Janine was over Angela and Eric's yesterday when I stopped by to drop off Jeremiah. I overheard them talking about a guy. Then I watched you over there pressing my sister to make a call." He shrugs. "I put two and two together."

"I don't need your advice."

"Good. I'm not about to give you any. I'm the last fucking person to give another man advice on relationships. Not when the one with my son's mother is all fucked up." He shakes his head in disgust. "I will say I think Janine is good people, and if it works out between you two, I'm happy for you."

"This conversation is way too fucking emotional," I grunt, picking up my half finished beer and chugging the rest.

He chuckles. "Who says firefighters don't have feelings?"

"Not anyone I know," Carter remarks as he interrupts the conversation.

"Emanuel, you've met my fiancée, Michelle," he introduces.

"Please don't stand for me," Michelle insists, waving me off as I began to rise.

"Good to see you again, Chaos."

We all laugh at my old nickname.

"How's Rescue Four treating you so far?" she inquires as she shifts down the inside of the booth, Carter taking his position on the outside and wrapping an arm around her.

"I haven't had to kick anyone's ass so far."

"Watch your mouth. You're in the presence of a woman," Carter growls.

Sean and I glance at each other and bust out laughing.

I'd been told on more than one occasion how overprotective he was of his woman.

Speaking of which ...

My gaze goes to the door again, and I sit up straighter when I see Janine coming through the door. Not even bothering to end the conversation, or explain my necessary absence to the rest of the table, I stand and make a beeline for the door.

I head toward her slowly, letting Janine greet Angela who's behind the bar serving drinks.

"Thanks for the invite. I'm feeling a little less stressed already." I hear her sigh as she removes the bomber jacket.

"Good. Let's see if we can move that process along. What're you drinking?" Angela questions.

"How about a mojito?" I intercept. I'm pleased when Janine gasps as she turns to me. I grin before glancing at Angela. "Why don't you make it two mojitos?" I look back to Janine. "For old times' sake."

"I didn't know you were going to be here," she says.

"I knew you would be."

Her perfectly arched eyebrows dip as she gives me a curious look. "How'd you know?"

I glance at Angela, who is at the farther end of the bar retrieving the mixes for our drinks. "Who do you think requested Angela to call you?"

A surprised then angry expression covers her face. "She

didn't ..."

"You're sexy as hell when you're pissed."

That seems to take some of the wind out of her angered sails. At that same moment Angela returns with our drinks.

"A fucking mojito," grunts someone behind me. It's another Rescue Four guy.

"Fuck off," I growl back.

He chuckles and saunters off. I shake my head just knowing I'm going to get shit for this drink of choice at work in the coming week. It's well worth it as I face Janine.

"I can't believe you set me up," she's saying to Angela.

"I'm sorry, I can't hear you over the music." Angela cups her ear as if straining to hear. She begins dancing to some Beyoncé song, I think, as she moves down the bar, taking other drink orders.

"I should go home."

"You can't. You've been drinking. Might as well enjoy the evening with me." I take her by the hand, pulling her away from the bar. I move closer to her until there is very little space between our two bodies. "You know you don't want to leave anymore than I want you to."

"How do you know what I want?"

"It's in your eyes, butterfly. They always tell on you." Wrapping my arm around her lower back, I escort her to an empty table, farther away from the bar, by the window. I pull out a chair, and she hesitates only for a moment before taking a seat.

Sitting across from her, I watch her intently as she sips at the mojito. "How was your first day of work?"

Her eyelids cover her pupils for a half a second and her lips form into a tight line. Her facial expression says more about her day than her any words she could speak.

"It sucked to be honest."

"What was so bad about it?" I lean in, resting both elbows on the table.

"I just hate being the new person. You know what I mean? Everyone around you knows what's going on except you. And there's this guy who's supposed to be training me or whatever ..." She pushes out a frustrated breath.

"It's only day one. Being the new kid on the block is supposed to be tough."

Her eyes bulge. "That's right. I'm complaining about my new job and you've just started a new job, too. How's it going?"

I shrug. "I'm not new to the job."

She swallows the sip of her drink she's just pulled through her straw and nods. A few strands of her straightened hair fall from behind her ear to the side of her face. I get the strangest urge to push it back, wanting to see the entirety of her face. So I do.

At my gesture, her eyelids flutter and a small smile

creases her lips.

"You're not new to firefighting but it's a new station, right? That means new coworkers, new boss, new location, all of that. How's it going?"

Her genuine interest warms my chest. "It's going."

She shakes her head. "No, no. You made Angela call me to get me down here, so you've got to give me more information than that. It's only fair."

I chuckle. "It's going well. Most of the guys I've known for a while from being called on the same scenes from time to time. There wasn't much overlap between Station Two and Rescue Four, but it happens sometimes. And Carter and I go way back."

"I remember you saying that. The Army, right?"

I nod.

Suddenly, I get the urge to be closer to her. To not have this wooden table, albeit small, separating our bodies. Being a man led by my instincts, I stand and move to her side of the table, holding out my hand.

"Dance with me." Grasping her hand, I pull her to stand.

"We can't dance here."

"Why not?" I've already begun moving my hips in time to the Celia Cruz song that's playing. Wrapping my arm around her waist, I bring our bodies together.

"Because there's no dance floor," she offers lamely.

I glance around. "That's not stopping anyone else." There's a small crowd developing around the empty spots in the bar, dancing. Angela's place, Charlie's, is well known among firefighters, and often a place first responders and young professionals go to let off some steam at the end of the day.

"That's it, butterfly. Just follow and let me lead," I say in a low tone, next to her ear. That little vein begins pulsing rapidly at the side of her neck.

"I told you this couldn't work between us." Her tone is soft as she says the words but she doesn't break away from my embrace.

"That's your fear talking, butterfly. And you should know something about me." I pull back to stare into her eyes.

"What's that?"

"I don't listen to fear. Especially when it's contradicting what you really want."

"How do you know what I really want? Whoop!" she yells when I suddenly spin her around before pulling her body back to mine.

"Because I want the same thing." I spin her again before she can respond. We continue to dance in silence for the rest of the song, Janine taking my lead. I can tell she's not totally comfortable with dancing but she's doing it for me. She wants to be more fluid and relaxed, but that overthinking mind of hers gets in the way.

Once the song is over, I wrap my arm around her waist from behind and tug her down onto my lap, taking a seat at the table we'd vacated to dance. "Go out with me this Friday."

"Emanuel—"

"That's a yes, right?"

She sighs. "What if—"

"No, butterfly, no what ifs. No overthinking. Just go with your gut."

She looks back at me, square in the eye, and says, "My gut says no."

I begin chuckling. "You're full of shit."

She giggles.

"See how much better your day just got with me?"

Sobering up, she pushes her hair behind her ear. For the life of me, I work to contain myself from licking it and sucking her earlobe into my mouth. Tension coils in my body remembering the way she shivered as she came when I did that in bed on our last night in Mexico.

"Why do you want this so badly?"

I frown, not at the question but at the suspicion in her voice that she tries to hide. It's almost as if she needs to convince herself that a man would be truly interested in her. Yet that just can't be the case. Janine might be a little stiff and overthinks everything but she has to know how goddamn sexy she is.

To give her that reminder, I lean over and whisper into her ear, "Because I'm pretty sure you broke my cock."

I can't help the grin that crosses my lips at her surprised reaction. She begins choke coughing, even though she hadn't been drinking anything.

"What?" she blurts out.

"Do you need me to say it again? You broke m—"

"No, I heard it the first time."

"Good, because I'm dead serious when I say it. You broke me for any other woman. It won't work for anyone else. I'm a firefighter, which means on any given night there are plenty of women throwing themselves at me. Before you I had no problem with it. Now, the only woman I want anywhere near my cock is you. You broke me after one fucking night. So all that bullshit about us not working goes in one ear and out the other."

Janine is speechless. Those golden eyes of hers halfway close as she sucks her bottom lip into her mouth. I know what she looks like when she's turned on, and this is it.

And just to add more fuel to the fire, I lean in and say into her ear, "And don't think I forgot about you lying to me about your name. You'll make it up to me eventually, on your knees in front of me, my cock sliding in and out of your mouth, tears of pleasure streaming down your face, your pussy soaking wet, and your belly filling from my come as you swallow it."

She is stunned into silence. That's fine. I didn't need words right then. Having her in my lap, my arm around her waist, and those lips only a few inches from mine, is enough for the time being.

Chapter Eleven

Janine

I don't know how the weekend got here so suddenly. One day it's Monday and I'm starting my new job, and the next moment I look up, it's Friday evening and I'm staring at myself in my full-length mirror, wondering if the gold chandelier earrings I've chosen for my night out are too much.

I twist and turn to look at myself at every angle in the wrap dress I've chosen to wear. It's not nearly as sexy as the dress I wore in Mexico on my and Emanuel's last date. I look over at the sliding white door of my closet, wondering what he'd think if I wore that dress instead. But I think twice, shaking my head. That dress is way too revealing for a night out on the town ... isn't it?

"No," I tell myself. Besides, it's mid fall, much too chilly out to wear it. I return my attention to the mirror, opting to leave the earrings in since they play well against my neckline due to my wearing my hair up in a high topknot. I play with the two tendrils I've curled with a curling iron at the sides to frame my face.

I peer down at the black dress and it seems ... off somehow. I wore this dress on a few dates with Matt, one of which was for a date out with his parents. I frown at the memory.

My attention is pulled away from the mirror by my ringing

phone. I move to pick it up, and checking the name of the caller, I groan. "Thinking of the devil really does make him appear," I grumble. "What, Matt?" I answer.

This is the third time he's called me this week. The second time I didn't answer and I erased his voicemail without even listening to it.

"What the hell are you doing?" His voice sounds irate.

"Um, excuse you?"

"I called and left a message two days ago. You haven't called me back."

Rolling my eyes, I move over to my vanity, picking up the eyeliner that I'd chosen not to wear earlier. But I rethought my decision as I stare at it.

"Were you really expecting me to call back?"

"Of course I was. What kind in idiotic question is that?"

I toss down the eyeliner and brace the phone tightly in my hand, placing my free hand on my hip. "So now I'm an idiot?"

"When you say stupid shit like that it really makes me wonder."

"Wow." I shake my head. "Don't call me again." I press the button to end the call and toss my phone back on the bed. Studying my reflection in the mirror again, I make a decision.

"This dress is boring." I don't want boring and safe, at least for one night.

Pulling the dress over my head and tossing it on the bed, I

slide open the door to my closet. I push back the long, red dress I'd worn in Mexico, and thumb through my other hanging clothes, most of which just don't feel right for the mood I'm in.

"Angela's right," I sigh. My wardrobe is so boring. She is always trying to get me to spice things up a little. If it hadn't been for her, I would've never taken half of the clothes with me to Mexico that I had.

I finally come to a gold, shimmery dress that feels perfect. I've had the dress so long, I totally forgot about it. I purchased it years ago on a whim. It had been during one of my dry spells with Matt. We weren't broken up at the time but it'd been a long time since I felt that spark when we initially got together. I thought it was because he'd been working so many hours, or that I was becoming too mundane. I wanted to spice things up. So on impulse, I bought the form fitting, long-sleeved dress that stopped at mid-thigh. The sleeves were loose and had slits from the end up to the bend of my forearm.

Two nights later while Matt completed another late night at work, I showed up with a picnic basket full of food and the dress with no panties on underneath. We actually had fun that night. It wasn't until three days later, when somehow his father found out what happened in his office, that Matt came telling me how irresponsible I was, and made him look bad.

I roll my eyes at that memory. "Matt is history but this dress isn't," I remind myself as I slip the dress over my head. I start to feel as sexy as the first time I wore it. I pair the dress with a gold pair of black high heels and leave the earrings I'd chosen in. Moving to my vanity, I pick up the eyeliner I had before, briefly looking over my shoulder when my phone rings again. Even though I'm across the room, I can see the name of the caller. I suck my teeth and go back to giving myself a winged eyeliner look for the evening.

"Go to hell, Matt," I mumble as the phone beeps to alert me that I have a new voicemail.

Stepping back, I smile in the mirror, liking the person I see staring back at me. I move to my bed, pick up my phone, and delete the missed call alert, along with the voicemail.

That's when a knock at my door sounds.

****

Emanuel

The muscles of my stomach clench as soon as she opens the door.

"Holy shit," I curse harshly.

Her eyes bulge. "I hope that means you like it."

I let my eyes trail down the length of her dress, examining her long legs before reversing my gaze to meet her face. "What's not to like?" Stepping closer, I lower my head, kissing her lips simply because of the force of an invisible pull between us. "You look great."

Smiling, she dips her head.

I step back and hold up the plant in my hand. "This is for you."

"A bamboo plant?"

"The woman at the store said these were for good luck, but that someone else had to buy it for you in order for the good luck to work …" I shrug. "Or whatever."

Her face widens on a smile as she reaches for the squared glass vase with three stalks of green bamboo stalks standing up out of the water. "Thank you. I think I'll take this to work to set up on my desk. I could use the luck there." A small frown touches those pink-tinted lips.

I narrow my eyes. "Had a rough week?"

She nods but then waves her hand dismissively. "At least it's Friday. I'm going to set this on the counter. Do you want any water or anything before we leave?"

I miss the question because I'm too busy staring at her legs and backside in that dress as she walks in the direction of the kitchen. The dress isn't too tight or revealing but it is sexy as hell, the gold color standing out against the dark brown glowing skin.

"Emanuel?"

I blink and lift my gaze to see her giving me an expectant look. "Is this dress new?" I question, stepping closer.

"Old, actually, but I've only worn it once. It's pretty,

right?" She looks down as if analyzing it.

"It wou—"

"If you say something cliché like 'it would look better on my bedroom floor,' I'm going to slap you."

Laughter spills from my lips because that's *exactly* what I'd been thinking.

"It's time to go."

"Where're we going tonight?" she asks as I place my arm at the small of her back and pull the door of her apartment open.

"Uh, uh, you'll find out when we get there."

She sucks her teeth and gives me what's supposed to be an angry expression.

As the elevator doors close behind us, I corner her and lift her hand to my lips. "You really look amazing tonight."

She sighs. "Thank you."

"And I still think this dress would look better on my bedroom floor." I wiggle my eyebrows, laughing as she takes a swat at my shoulder. I duck out of her reach.

It takes about fifteen minutes to get to the Spanish tapas restaurant I'd chosen for the evening. I know I've made the right choice when Janine's eyes light up as we pull into the parking lot.

"Angela told me about this place. She and Eric came her a few months ago. Says she loved it."

I nod as I pull up to the valet and put the car in park. After getting out, I give the valet my name and information before moving around the side door to pull it open for Janine.

"Thank you," she says as I assist her out of the car, and because her lips are so inviting, I lower and place another peck on them.

Pulling back before I can get too excited, I say, "I'm glad I could be the one to pop this cherry for you, too."

"Oh my god," she groans. "You're like a teenage boy sometimes. Do men ever grow up?"

"Hopefully not," I tease, but then get serious as I give the hostess my name for the reservation. I watch as Janine continues to look around as we're led to one of the round tables by a window at the back of the restaurant. The lighting in the restaurant is low and there's flamenco music playing in the overhead speakers.

"Tell me more about your week at work," I say once I've helped her with her chair and rounded the table to take my own.

Shrugging, she pushes out a breath. "Still trying to get the hang of everything and learn the system, and of course the work culture. There's a lot of little cliques in the office."

"You're surprised by that?"

"I shouldn't be, I know. Every place has cliques and whatnot, but I've only had one real job since I graduated college."

"What'd you study in college?"

"Business Administration with a concentration in marketing."

I frown. "Then how'd you become a teacher for seven years?"

She looks off into the distance, a sullen expression covering her pretty face.

Instinctively, I reach across the table for her hand, intertwining it with mine. She stares down at out clasped fingers and smiles.

"I went to college in Boston, and afterwards I didn't want to leave. I started looking for jobs my senior year in my field by couldn't find anything beyond a receptionist position. A friend who'd graduated a year ahead of me told me about this program that helped college graduates become teachers even though they hadn't studied teaching in school. I looked into it, and they were going to be interviewing on my campus, so I applied. Next thing I know, a month after my college graduation, I'm taking the qualifying exam to become certified. I passed and then spent that summer training under teachers in my school district. That September I began my career. I had to continue with master's level classes in teaching for my advanced degree in order to maintain my certification."

"But you didn't enjoy it," I remark as I continue playing

with her fingers in mine.

Before she can answer, our waitress comes to the table to take our drink orders. Janine orders a glass of red wine while I order one of the beers they have on tap.

"I enjoyed it at first. I taught second grade and the kids were great. But after a while it became …"

"Stagnant?"

"How'd you know?"

"Lucky guess. So now you're working in advertisement?"

She nods as she moves her arms from the table so the waitress can place our drinks in front of us.

I reluctantly let her pull her hand away, but as soon as her hand lands back on the table I cover it with my own again. For some reason I need the connection of physical touch.

"What about you?"

I raise my eyebrows. "What about me?"

"What made you become a firefighter?"

"I had the skills, so it seemed like a natural choice."

"Don't give me that," she laughs. "And you call me full of shit."

I chuckle because she's right. "I was never the type to work a typical nine to five."

"You don't say?"

I laugh at the sarcasm in her voice. "There's a lot of

overlap between being in the Army and being a firefighter."

The waitress returns to take our orders. We order a number of different tapas to try between the two of us, including cured ham, grilled bread topped with capers and mushrooms, and fava beans in some type of aioli sauce.

"What's the overlap between the Army and being a fire department?" she asks once our orders are taken.

"In the Army, because of my role in special forces, I had to know a wide range of information, even though I was assigned a specific role. There's also the rank. It's less structured in the fire department, but both the Army and department follow strict codes of rank and who is supposed to be in charge and whatnot. And then there's the camaraderie."

"I've always wondered if the television shows and movies portray the relationships between firefighters as true. They always seem so close."

"It's true. Every day we walk into hell and have to have one another's back in total darkness. A bond develops out of that."

"Like going to war with fellow soldiers."

I nod. "Something like that."

"So what made you leave the Army?"

"I wanted to put down roots, finally. After years of having to pick up and move or being deployed, I wanted to be in one place for a while."

Her lips twist up in a funny way and a contemplative expression crosses her face. "I can understand that."

I want to interrogate that more. The sincerity in her voice convinces me that there's something deeper with her understanding.

"Here you go," our waitress chimes as our food is delivered.

The conversation about work is put on hold for a while as we begin enjoying our meal which is a relief for me. After about two weeks at Rescue Four I feel I've earned the respect of most of my fellow squad members. I knew the respect wouldn't come automatically. One has to prove themselves to become an accepted member of the team. That I understand, and respect, honestly. I even realized some would have trouble accepting me onto the team because of the way my current position became available.

A teammate had been severely injured in a fire.

Most of the guys had come around. Figured out that I wasn't the enemy. The ones who didn't I couldn't give a shit about. I just needed them to be reliable in the middle of a fire or a rescue. Other than that, they could fuck off. All except one. Don.

He's been a thorn in my side since my first day. And it wasn't his standoffish attitude. That, I could let roll off my back. It was the fact that he, of all people, had me feeling like there was some information being withheld from me. As if there was a secret almost everyone in the station knew that I didn't. I hate being kept out of the loop, and I already made a decision to do something about it.

"We have to get the churros! With the chocolate sauce," Janine declares as we peruse the dessert menu.

"Churros with chocolate sauce and the flan," I say to the waitress as I hand her back my menu.

"The music's getting louder," Janine notices, looking around the restaurant dining area.

"That's because their dance lessons start soon."

She turns to me, surprised. "Lessons?"

I nod. "They just added flamenco and salsa lessons on the first Friday of the month."

"And of course you chose this Friday to bring me here."

My smile grows. "Naturally."

"I'm not dancing," she declares as our dessert is brought to us.

I wink and toss her a cocky smile.

****

Janine

I specifically said I *wasn't* going to dance. So how the hell am I front and center of the dancefloor, with my arms in the air, listening intently for the next instruction of our dance instructor? I wanted to say no, but when Emanuel pulled me onto the dance floor and whispered in my ear that he wanted to see my hips swaying in this dress, how could I resist?

Now if I can just get past my fear long enough to let loose a little bit and move to the beat of the music, I might not actually make a fool of myself.

"Tuh," I push out on a breath. I am the queen of overthinking, especially when I feel out of place and as if everyone is watching me.

"It's just me and you, butterfly," his warm, deep voice soothes in my ear.

How does he know exactly what I need to hear?

His hands slide to my waist and I feel his hips pressing against my backside. "No one else is here, but me, you, and Marc Anthony."

Our laughter melds together as Marc Anthony's "Dimelo" continues to play. I grow warm inside when the sound of the famous salsa singer is replaced by Emanuel's voice. He's singing in perfect Spanish, serenading me as he manipulates my body to dance in time with the music. We've stopped listening to the directions coming from the front of the dance floor. There is an ease that comes over me in Emanuel's arms. One I hadn't even noticed I needed or wanted but it's there. He's made my confidence grow, and with it, the hesitation is removed.

I begin moving in time with the music almost effortlessly. Emanuel spins around to face me and it truly becomes just the two of us in the room. My steps lose their hesitancy and resistance to the music. When Emanuel twirls me around, I go with ease, knowing I'll end up right back in his arms, where I belong. He is a natural at this ... either that, or he's had lots of practice. But I don't concern myself with thinking about the different women he's performed these same dance moves with. It's just us, here and now, which is right where I need to be. And I get the suspicion it's where he needs to be as well.

"That was so much fun," I sigh as Emanuel gets behind the driver's seat of his car. Pressing my back against the cool leather seat, I squeeze my hands at my sides, still feeling the energy of dancing vibrating through me. "I don't think I've ever felt that good after a night of dancing."

He gives me a strange look. "You didn't go out dancing with your girlfriends in college?"

I frown, thinking back to my time in college. I shrug. "Sometimes, but I don't know ... that was different." I keep to myself that I met my boyfriend mid-way through my sophomore year at Boston College, and after that, going out dancing with my friends became a rarity. Matt didn't like going out with my friends, though I often tagged along with him when he went out with his, at his request. Those nights weren't very enticing when it came to letting down my hair and enjoying myself so much.

"*He* got in the way, huh?"

I glance over, not understanding the almost possessive tone in Emanuel's voice. His eyes are narrowed as he stares me down.

"How do you know there was a *he*?"

"Same way I knew there was a he behind your being in Mexico alone. Is it the same guy?"

I push out a breath. "Yeah, but I don't want to talk about him."

"Good, because he's old fucking news anyway. Do you need to go straight home?" he questions, changing the subject.

Looking at the time on the dashboard, I blink. It's close to eleven-thirty. Way past my usual quitting time, but my body still buzzes with adrenaline. I shake my head. "No."

"Good, let's take a drive."

It's on the tip of my tongue to ask where we were driving to, but I refrain. I don't need to know the plan. I don't *want* to know the plan. I just want to *be* with Emanuel.

"What are you thinking about?" He makes a right, heading toward one of the main highways leading out of the city of Williamsport.

"How good it feels to be with you," I say honestly.

He gives me a quick glance, and I see mischief in those

eyes of his.

I gasp when he hits the gas pedal and his Mustang begins picking up speed. I giggle.

"What's that about?"

I turn to him. "I knew you'd have a car like this." I pause, making sure I want to verbalize my thoughts. "I imagined what kind of car you drive, how you decorate your apartment, all of that."

"And you pictured a Mustang?"

"Either that or a Thunderbird."

"That's on my list to get whenever I buy a home with a garage to fit both of my babies."

I laugh, tossing my head back. "I should've known."

There's silence for a little while but not an uncomfortable silence. It's one that doesn't need filling. I lower the window to get some air even though it's fall and the night temperatures are dropping. I watch as we pass a sign on the road that says "Leaving Williamsport." We continue driving into a more secluded wooded area. Emanuel picks up speed.

"Do me a favor?"

"What's that?"

"Lift up your dress."

My breath hitches and I go to ask him if he's serious but the look in his eyes tells me he absolutely is.

"Emanuel, I can't," I say.

"All you have to do is use your hands to bunch up the sides of that dress, show me those sexy little thighs of yours."

I swallow the lump of lust and tension that has formed in my throat. I don't even realize what's happening before I look down and see my hands doing exactly as his instructions dictated.

"That's it, butterfly. Pull it up to your waist."

I do so, lifting my hips to pull my dress up until it bunches at the sides of my waist.

"Bikini cut panties. Sexy," he growls. "Put your hand into them."

Never would I have ever imagined myself doing something like this with a man I was technically on a first date with. At least, our first date here at home.

"Is she wet?"

"Y-yes," I moan. I don't know how it happened. Maybe it's just a natural byproduct of being around Emanuel, but I am already feeling the moistness of my arousal soaking the seat of my panties.

"Is she hot?"

I nod.

"Uh, uh, butterfly. Words. Use that pretty little mouth of yours. Is she hot?"

"Yes."

"Good. Play with your clit for me."

Again, I do as instructed because I need the release.

"Not so fast, slow down. That's it, small circles. Now move down to that tight hole of yours."

My eyes drift shut as I let the sound of his voice be the beacon that summons me to my orgasm. Doing as he tells me, I insert my pointer finger into my wet canal. I moan but then bite down on my lower lip, cutting the sound off.

"What the hell was that?" his demanding voice booms.

I turn in his direction. "Wh-What?"

"Don't you dare try to hold back from me. I want to hear every moan, every squeal, every sound that beautiful mouth and body of yours makes when you're enjoying yourself." For good measure, he reaches over with his right hand, taking my chin in between the grasp of his thumb and forefinger, pulling it so that my lower lip pops out from between my teeth. "Let me hear it, butterfly," he growls.

I am literally dripping into my hand from the words that've just spilled from his mouth. I swallow, trying to get rid of the dryness in my throat, and uncertainty weighing my chest down. I hate to admit it even to myself, but I do hold back during sex. My ex hated when I got too loud. He said real ladies didn't moan loudly, or curse during sex. After ten years together, I changed so much for him.

"Fuck him," Emanuel growls, firmly holding my face by the chin. "Look at me. You're with me now. Let me hear you."

I stare at those golden eyes of his as he briefly takes his eyes off the road ahead and pins me with his powerful gaze. I am drawn back to that night we shared in Mexico. The night I wanted to let all of my inhibitions go but was still too afraid. In this moment, I decide to let go of that fear.

Lifting my hips up, I begin working my body with one and then two fingers, also using my thumb to run circles around my clit just the way Emanuel had that night. A moan breaks free, and instead of cutting it off, I let it rise all the way from my belly and flow out of my lips without apprehension. I can barely catch my next breath before another groan escapes.

"Shit!" I curse when I feel the engine of the car revving up, and we suddenly pick up speed.

I glance from Emanuel to the speedometer. We're going ninety miles an hour and gaining speed. Fear seizes my body for all of a heartbeat before I look to Emanuel, whose face is totally relaxed and in control as his gaze moves between me and the windshield. The only time tension arises in his body is when his eyes roll over my body to see my stilled hand.

"Keep going."

I don't hesitate at his command. I begin working my body, strumming it like a guitar. My hips rise and fall from the seats, begging for more.

Emanuel rolls the windows down a few inches to let the night air inside of the car.

I gasp as the sensations from the rushing wind, the pressure from my fingers, and the knowledge of Emanuel's eyes on me as I work myself over become too much. Tossing my head back against the seat, I squeeze my eyes shut and let the orgasm have its way with my body.

I don't recall screaming or making any sounds with my mouth, but when I finally come back to myself, my throat is raw.

Not only that, but we've finally come to a stop. We're somewhere on a long stretch of road, surrounded by woods on either side. I have no idea where, and it is the dead of night so very few cars are around. I'm not given much time to analyze the situation when Emanuel throws the car in park.

"I need to taste you," he growls.

He pushes his seat back and it takes some maneuvering, but somehow I find my head laying on the lowered window sill, halfway out of the car, while my body is now fully turned toward Emanuel in the driver's set. My legs are over his shoulders as he buries his head in between my thighs. He first uses his tongue to lap at the soft skin of my inner thighs. I begin panting in anticipation of another orgasm, and he hasn't even touched my pussy yet.

By the time he does finally reach my outer lips, I'm already calling his name. It sounds so perfect spilling from my mouth that I continue saying it almost as if on a chant. Emanuel is not immune to hearing his name being moaned from my lips, either. He rolls his tongue against my clit, massaging and tickling it, sending tingles throughout my body. His hands move underneath my thighs until my ass is fully clasped in them. He squeezes and pulls the flesh of my skin, bringing me closer to his mouth. I swear he is trying to consume me from the outside in.

I am so overcome by the feeling flowing through me and the warmth of his tongue and mouth that the awkwardness of my positioning barely registers with me. I have but a passing awareness of my head against the hard metal door frame. The only thing that matters is that my second orgasm is being wrung out from my body.

Letting my head flop backwards, all of the way outside of the window, I yell out Emanuel's name, loud enough to wake the dead.

It takes me a long time to catch my breath after that soul snatching orgasm. My vision is blurry, as I blink, staring around at the inside of Emanuel's car, still trying to get my wits about me enough to remember where the hell I am. With my dress up around my waist and my panties ... gone, I should be embarrassed. Or ashamed.

I'm neither of those things.

When I focus on the expression on Emanuel's face, and the glistening moisture of his lips, I only have one thought.

I want to taste it.

I move so quickly, I surprise even myself. Wrapping my hands around the sides of his face, I pull him to me, and devour his lips with the same fervor and energy he'd used on me. I lick his lips, tasting myself on him and liking it. I moan aggressively into his mouth. Our tongues collide as he kisses me back with the same amount of enthusiasm. The thing that forces us apart is my need to breathe again. It's only when my lungs feel as if they're going to explode from my chest, do I pull back, and that's when I realize that I am now straddling him in the driver's seat.

"There's my butterfly," he croons as he peers at me with those piercing eyes of his.

My chest wells up with a sense of belonging. I don't have the words to form what it is I want to say. I don't even have the comprehension to understand just what it is that I'm feeling right now. All I can do is lay my head against his shoulder and pull him to me.

A sense of relaxation overcomes me when his strong arms encase my body, holding me as tightly to him as I am him to me.

It's right at this very moment that I know all of that stuff I said about Emanuel and I not working was a complete and total lie.

Chapter Twelve

Janine

I feel refreshed. Almost the same way I felt right after my return from Mexico, but somehow I feel even *better.* Emanuel and I spent the entire weekend together. Well, at least most of it. He had to go into work on Sunday afternoon. But from Friday night, until Sunday we didn't spend more than an hour apart. And that was only because after spending the night at his place on Friday, I had to go back to my place to shower and change into fresh clothing.

I can't believe I spent two nights at his place. And the biggest surprise was that we didn't have sex. Sure he gave me a mind-blowing orgasm with his mouth in his car, after watching me masturbate, but that was the furthest we went. Even as I laid in his very comfortable and cozy bed, he'd done nothing more than wrap his arms around me until we fell asleep.

Now, as I walk into work on this Monday morning I'm feeling ready to tackle anything that comes my way.

"Good morning, Shelah," I sing-song as I wave to her on my way in.

Shelah, the office receptionist's face lights up. "Someone's sounding chipper on a Monday morning." Her almond-shaped, brown eyes narrow as she gives me a mischievous smile.

"What's not to be happy about?"

"Uh, that fact that it's Monday?"

We both giggle. "Mondays are for new beginnings, Shelah. Great things can happen on a Monday." I wink at her, and head back to my desk.

"Sounds like someone got some this weekend," she mumbles loud enough for me to hear.

I grin but don't turn back to confirm or deny her statement. I'm not the type to share my personal business at work. Besides, part of her statement *is* true to an extent, at least. I did have a great weekend with a great guy, and yes there were some orgasms involved. Who wouldn't be feeling better after that? But that's not what all of my cheeriness is about. After Emanuel left for work on Sunday, I sat down, ready to catch up on a couple of episodes of *Game of Thrones,* when an idea of a new tech company Lux Advertising was working for popped into my head. I spent the better part of an hour writing out my idea and coming up with a few different campaigns and ways to approach the rollout for the new product.

As I pull out my notebook with my ideas written out and boot up my computer, I notice my boss walking in my direction. Too anxious and full of excitement, I jump up from my desk and meet him at his office door.

"Good morning, Danny, how was your weekend?" I question, trying to ease into the work conversation.

"It was great. How about yours, Janine?" He barely looks at

me as he passes over the threshold into his office and sets his cup of coffee and briefcase on the desk.

I can already tell that I only have about fifteen seconds before I completely lose his attention and he's onto something else.

"So, Danny, I was thinking about the new tech client we're working with and the app they're trying to roll out."

"Oh yeah?" He's now searching for something in his briefcase.

"Yes, and I think the app is a wonderful tool that will really be a boost to millennials. In particular millennials who are working and raising families."

He snorts.

I can't tell if it's due to something I've said or at the file he's now holding up as he skims over it.

"But the thing is that in today's day and age most people are inundated with new technologies. We need to find a way to make it relevant to them. To their lifestyle. Which is why I think focusing on the parental aspect is the way to go with this particular app."

"That route isn't what the company was thinking with this project," he states flatly, frowning, as he briefly lifts his gaze to me.

"I know." I move closer, ready to make my hard sell. "It's completely different. Many of the company's ideas center around the young, hip millennial who's a mover and shaker, but I think that's the wrong way to go. Speaking as someone in that generation, we're constantly—"

"Janine, that sounds interesting. Look, talk it over with Zeke. You two hash out a couple of ideas and we'll reconvene on Wednesday to decide what to go with. Marvin and his team will be back in the office on Friday to see what we've come up with." He nods and picks up his phone to begin placing a call.

Feeling slightly defeated, my shoulders slump as I turn to head out of the office. It's obvious I'm being dismissed. However, as I retrace my footsteps to my desk, I am buoyed by the knowledge that Danny didn't give me a hard *no*. He may not be as enthused by the idea as I am but maybe it's just because I didn't have the chance to present the research just yet.

"Good morning, Zeke," I say as he approaches his desk.

Pausing to pull the over-the-shoulder strap of his cloth briefcase over his head, he gives me a curt nod, I guess as an acknowledgement, but no words actually spill from his lips.

I'm undeterred. "I know you're just getting settled in, but I wanted to run something past you."

"I need coffee," he sighs and turns, heading back toward the front of the open office space where the kitchen area is.

Gritting my teeth, I patiently wait for him to return by pulling open my notebook and carefully reviewing the notes that I took the day before in preparation for this campaign.

This time when Zeke returns, I give him a few minutes to settle in first. I realize that with Danny my approach needed to be a little different. He is typically on the phone or with clients, or in some type of meeting at all hours of the work day. If you don't catch him first thing in the morning, it's difficult to find another time to approach him unless you're already on his schedule.

Zeke—being my desk partner—is different, although he likely says fewer words to me throughout the day than Danny does.

"Zeke," I say, moving my head around my computer after checking and returning some emails, "I spoke with Danny this morning about the Digita Technologies campaign. I—"

"Why would you do that?" he questions in a clipped tone.

I blink and gather my thoughts, pushing down the anger that rises in me at his lack of patience. "Because I think I came up with a really great way to approach this rollout." Before he can reject or interject with anything, I stand and bring my notebook around to his side to show him what I am talking about.

"Danny said to discuss my idea with you—"

"Probably because he didn't want to hear it."

I glower at him. But I refuse to let him take me out of my good mood. "Or because he was busy and he wanted you to do your damn job to help train me."

"What did you say?"

I shake my head. "You heard me the first time. Look, I've been researching, and the stats say that about fifty percent of millennials are parents. More than one million millennial women become mothers each year. That is a huge market. Of course, we can narrow it down further, but I believe focusing on the momprenuer—"

"What the hell is a *momprenuer*?"

"It's a mother, obviously, but she is starting or is currently running her own business from home. Many millennial mothers are learning to not only stay home with their kids while they're young, but also bring in extra income while doing it. The internet has—"

"And what does this have to do with Digita?"

"Well, their new app is perfect for this type of person. It combines scheduling, finances, project management, and even social activities all in one. This is exactly the type of app a momprenuer would love to get their hands on."

Zeke pauses and looks over my notes.

Just when I think I'm starting to get somewhere, he lifts his head and rolls his eyes. "This is ridiculous. Digita came in and specifically gave us the marketing research they've done. They know who they want to appeal to, and the *momprenuer*." he says mockingly, "isn't it."

He tuts, shaking his head and pushing my notebook out of his line of sight.

Taking a step back, I lift my notebook from his desk and look over my notes, swallowing the lump of embarrassment in my throat.

"But what if—"

"You really want to know how you can be of help on this campaign?"

My ears perk up as I ready to hear any suggestions Zeke might have for improving this idea of mine. My hopes are dashed when I peer down at his narrowed hazel eyes and wrinkle in his forehead.

"Don't bother showing Danny anymore of that." He juts his head toward the notebook in my hands. And rolls his eyes dismissing my idea. "I've already picked out a campaign that I know Digita is going to love. All you need to do is back me up in the meeting with Danny on Friday. Better yet, all you need to do is sit there and smile. It's probably what Danny hired you for anyway," he mumbles the last part before turning around.

"What is that supposed to mean?" I ask before I can think better of it.

"Nothing."

"No, it's not nothing," I insist placing my hand on my hip, glaring at him. "Something's been up your butt about me since I walked into this office on my first day, so let's just get it out in the open."

"Okay, fine. Everyone in this office knows why Danny hired you."

"Because I'm a hard worker and—"

"Right," he says mockingly. "It's this whole *diversity* nonsense being pushed down everyone's throats these days. I was on the committee that checked resumes to interview for your position. You don't even have experience working in advertising."

"I have a degree in—"

"Marketing and business admin. Right. You and everyone else who applied. What they also had was experience in this type of work. Regardless, the politically correct agenda of the day dictates hiring practices. Everyone wants *diversity and inclusivity,* forcing good managers to hire less than adequate employees." He makes sure to hammer his point home about who he's referring to when he slowly looks me up and down. No more is said as he turns back to his computer and continues typing out the email he'd been working on.

I stumble backward, bumping into someone behind me. "I'm sorry," I say just above a whisper to a blonde-haired woman named Jennifer. She's been polite to me since I began working at Lux Advertising, but in this moment, her perfect Barbie-esque appearance is a little too much to handle.

I move away and glance around the office, taking in my

coworkers, none of whom are paying any attention to me. It slowly seeps in that Zeke is correct. Aside from Shelah, who is our receptionist, I am the only person of color in the office. Not only that, but we're all around the same age, and there isn't, from what I can see, anyone facing a disability of some sort.

Was I hired as a token?

After placing my notebook on top of my desk, I make a beeline for the bathroom. My day went from sunshine to downpour in less than an hour.

****

Emanuel

"Allende, you're driving tonight," Sean states, pointing at me from across the kitchen.

I glance up from the pasta primavera with shrimp that I'm cooking. "Not a problem."

"That smells good. What's in it?" Sean reaches in to swipe a shrimp. "Shit! What the fuck?" he growls as I slap his hand with the wooden spoon.

"Learn some fucking manners. You don't stick your dirty ass hands into my food!"

"That's what I've been trying to tell him since we were kids."

We both turn at the sound of the feminine voice to see Angela standing there grinning as she gives her older brother a *that's what you get* expression.

"What are you doing here?"

I look at Sean, lifting my eyebrow. He's not simply asking out of curiosity. His tone is clipped, angered almost.

"Well, hello, too, big brother. I'm here to see my husband, of course," Angela replies with her hand on her hip.

"Eric's upstairs," I say.

"Thanks, Emanuel." Angela nods and moves in, giving Sean a quick hug before exiting the kitchen to head up the stairs, I assume.

I turn to my lieutenant. "What was that about?" I get the feeling it isn't strictly family business that has him so anxious. I've been feeling it for weeks, here at the station. As if there's some hidden danger that everyone knows about but no one is actually saying. Not the typical danger, either. We're firefighters, our job puts us in some very precarious situations routinely. It's a part of the job and we all know it. And more than that, we all *embrace* it. But the type of unspoken danger I'm talking about seems like something else.

"Nothing." Sean shakes his head. He turns, but is stopped when I grab him by the arm. His expression turns serious when he glances from my hand to my face.

He can be pissed all he wants. "What the hell is going on?"

He snatches his arm from me. "Don't put—"

"Yeah, whatever." I wave off the threat I assumed was

about to spill from his lips. "You've all been skirting around something for weeks now and I want to know what the fuck is up." I work to control my anger.

"I—" He stops when footsteps can be heard coming down the stairs. "We'll talk about it later."

I'm ready to tell him later isn't good enough when the alarm sounds for an incoming call.

"Rescue Four, two young men trapped on the scaffolding of a building. Address ..." the operator's voice sounds throughout the entire station on the speakers.

Whatever I was about to say to Sean is forgotten in an instant as I turn off the stove and race behind him toward the garage. I easily step into my turnout gear, pulling the suspenders over my shoulders, and grab my jacket but opt not to throw it on at this time.

I head straight for the driver's seat since I'm driving that shift. Sean hops into the passenger seat since he's the highest ranking member on the squad for the night. Don and Carter get in the back of the rig. Once I do a quick head count to make sure we're all in, I look over at Sean who gives me a quick nod, granting me the okay to pull out. I raise my hand and pull on the wire that is attached to the horn, alerting all surrounding vehicles and personnel that we're on the move.

I make a right out of the station, checking the GPS locations at the front of the steering wheel that shows me we are about eight minutes out from the location.

"Dispatch says two young men, early twenties, were hanging out on a scaffold and now it's hanging from one side."

"What the fuck were they doing out there in the first place?" Don growls, angrily.

"You can ask them when we get there," Sean retorts.

"Emanuel, you're going to be strapped into a harness just in case we need it, and Carter is going to be the point man on the ladder ..." Sean continues to call out directions.

I take it all in, while still navigating the rig around some tight corners, finally bringing us to our final destination.

"Shit!" everyone in the truck says simultaneously when we look up and see two pairs of arms flailing for help about fifteen stories off the ground.

"Help! Help!" Their yells get louder once they notice the fire truck pull up. The only problem with that, is with their increased volumes comes more exaggerated flailing and body movement, causing the scaffolding to sway even more.

"Let's get this done!" Sean yells.

Everyone begins moving in their respective positions. Stepping into my harness, I silently say a prayer that I won't have to be delivering any bad news tonight.

The initial plan was to try to get inside the building to head up to the fifteenth floor, open a window, and pull the boys inside, but by looking up at the building, I know that plan is a wash. There's no way we'll have time to wait for a building manager to make it down here to unlock it and let us in. We have to get them from the outside.

"Emanuel, you're gonna have to go up on the ladder," Sean instructs.

I was already climbing to the top of the rig to turn the ladder on.

"Your harness on correctly?" Don questions.

"Yeah."

"You sure?"

I give him a look. "I've been tying harnesses for a decade. I know what the fuck I'm doing."

He frowns but doesn't say anything.

Right now isn't the time to question him on it either. I start to hear the sound of the ladder being raised but that's followed by another loud, crashing sound.

All of us look up to find that another piece of the scaffolding has fallen off, crashing to the sidewalk only a few feet from the rig.

"Shit! Carter, get that ladder up there faster!" Sean orders.

We all know Carter is moving as quickly as he can, but right now yelling is about the only thing we can do.

I move to the bottom of the ladder and start to climb even though it hasn't reached its full height yet. I hear footsteps behind me and I can tell by the sound that it's Don bringing up the rear.

When the ladder finally reaches its full length and is safely resting against the side of the building, I run up the steps as quickly as possible to reach the two young men.

"Oh god, you gotta help us!" one of the terrified young men shouts.

"It's okay. You're going to be fine, but you have to stop moving so much. Every time you move, this scaffolding gets more and more unstable. All right?" I say in my calmest but most stern voice.

"My friend. He's stuck!"

I glance past the man to see the second guy not moving nearly as much. Briefly, I see a thick rope entangled around his waist and leg.

Turning back to the first man. "You're going to have to jump, okay? I can't bring the ladder any closer."

"I-I can't!"

"Yes you can. Take my hand." I stretch my hand out to meet his. "On the count of three. One ... two ... three!" I pull him by the arm as he leaps from the scaffolding onto the ladder.

The ladder shakes and shifts a little, startling the young man.

"It's okay, I got you."

He's fine. I look down to see Don.

"You got him?" I yell.

"Yeah." Don grabs the kid and begins helping him down the ladder.

I look back to the second guy who I know isn't going to be as easy as his friend to rescue. Again, the second guy isn't yelling for help or moving much at all, which in this case isn't a good sign. I can see blood marks on his ripped blue jeans.

"Fuck!" I curse when I trace the cause of the blood to a cut on his leg. "What happened?" I question.

"C-Cut myself trying t-to get out of the r-rope," he stammers while holding up a pocket knife.

Doing a quick assessment, I realize that he probably got his leg entangled in the ropes of the scaffolding and tried to free himself using the knife in his hand but only made matters worse by cutting himself. *Shit,* I swear to myself when I see the amount of blood he's losing. He could've cut his femoral artery. That rope around his leg might be the only thing keeping him from bleeding out.

"Shit!" I grunt.

Don has just passed off the first guy to Carter who helps to lower him to the awaiting paramedics.

Don peers up at me, expecting the second young man to be coming down. He doesn't know the situation up here it dire.

"I have to go get him," I yell down.

"What? No!" Don retorts as he begins running up the

ladder.

I don't have time to wait or to waste. I can't reach all of the way over from the ladder to pull the kid off, and he can't jump in his condition. I have to go get him. I don't think about how secure the scaffolding might be. I ensure that my harness is firmly secured to the ladder, but just as I'm about to leap, Don grabs onto my turnout gear.

"What the hell are you doing?" he growls.

"He's stuck on there." I point to the kid's leg. "He's bleeding out and can't move."

Don does a quick assessment of the situation, seeing what I've already seen.

"Fine, I'm right here," he says.

I nod, actually feeling safer knowing that he's not moving but also not standing in the way of my doing what I need to do.

I move quickly, reaching for the scaffolding and trying to assess how secure this thing is. Unfortunately, I find that it's not secure at all.

I turn to Don. "This isn't gonna work. You'll need to hang onto me while I cut him out."

He nods.

I stretch as far as I can get my body to reach to grab the rope around the young man's leg. Using my own knife, I begin cutting at the rope, hoping that the scaffolding doesn't give way before I can free him. There's also the matter of ensuring that I don't remove the rope that is serving as a tourniquet for the boy's leg. One false move and this young man's life is over before it truly ever began.

"Got it!" I say as I free the rope from the scaffolding ... right before more of it gives way, falling lower. "Shit!"

"I got you," Don assures.

Without thinking, I wrap my arms around the struggling guy and pull him with me back to the ladder. Don is there to help relieve the pressure of the boy's limp body. We awkwardly maneuver carrying his body down the ladder until we reach the bottom. He is gingerly brought down the rig to the paramedics, who quickly assess the delicate situation he's in, and whisk him off to the ambulance and then to the hospital.

Pushing out a breath, I silently hope the boy makes it to the hospital alive and the doctors are able to save him. A dark cloud begins to fall over me. My fingers tense as I ball them into fists. It's the same feeling that's come over me for months now. Blinking, I try to shake the mood off but it's no use. Especially when I look up and catch sight of Don grilling me with his glare.

I narrow my eyes on him, already feeling primed for a fight due to the excessive energy coursing through me.

"You're dangerous," he growls, moving closer. "You don't wait for direction, you don't wait for your team, and you don't give a fuck about anyone but yourself."

"And you're a fucking empty shirt who needs to stay the fuck out of my way."

"Fu—"

"Hey, hey!" Sean breaks us apart. "Let's pack up this equipment and go," he orders.

I give Don one last glare and turn, only to come face-to-face with Carter.

His eyes move from me to Don, over my shoulder, and then back to me. "He's not an empty shirt."

"Then what the hell is he?" I question, feeling pissed off all over again.

Carter looks away, shaking his head. "There's a lot you don't know."

"Then why don't you fill me in?"

"Eventually," is all he says before he turns and heads back inside of the truck.

Glowering at my entire team, I begrudgingly gather my belongings and put everything in the truck away before getting behind the wheel again.

Chapter Thirteen

Emanuel

"What?" I growl into the phone without looking to see who's calling.

"Hey," Janine's soft voice moves across the line. Somehow, that short, one syllable word has a calming effect on me. The strain that moves through my body isn't completely pushed out but the ragged edges are just a little smoother.

"Are you all right?"

"I'm fine, why?" My tone continues to be clipped.

"I, uh, your voice just sounded off."

I clear my throat as I turn to face the entrance doors of Williamsport Hospital's emergency room.

"I'm fine."

There's a long pause on the other end. I want to reach through the phone, cup her face, and bring her lips to mine. Both for her comfort and for my own. I want to reassure her that my mood doesn't have anything to do with her or my desire to talk to her. However, I don't allow those words to spill from my lips.

Maybe she's better off without you, that sudden voice of doubt shouts in my head.

"I know it's late but you said to call you after your shift. It's after eleven. Did you still want to talk?"

Pausing at the side of my car in the parking lot, I squeeze

my eyes shut before blinking them back open. Her voice does things to me that I still can't explain. But I still don't want her to be affected by my mood at the moment. I don't want this ugliness to settle over any part of her.

"No … yes. I did want to talk but I got caught up at the station. I got called into an extra shift, so I'm still not off. I'll call you tomorrow." Hanging up without another word, I climb into my car, slam the door shut, and pound on the steering wheel.

I'm so pissed I don't know what to do with myself. I just left the hospital after finding out that the second young man I pulled off the scaffold didn't make it. He'd lost too much blood by the time the paramedics got him to the hospital. He was only twenty years old.

It took a few minutes after hearing that for the flashbacks to start coming. Memories of me checking and rechecking a little boy's bedroom, only to find him hidden in his closet, burned and barely breathing.

Pushing the palms of my hands into my eyes, I try to make the memories stop but it's to no avail. When I open my eyes, I blink and recognize where I am again. I start the ignition to my car, and a minute later am driving out of the hospital's parking lot.

It takes me fifteen minutes to make it across town to the Williamsport Fire Department's headquarters. I hang a left into the parking lot. Even though it is close to eleven thirty at night, there are about eight cars parked by the back entrance of the building. I park next to a familiar vehicle and hop out without thinking. Taking long strides, I reach the side door and punch in a code that very few people in the department know about. The lock unhinges and I pull the door open.

At the end of the long hallway on the right is a classroom that's used during the day for new recruits in the training academy. However, at night, seven days a week, it's used for other purposes.

"Man, a part of me still wishes I'd never been there," a red-haired guy says.

I know him as Jason. He's a ten year veteran of the department and works at station house eight, I believe.

"But, on the other hand, I'm glad it was me and not one of my other guys there to see it, ya' know?" Jason looks around the circle of men with his dark brown, watery gaze. With slumped posture, elbows on his knees, he shakes his head pushing out a heavy breath, looking as if the weight of the world rests on his shoulders.

The other seven heads in the room nod in unison. I do, too, knowing what it's like to both hate and appreciate that you were the one to witness what you'd seen.

"Thanks for sharing, Jason," the leader, Terry, says. He glances around, his eyes widening when he sees me. "Emanuel," he calls. "It's been a while since we've seen you here. Would you like to share?"

I want to tell him to go fuck himself, to demand to know why he decided to single me out. But the answer to that question is obvious. I haven't been here in months. I glare at the other men in the room, looking at my fellow firefighters. Their faces are sympathetic as they stare. I hate that fucking expression. We aren't a sympathetic group as a whole, but in this room the mask is removed. In this room, many of us, who ordinarily wouldn't, reveal our souls.

"It happened again." I run my hand through my hair, trying to find the right words. "My woman just called me." I pause, realizing what I just called Janine without even thinking about it. I inhale a deep breath. "She doesn't know this side of the job. And I haven't revealed it to her on purpose."

I sigh heavily.

"I was coming out of the hospital when she called. A young guy I pulled from a scaffold earlier today died from bleeding out. That's bad enough, but it's the memories that come back. I can't shake those fucking memories when shit like this happens."

I shake my head.

"Keep talking," Jason urges. "It's good to talk."

"Jackson," I say on a sigh. It's the first time I've said his name since that night. "He's my one."

"We all have a one," another guy across from him

interjects.

I nod, thankful I don't have to explain what I mean in this room. Every one of us has an incident, a rescue, a death that brought us to this room. To this group.

"He was five fucking years old," I grit out. "A kid. And I missed him on the first sweep of his bedroom. If I would've caught him the first time—"

"You would've missed his mother and his baby sister," Larry, another Station Two guy says. "I was there that night, remember, Emanuel? I was outside but I was there. You pulled that mother and her sleeping newborn out before going back in for the kid."

"I know but—"

"But nothing. That's what this shit does to us. This guilt. It eats us alive. But it's a fucking liar. The truth is that that fire was too hot for anyone to go into. All three of those people in there should've been dead. But two are still alive because of you. That little boy got to say good-bye to his mother before he died because of you. I know what those memories are making you believe. I've got my *one,* too. But the only way to survive it is to tell the truth. The truth is, someone was gonna die that night. You're not stronger than death, no matter how badass you are. None of us are. You did what you needed to that night."

I don't say anything. I stare down into my hands as I sit

forward in the folding chair, my elbows digging into my thighs.

"We all get it, Emanuel," another guy says. "My one doesn't involve a kid. It was an elderly couple ..." he starts.

I'm glad he begins talking. It takes me out of my own head and allows me to focus on his words. The specifics of our stories are different. Disparate times, locations, dates, and events, but the feelings underneath are all the same. The feelings of failure that come with knowing at that particular time you weren't strong enough, fast enough, big enough. Just plain not enough for the situation you were in.

It's a tough fucking pill for a firefighter—a person tasked with walking into hell and making it out alive time and time again—to swallow.

By the time thirty minutes has gone by the group is over and we all begin heading out. That's when I realize there is someone sitting by the door. I was so focused on the guys in the circle I hadn't heard him come in.

Squinting, I watch him as he struggles to stand. Someone rushes toward him to help him up.

"I got it," he says impatiently, pushing Larry away.

Hearing his voice is when it clicks into place.

But he moves too quickly, using a crutch as he pushes through the door that's being held open for him.

I hurry out of the room as well to catch up with him.

"Corey!" I call out.

His back stiffens and he stills.

The guys from the group move past us in the hallway, nodding their heads in acknowledgement.

Corey doesn't turn to face me.

"Corey," I say again, lower this time since I'm much closer.

"What the fuck do you want?" he growls, only looking at me over his shoulder.

I get that he's not going to turn around so I move around to his front.

He's damn near snarling at me. Can't say that I wouldn't be as pissed if I were in his position.

"This your first time here?"

"What the hell is it to you?"

I'm not taken aback by his tone.

"It's a lot to me."

"Why, so you can run back to the Rescue and tell everyone how fucked up I still am?" He tries to move around me but I step in his way.

"I just might do that."

"Get the hell out of my way."

"I will ... when I'm good and goddamn ready."

He tries to step to his right and nearly crumbles to the ground.

I help stop his fall, but once he's uprighted again he

pushes away from me.

"Don't touch me. I got it!" he yells.

I hold my hands up, taking a half a step backwards, giving him some space. "You know you're not the only one fucked up over what happened to you."

"How the hell would you know? Oh yeah, you *are* my replacement."

"I am." I nod.

His face grows angrier as his dark eyebrows narrow.

I move closer. "It's not me you're pissed at."

"You sure about that?"

"I am. I get it. You—"

"You get what? You get what it's like to walk around without a fucking leg?" he demands.

I tilt my head in concession. "No, I don't get that, and it wasn't my intent to imply that I did. You're a firefighter, and from what I've heard you're a damned good one."

"*Was,*" he scoffs.

I shrug. "You still might be one. But it's up to you."

"Whatever, man. I didn't come here for a fucking lecture." He huffs and moves past me.

This time I let him, stepping out of his way and pivoting to watch as he limps, leaning on the crutch toward the door at the end of the hallway. I don't fault his anger. I can't say that I wouldn't be half as pissed if I were in his situation.

Looking back toward the classroom I exited not too long ago, I recognize I have my own scars from this job. Mine might not be as visible as Corey's but they're there. Nobody walks away from this job unscathed. And most people who do what we do and see what we see on a daily basis, couldn't find it in them to keep showing up everyday. Regardless, that's the job and the life I signed up for.

****

Janine

"Matthew, why are you calling me?" I demand into the phone as I answer. It's the third time he's called me this week.

"What has you so pissed off?" he questions, sounding surprised.

"The fact that you obviously can't take a hint couldn't possibly be it." The sarcasm drips from every word.

"What magazine or book on relationships have you read that is making you believe this playing hard to get thing is going to work on me?"

I pull the phone from my ear and stare at it, mouth ajar.

"Matthew, I'm going to speak really slowly as I ask you this. Have you fallen and bumped your head?" I question in the same voice I used to speak to my first graders when trying to calm them down.

He actually chuckles into the phone. His laughter used to

have me all mushy inside but now I just find it annoying. *Why the hell do I keep answering the phone for this man?*

"That was cute, Janine. But I should be the one asking you that question."

Sighing, I pinch the bridge of my nose as I pace my apartment living room. "Look, there's really nothing for us to talk about, so why don—"

"There's plenty for us to discuss. Like, why you're still behaving like an entitled brat and refuse to move back home? And why you refuse to answer my calls?"

"Because we aren't together anymore. And seriously, after the day I had at work, I really don't want to talk to you anymore."

"See? That's what I'm talking about. You've taken on a job that is obviously too much for you to handle in a city that you barely know. You know you want to come back to Boston, it's just your pride has gotten in the way and—"

"Good-bye, Matthew." I hang up the phone in the middle of his rant. I really didn't need to hear whatever he was talking about. Like I said, I had another shitty day at work. It's been over a week since I tried to approach Danny about my idea for the new Digita app, and since I got my ass handed to me by Zeke and his little confession about the real reason I was given my job.

The people at Digita had some type of issue come up, so

they had to push back their meeting with Lux by a few weeks, giving us more time work out a campaign they would like. However, my confidence has waned so much that I can't find it in me to bring up anymore ideas. I've been feeling completely inept and incompetent at work. Truth be told, Matthew's words got under my skin more than I wish they had. It's starting to feel like he's right, I'm feeling way over my head.

I startle when my phone begins buzzing in my hand again. Without checking, I answer and say, "I told you not to call me again. What part of I don't want to talk to you, do you not get?" I seethe, chest rising and falling rapidly as I pant.

"Those aren't the exact words I remember hearing the last time we talked," Emanuel's voice croons through the phone.

I relax my shoulders and stop pacing, looking around my living room as if he's there.

"Sorry," I mumble. "Thought you were someone else."

"Someone giving you trouble?" His voice is suddenly on high alert and I get an image of him glancing around for who or what he can attack.

A feeling of comfort begins to take hold in my chest, but I clamp down on it, remembering back to the last conversation we had.

"Why would you care?" I ask.

There's a pause on the other end of the phone.

"What's that supposed to mean?"

"It's not *supposed* to mean anything. It was an honest question. Because the last time we spoke you didn't seem too thrilled to talk to me."

"Janine, I—"

"And look, it's fine if you're getting bored with me or whatever. I just ask that you be honest about it. I've had enough relationships with people who weren't particularly interested in my hanging around long-term but strung me along—"

"That's what you think this is?"

"I don't know, Emanuel. Is it?"

"No."

"Are you sure because if you're not—"

"I'm certain."

"Are you seeing someone else?" The question comes out of nowhere but it's one that's been lingering on my mind for a while.

"No." There's no hesitation in his voice. "Are you?"

His voice sounds tight, and if I'm not mistaken, there might've been some anger in that question.

"No. I'm more of a monogamy kind of girl." I swallow, hoping that I hadn't just shown my hand.

"I'm starting to think I am, too ... well, a guy not a girl."

I crack a smile for the first time since this conversation

began.

"It's been a few days since we talked and I haven't seen you. I was getting worried you might be done with me already," I admit. My gaze raises to the ceiling as I tense up with embarrassment.

"What the hell would make you think that?"

"The last time we talked …"

There's a heavy sigh on the other end of the phone. "That was my fuck up."

I don't say anything, simply remaining quiet because it feels like he's gathering up the nerve to reveal something important. My ears perk up in anticipation of what it might be.

"That night you called, I was just leaving the hospital."

"Oh my god. Are you okay?"

"Yeah, it wasn't for me. We had a call of two young guys hanging from a scaffold. One made it off okay. The second was much worse."

I listen as Emanuel explains what happened to the second young man and how he succumbed to his injuries.

"You know the scars on my arms and chest?" he questions.

"Yes."

"Those are from a rescue last year. When I was still at my other stationhouse. A little boy died … and I got a fucking medal." His voice is tinged with guilt, shame, anger, and disappointment.

"Oh, Emanuel." I didn't know what else to say. Not only was my heart breaking for the young people who lost their lives, but for the fact that I was so selfishly thinking of myself when he was dealing with all of this heaviness. "Why didn't you tell me?"

He pushes out another breath. "I didn't want to put all of that shit on you. I signed up for this job. I do it proudly but you didn't ask for this. And I didn't want to fuck up what we have going by telling you all of my shit."

A small smile touches my lips. Emanuel isn't the suit-wearing, clean-cut, MBA graduate, never curses guy that my ex was, but within a few words he had the ability to make me feel more cared for than my ex ever had.

"You shouldn't have to bear all of that alone, though."

"I don't. I go to this group sometimes ..." He tells me about a group formed by the Williamsport Fire Department that allows firefighters to meet and discuss with one another all of the depressing, horrible, trying things they see on the job day in and day out. "It's still growing. Many of us are too proud to go to a group like this but it does help."

I nod even though he can't see me. "I'm glad. Regardless, I'd still like it if you would share some things with me ... When you're ready to."

"Noted."

My smile widens.

"Now, I have a more important question to ask you."

"What's that?"

"What color panties are you wearing?"

I burst out laughing.

"Why are you laughing? I'm serious. What color are they?"

I shake my head. "You're insane."

"Hell yeah, I am. I'm going insane waiting to get off shift so I can get home to see that pretty face of yours."

I sway a little bit, feeling like I'm floating from his compliments.

"They're black," I say, referring to my underwear. I don't even have to think about what color they are because all of my panties are black. I keep it simple that way.

"Not a bad color at all. What are you up to this weekend?"

"Whatever you have on the agenda for us."

"Now you're learning, butterfly. I'm off the entire weekend, plan on spending it with me."

I didn't even bother asking what he had planned. Either he didn't have anything planned as of yet and would have to get back to me, or he did have something planned that he was just unwilling to share with me before he was ready. I'm learning to go with the flow when it comes to Emanuel, and become pleasantly surprised with whatever happens when we go out. Now, if I could just be like that in the rest of my life.

Chapter Fourteen

Emanuel

Getting the urge to call Janine, I pull out my cell phone and stare down at it. It's after six so she should be home from work by now. Calling her in the evenings when I'm at the station has become a routine over the last few days. We just got back from a call and I was feeling anxious. Nothing had gone wrong on the call, but it often took me a little while to calm down after getting back to the station. I figured I'd give it some time before I called her.

"The hell?" I growl when I feel a force hit my shoulder, pushing me backwards a little. Lifting my gaze, I lock eyes with Don. "You got something to fucking say?"

"What the fuck is wrong with you? Captain told you to wait on that last call."

I glower at him. "And I fucking waited just as I was told."

"The problem is you *had* to be told to wait. You run ahead of everyone else, thinking you're some fucking hotshot. You're going to get yourself killed."

"Look, if you want to sit around on your ass and watch shit burn, that's up to you. But I took on this job to actually save lives."

"Fuck off!" He pushes me backwards by the chest.

I shove him as well and ball up my fist, taking a swing at him but only catching air when he ducks.

"Hey! What that hell?"

I hear a number of our teammates running over to get in between us. I'm pissed when Carter's face gets in my line of sight. At that point, I don't give a shit who's in my way. I want a piece of Don.

"Chaos, calm down," Carter implores, but keeping his distance, holding up his hands in between Don and I. Sean is standing next to him, to help put space between our two bodies.

"What the hell is this shit?" Sean demands.

"Why don't you ask him?" I point at Don. "He's been on my fucking case since I got here and I'm just doing my damn job!"

"He's a fucking hothead who doesn't listen!" Don snarls.

"I do my goddamn job!"

"Yeah, and the next time you run ahead of us and a beam fucking falls on you, who the fuck do you think is going to be pulling your sorry ass out?" he yells.

The room goes silent as everyone pivots to Don.

"That's what this is about," Carter finally says, breaking the silence.

"What?"

"Corey."

"Fuck this." Don angrily stomps off in the direction of the garage where the fire truck is parked.

Sean and Carter turn to me, sympathy in both of their

expressions. They exchange a look between the two of them and then back to me.

"Listen," Sean starts, "Don is a hell of a firefighter, and Corey is his best friend."

"I get that. It's tough his friend not being here and I'm his replacement, but—"

Carter shakes his head. "That's not it. Not entirely." He looks to Sean.

Sean shrugs. "I'm going to go talk to Don. You fill him in," he tells Carter.

I watch as Sean heads off in the same direction as Don had.

"Do you know how Corey was injured?" Carter questions, turning to me.

"A collapse, right?"

He nods. "Yeah, Don, Corey, and I entered a two-story home. There was a mother and her children inside. We search, and I tell Corey to check the end of the hallway where one of the bedrooms is located. Don and I head in the opposite direction. Minutes later there's a loud crash from down the hall. We run and find Corey trapped under a beam. It pinned his leg and hit is head pretty good. He had a concussion and had been knocked out. It took a while to pull him out but we did. Unfortunately, the hospital couldn't save his leg."

Inhaling, I take the story in as I rub my hand down the side of my face. I get it. Don seeing his best friend in that predicament, knowing you couldn't get to them.

"But that's not it," Carter says. "Don should be the one to tell you the next part."

****

I move into the garage behind Carter to see Don and Sean standing at the far end of the truck. Don's arms are folded over his chest and he stares at me. Then he looks between Sean and Carter, the four of us are standing in a circle.

"Look, man ..." Don pushes out a heavy breath. His shoulders appear weighed down by the weight of whatever's on his mind. "I'm sorry for that shit. You're a hell of a firefighter."

I nod, pushing out a heavy breath, deciding to let it go. "Water under the bridge."

He nods. "Did you tell him everything?"

"Not the investigation," Carter replies.

My ears perk up. I have no idea what investigation the three men are talking about, but I have a feeling I'm about to find out.

"The department doesn't want this to get out so it's your job to keep your mouth shut about this."

"I don't even know what *this* is," I remind him.

"The night that Corey got hurt is when we began putting the pieces together. There's an arsonist in Williamsport."

My anger growing, I fold my arms over my chest but remain silent, waiting for Don to explain.

"He typically targets women home alone with their young children, most of the time when they're sleeping. The fathers are often away on business trips or work overnights. We got a couple of calls, and as the investigator I started noticing a pattern. But as we honed in more and more on what was happening, it became obvious that Rescue Four was a target. The beam that fell on Corey wasn't an accident. Wasn't just a happenstance of the fire. Someone had intentionally disrupted the beam. Cut it to weaken the structure. It looked as if they were trying to cause a total building collapse but failed."

I look around the circle at the faces of Don, Sean, and Carter. Their expressions range from serious to pissed off.

"So you're saying what happened to Corey wasn't an accident, and there's an arsonist specifically targeting the firefighters of Rescue Four?" Hot anger begins coursing through my body.

"We believe so."

"*Believe?*"

"There hasn't been anymore instances in some time. What happened to Corey could be just a fluke. At least, that's what the brass at the department is pushing. Many of the fires I suspect are arsons were made to look like they're the result of faulty electrical wiring or a negligent parent forgetting to turn off the fireplace before heading to bed."

"Or not putting out a cigarette," Sean adds.

"That too. They're difficult to pin down, and we're not getting any movement from above. There's no way to prove it."

"Wait." I hold up my hand. "Did you say this person intentionally looks for mothers with young children while they're sleeping?"

Don nodded. "Yeah, the problem is that it's typically only Rescue Four that gets those calls because they're in our district."

"Station Two got one of your calls," I say out loud but not to anyone in particular. I feel their gazes shift in my direction but I'm staring at the concrete floor in front of me. "It was a late night about eight months ago. For whatever reason, Station Two was called on the job. I think all of the Rescue Four trucks were out. A mother, her three-week-old infant, and five-year-old son were home sleeping in bed ..."

The memory of that night comes back in full force just as it always does. I can practically feel the smoke surrounding me as I mentally walk through every step I took that night.

"I pulled the mother and baby out. That's when she said her son was still inside. I'd done a sweep of his room the first time around. But he was hiding in the closet. I found him the second time I went in, but by then he was so badly burned and had so much smoke inhalation ... he died at the hospital four hours later."

I raise my gaze to look across the circle at Don. "I earned a fucking Webster for that rescue. Are you telling me that that night was the job of an arsonist?"

Don's eyes widen as he glances between all of us. "How the fuck did we miss that?" There's pain in his voice.

"It wasn't our call," Sean consoles.

Suddenly, Don's eyes widen and his mouth momentarily falls open. "It was the night of Eric's wedding."

The three men's eyes widen as the memory comes back. Rescue Four was down to only a few firefighters that night due to the wedding. Their calls were rerouted.

"Shit," Carter curses angrily. "We thought ... fucking *hoped* that the son of a bitch had just given up. But he's still at it."

"That was eight months ago. Why hasn't the department done anything?" My voice is dripping in anger.

"Those fuckers don't believe we're dealing with an arsonist or that we're being targeted. Like I said, he makes it appear as if they're accidents."

"So what are we doing in the meantime?"

"We're watching each others' backs," Don says before stepping forward, moving closer to me. "I know you think Captain Waverely is being overly cautious or another empty shirt like your last captain. He's not. He's the real fucking deal.

But he's known something was off for a long time. That's why any call we go on, we don't split up unless it's absolutely necessary."

Getting Don's meaning, I nod. "You checked into my former captain?"

He gives out a half chuckle, half grunt. "Captain fucking Rogers? Yeah, I looked into him a little while researching you."

I lift an eyebrow. "Now, there's a surprise."

"Tell him why, Don," Carter urges.

Don's frown deepens. "We think this fucker is a firefighter."

"What the hell?"

"Yeah, tell me about it," Sean adds to my shock.

"He's too good at this. He's always a step ahead of us, and making the fires seem like accidents isn't easy to do."

I nod, knowing that's the truth. Fire investigation has come a long way in recent decades. At the academy, we're taught basic fire investigation. It's imperative to know how a fire began to be able to pinpoint the best way to put it out or trace its next move, if need be.

"This is fucking crazy," I sigh.

"Tell us about it. Now that you know, it's up to you to keep this within the station. We think the more gets out, the more dangerous this situation could get."

"I won't say shit."

Don tilts his head. "Now, here are the things you should be on the look out for ..." he continues as he goes into what I need to keep an eye out for whenever we get a call. Particularly, on calls that involve house fires with mothers and young children.

Chapter Fifteen

Janine

"An escape room?" I question as we pull into the parking lot of a plain looking brick building that reads Williamsport Escape Room Tour. We just finished lunch at a local Thai restaurant, and now apparently we were going to work it off by hunting something or escaping from somewhere.

"What is this?" Emanuel helps me out of the car. It still gets the butterflies in my belly flapping when he demonstrates his chivalry.

"Exactly what is says. You've never been to an escape room before?" he questions.

I shake my head.

"Good. Popping another—"

"Don't say it," I warn, making him laugh. The sound of his deep chuckle moves through my body, causing me to tingle as he takes my left hand into his.

We enter the building and I glance around to see a few other patrons talking with a staff member.

"Good afternoon," the friendly older man behind the counter greets.

"Good afternoon. Two for Allende," Emanuel says.

The man pulls up his tickets in their system. "Ah, here you are. You get to choose which of the three rooms you want to try."

I look up at my date.

"There's the bank heist, zombie apocalypse, and the dig," Emanuel says before explaining what the different escape rooms entail.

"Bank heist," I answer excitedly.

"I was hoping you'd choose that one."

We're paired up with six other people and are herded into a room that has been created to look like a bank from the 1920s. There's a man standing behind one of the closed-off windows, smiling and waving at us. We're given instructions on what to do and what the objective for this particular room is. Within minutes we are all splitting off into our different assignments and tasks, trying to work with one another to achieve our objective. We're on a time limit and the clock is posted at the top corner of the wall, counting down to create a sense of urgency.

There are many different scenarios that pop up out of nowhere while we're all trying to figure out how to get out of the room with the money we've now stolen. When running down one hallway a man jumps out of nowhere, scaring the hell out of me.

"Ah!" I stumble backwards right into the arms of the person behind me. I don't have to look back to know it's him. The warmth that fills my body as he braces me tells me enough.

"I got you, butterfly," he coos in my ears. He pushes the man out of the way and keeps his arm at my back while we make our way from the hallway to another room. There, we are given clues on to how to break out of that room. This continues and the hour flies by. I would say I can't remember a time where I had so much fun but that would be a lie. Because the truth is anytime I'm with Emanuel it's fun. He manages to keep a smile on my face or keep me laughing.

"That was great. Let's do another one. My treat," I say, squealing as we emerge from the final room of the bank heist.

"Which one do you want to do?"

"The zombie apocalypse." Feeling giddy, I start to reach for my purse to pull out my card to pay for the two tickets but by the time I look up to where the register is, Emanuel is already paying to add our names to the list.

"Hey," I frown, tugging on his shirt for him to look back at me. "I said it was *my* treat. You've already paid for lunch and the first room."

"And now I'm paying for the second. Don't argue," he orders while smacking me on my jeans covered behind.

I can't help the giggle that pours from my lips.

The second escape room is just as much fun as the first, albeit scarier. The zombie room is darker, more difficult to see, however. But Emanuel has no problem navigating his way around and finding the clues we need to find in the midst of all the chaos, to lead the way out.

"That's not fair!" I argue in the car on the way home.

He chuckles. "What? I can't help it if my career prepares me for this sort of thing."

"It's not fair that most of the people in that room, including myself, spend forty hours of our week in a well-lit office staring at computer screens all day. You, on the other hand, have to practically learn to walk blind, feeling your way through strange houses and buildings. It gives you an unfair advantage at this sort of thing."

"Not my fault they chose piss poor careers."

I giggle out loud. "What if they really like their jobs?"

He shrugs while keeping his eyes on the road. "Sucks for them."

I shake my head.

"How about you? Do you really like your job?"

My heart sinks a little and my smile falters. "I'm still learning," is all I say before changing the subject to something else.

We're headed back to Emanuel's so he can cook us dinner. Of course, he won't tell me what he's preparing. It's the perfect ending to a great Saturday.

****

Emanuel

"That was delicious." Janine sighs as she places the dishes from our dinner into my dishwasher.

I take her by the wrist to stop her. "You don't need to put those away. I can do that later."

She immediately begins shaking her head. "No way. After you prepared that delicious chili, and the apple crumb pie and ice cream to go with it …"

"I didn't exactly prepare the pie and ice cream."

Smiling, she lifts on her toes, pressing a kiss to my lips. I deepen the kiss because my bodily instinct takes over.

She pulls back. "I know, but they were delicious nonetheless. I'm going to have to walk to work this week or something to work these calories off."

I frown, disliking the way she's patting her belly as she says that bullshit.

"I'll show you how to work it off," I growl, lowering my head and licking the side of her neck as I press her back against my kitchen sink.

"Mmm," she moans, and the sound goes straight to my dick. I instantly get an idea.

I take a few steps backwards. "We're going to work those calories off by the end of the night."

She lifts an eyebrow, giving me a curious look.

Rounding the bar area that separates my kitchen space from the living room, I lift the remote to turn off the Netflix movie we'd been watching.

"Let's play a game."

My grin widens at her expression.

"You put one more dish in that damn thing and I'm going to bend you over my knee," I tell her as she attempts to place another bowl into the dishwasher.

Her eyes widen and that pretty mouth of hers opens. And suddenly, I'm assaulted by visions of her making that same face as my erection slides in and out, between those lips.

"Two truths and a lie," I say before I can go any further with my daydream.

"I've never played."

"How'd I know you'd say that?"

She shrugs, frowning.

"All you gotta do is throw out three different scenarios, one of which is a lie, and I have to guess what the lie is."

"That's it?"

Tilting my head, I give her a smirk.

She giggles and looks up at the brick ceiling. "Of course that's not it."

"You catch on quick. This is strip two truths and a lie. Whenever you guess the lie correctly, I strip. If you guess incorrectly, you have to strip, and vice versa."

She silently laughs and shakes her head before shrugging. "Fine, but I'm going first."

"Ladies always go first. They come first, too." Laughing, I duck as she balls up and tosses the kitchen towel she was holding onto in my direction. It goes right over my head.

"All right, let's see …" She pauses, thinking. "Can these be about anything?"

"Anything at all. You just have to make sure two scenarios are true and one is a lie."

"Okay," she says after thinking for a moment. "I'm afraid of the dark, I'm afraid of snakes, and I'm afraid of clowns."

"That's easy. The dark is the lie. Take your shirt off."

She frowns. "How'd you know?"

"I've slept with you in the dark, remember? And you happily chose the zombie room earlier today knowing it was going to be dark. So snakes and clowns, huh? Take off the shirt," I order again, moving closer.

She holds up her hand. "Yes, snakes and clowns." She shivers. "And you didn't say that you get to choose what item of clothing I take off." Reaching up, she pulls the decorative scarf that's tied around her neck off. She sets it on one of my wooden stools and gives me the eye.

"Okay, I see how we're going to play this. I grew up in Williamsport, I grew up in foster care, I grew up with an older brother."

"You grew up with an older brother is the lie." She moves closer. "You've never talked about any siblings."

I nod and pull off my shirt, tossing it on the couch to my left. When I face forward again she's standing right in front of me.

"I didn't know you grew up in foster care."

I incline my head, feeling uneasy about sharing my truth with someone but also feeling relaxed about it at the same time. I want her to know more about me. Not the superficial, what I do for a living, what kind of car I drive type of bullshit. But all of me.

"From how young?"

"Since nearly two years old."

Her eyes widen and her hands press softly against my stomach.

"My father abandoned my mother, when I was a kid my mother loved to bake cookies, and I lived in ten different cities throughout my childhood."

I could see in her eyes which one was the lie. If I was a fair man I would've chosen the one I knew was a truth just to let her win a little.

I'm not a fair man.

"Your mother making cookies." I don't even finish the sentence before I'm easing the light-colored, button-up blouse she wore for our date up and over her head. I toss it onto the same couch my shirt now haphazardly hangs from.

"You lived in ten different cities growing up?"

"At least," she replies just above a whisper. "I stopped counting after ten."

Lowering my head, I drop a kiss to her bare shoulder. The skin there is silky and smooth, just like the rest of her body. I drop my hands to her waist.

"Your turn."

"I want a lot of kids, I want to retire as a firefighter in my sixties, and I want *you* in my bed now," I growl, picking her up underneath her thighs, forcing her legs to wrap around my waist as I stalk off down the hallway to my bedroom.

When she nips my bottom lip with her teeth, a growl escapes my lips. "You want me in your bed, that's the lie," she says, grinning as I kick open the bedroom door.

"Trick scenario. All three are the truth," I tell her right before covering her lips with mine.

****

Janine

His words aren't given enough time to process before the feeling of his warm tongue licking the roof of my mouth takes over all of my ability to think. Needing to get as close to his body as possible, I tighten my arms around his shoulders.

I feel our bodies lower as Emanuel drops us to his low sitting bed. I am pushed back against the comforter of the bed, but I continue to hold onto his body, not wanting to lose the body heat he gives off. It ignites every nerve ending I have.

"Next time we'll play truth or dare," he growls after pulling back.

I watch his strong hands go to his belt buckle and he begins to undo them but I'm feeling brave. My hands cover his as I sit up.

I look up and meet those honeycomb eyes of his. "Can I?"

He nods.

I use my hands to undo the belt and then the button of his jeans. Slowly, I slide the zipper down, and reach inside to begin running my hand along the length of his cock. I run my thumb over the tip and am surprised to find that he already has precum seeping out. My mouth waters and I instantly know exactly where I want to put him.

Emanuel must sense my hunger because with his right hand he reaches up and cups my chin, pulling on it a little to widen my mouth.

"Right there is where I want to put my cock. Will you let me do that, butterfly?"

I nod without hesitation. I assist him in pulling his jeans and boxer briefs all of the way down to his ankles. He is so long and thick that I hesitate for a heartbeat. I remember back to that night we spent together in Mexico when I briefly wondered if he'd even fit inside of me. I hadn't even thought about my mouth.

But I don't waste too much time thinking about it. I want to taste him. I need to make him feel as good as he makes me every time he puts his mouth on me. Standing, I move from the bed and go to my knees in front of him. I use the tip of my tongue to taste his precum and a moan instantly escapes my lips. At first, I go to suppress the moan but then I remember who I'm with. He doesn't want me to hold back.

That reminder emboldens me and I wrap my lips around the entirety of his cock, using my tongue to make sure I wet every part of his erection. Pulling back, I use my hand to tug and massage the part of him that my mouth can't reach.

I go to wrap my lips around him once again, and he says, "Eyes on me, butterfly. I want to look you in your eyes when I come in your mouth."

A shiver runs through me. Slowly, I allow my gaze to travel up the length of his rippled abdomen and hard chest before reaching those sexy as sin eyes of his. There's an intimacy I've never experienced before as I stare into his eyes while taking his length into my mouth. I begin bobbing my head on his rod while maintaining eye contact. His gaze never wavers from mine. His eyelids become heavy, halfway closing as he grows closer and closer to his orgasm. The groans coming from his lips are like a direct line straight to my pussy. My lips clench every time one of those sexy sounds spills from his mouth.

His body starts to shiver on a loud groan and I feel him tighten up. The orgasm moves through him, and I feel him spilling into my mouth. As I stare into his eyes, which continue to capture my attention, I swallow every bit that spills out.

Moving back, I go to wipe my lip and chin with my hand but I am quickly pulled up from my knees to my feet by Emanuel's capable hands. His lips cover mine in a demanding kiss that steals my breath. I struggle for air but he doesn't give me any pass. Finally, I give in to the kiss and give back as much as I get.

His hands are at my waist, undoing my high waisted jeans and tugging them down to reveal the black cotton panties of mine. I finally break free from the kiss to look down and watch him as he continues to undress me.

A pang of guilt or unease moves through me as I stare at the plain jane panties I often wear. For his part, Emanuel doesn't seem to mind as he works until we are both stripped naked of all of our clothing. He bends low, going to the black nightstand at the side of his bed, pulling out a brand new pack of condoms. He tears one of them open with his teeth and quickly sheaths himself.

"I want to watch you as you ride my cock," he says, positioning both of our bodies on his bed.

He moves underneath me and I am left to straddle his

hips.

I shouldn't be as clueless and embarrassed as I am. This isn't the first time Emanuel and I have been together like this. But this is the first time I am on top, and I'm unsure of myself.

He must be aware of this because he begins giving me instructions.

"Take me into your hand."

I wrap my hand around his still erect cock. I silently wonder how the hell he's still erect after having one orgasm already but I try not to get too distracted from the task before me.

"Lift your hips ... that's it. Now slide down onto my cock." His voice is tight and rigid, as if he is fighting to maintain control. I can hear the need and want in his body. That alone has my nipples pebbling and aching

"Oh god!" I let out as I slide down onto him. I feel him stretching me as this part of my body gets reacquainted with his size and girth. "Emanuel," I say his name on a plea.

"You feel so good, baby," he breathes out through clenched teeth. "Ride that shit for me, butterfly."

I raise my hips and then come back down on him while holding him by the wrists as his hands grip my waist.

"Pinch your nipples. I can see they want some attention," he orders.

Lifting my hands, I do as he instructed while circling my

hips, grinding on his shaft. My head lolls backwards at the pleasure that rolls through my body. I tighten my pelvic muscles round his cock.

"Fuck, baby!" he groans.

I do it again, obviously feeling how turned on that made him. Over and over I rise and fall, and then swivel my hips on his cock, pushing both of us to higher and higher altitudes. Soon my body is begging for a release. Every part of my body feels sensitized as if a light stroke across my skin could send me reeling.

Emanuel provides just what I need when one of his hands moves from my hips to my clit, pinching it before letting it go and running circles over it with his thumb.

Tilting my head toward the ceiling, I let out a piercing scream as my orgasm tears through my body. All of the muscles in my body tighten up and clench as they are wrung out.

At some point I manage to stop screaming just so I can breathe again but Emanuel isn't quite finished. I soon find myself on all fours while he is behind me, pressing himself into my pussy from behind. I bite down on the pillow beneath my face and beat against the bed with my fist as he begins pounding me. The bed, nightstand, and my sanity all begin to jostle about and shake.

His large hands are at my waist, pulling me onto his

shaft over and over again. It doesn't take long for my second orgasm of the night to be wrung out of my body. That orgasm is accompanied by a muffled scream since I am face down into the pillows. I feel Emanuel's body shudder and shake behind me as he, too, experiences his second orgasm of the night.

And just when I thought he was as done as I was, he has the nerve to pull out and then use his hands to separate my asscheeks. I soon feel a wet warmth and realize it's his tongue, circling my clitoris from behind.

"No more," I plead, not sure I can take anymore.

"Come again for me, butterfly," he growls. "I need you on my fucking tongue."

My heartbeat begins to increase at his urging, and I feel two of his fingers sliding into me while his tongue continues to pursue his ultimate goal. And again, I find my body shuddering and ultimately, giving him what he demands. The third orgasm starts in my toes. The sensation moves up my legs, exploding in my center, and then ripples down my spine. There are sounds that emanate from my mouth, but for the life of me, I can't make them out. I'm pretty sure it's not an actual language that I'm speaking at the moment.

By the time I come down from my orgasm, I've collapsed onto the bed next to Emanuel, sweaty and panting. When I feel the tips of his fingers caress my cheek, pushing my hair out of my face, a shaky smile touches my lips.

"You were loud tonight," he says, sounding impressed, causing me to giggle.

"Is that a problem?"

"Not ever."

Chapter Sixteen

Janine

"Were you really raised in foster care?" I ask as I lay on top of Emanuel's chest in his bed.

We're both naked, wrapped in each other's arms with his white blanket partially covering our bodies. I find myself tracing the rim of his pectoral muscles, loving the way they jump and respond to my touch.

"Yes."

I continue to stare at his chest instead of looking up at his face as we talk.

"What happened to your parents?"

He adjusts in the bed, shifting his body weight and tightening his arm around my shoulders before responding.

"Dead. Both of them."

"I'm sorry."

"Don't be. I didn't know them. They didn't know me. They gave me up long before they died." There was a rigidity in his voice as he spoke of the parents he never knew.

"I never knew my dad either," I confess. "He was married, and not to my mom, when she got pregnant with me. According to her he gave her some money but never wanted anything to do with us."

"Is that why you moved around so much?"

I shrug and push out a breath. "I used to think so. Thinking she was moving away from the memories of him, but as I got older I realized that wasn't it at all. My mother is the quintessential party girl who never grew up. She never *wanted* to grow up, even with a baby on her hip. By the time I was thirteen, our roles were effectively switched. I was the one waiting up at home, alone, for her to return, asking where she'd been all day and night. On more than one occasion I found myself waiting in the dark because she'd *forgotten* to pay the light bill with the money she got from random men. I don't remember her working much."

"Where's your mother now?"

"Psh. Your guess would be as good as mine."

"You don't speak to her?"

"A few times a month when one of us calls the other. I spoke with her a couple of weeks ago. She knows I've moved. She mentioned possibly coming for a visit." I roll my eyes. I wasn't going to hold my breath. My mother often talked of visiting while I was in Boston. Out of the eleven years I lived in the city, she visited a total of maybe four times.

A comfortable silence grew around us until Emanuel's chuckles broke it. That's when I look up at him.

"I want in on the joke."

He grins as he stares down at me. "We both had some fucked up childhoods."

A smile cracks open on my face and I turn my head into

his chest, giggling. It feels comfortable to laugh about the craziness of my past with someone who got it, at least on some level. For years the two people who were closest to me had more or less of an idyllic childhood. Angela was the princess in her family, who was very close with both of her parents, who provided a stable home life for her and her brother, Sean. Matthew was an only child to two of Boston's elite. He was given just about everything he wanted, and had a cushy job at his father's hedge fund waiting for him once he graduated with his MBA from one of the top schools in the nation.

I loved Angela, and even Matthew when we were together, but neither one could relate to what I went through growing up. Or the desire for stability that drove me, as a result of it.

"How many homes were you in?" I question.

"Six or seven ... I lost count."

I continue asking questions about his growing up in foster care. I want to know more. But some of the answers are hard to listen to. I begin to understand why he chose to drop out of high school and enlist in the military at seventeen, given his experiences.

The last thing I remember is wrapping Emanuel even tighter in my arms, holding him close, as I drift off to sleep to the sounds of his breathing.

****

"Janine! Are you still asleep in there, girl? Open the door!"

I groan and turnover, hating the dream I'm having and hoping it will go away so I can continue to lie snuggled up in Emanuel's arms.

"Janine!"

"Butterfly, I think that's for you," his deep, raspy morning voice says in a low tone, piercing the thin veil of sleep I'd been under.

My eyes pop open. "It can't be," I groan.

"Janine! Open the door."

"Holy shit!" I sit up in Emanuel's bed and toss his blanket off of me. I don't even think as I start toward the front door.

"You're going to answer naked?"

I glance down at my body, and sure enough, I am one hundred percent in the nude. Looking around the floor I spot my jeans from the previous night and Emanuel's button-up shirt. I quickly snatch both off the floor and put them on, still buttoning the shirt as I race to the front door, just in time to hear loud banging from across the hall.

"Janet!" I hiss as I pull the door open, trying not to be too loud as it's early in the morning on a Sunday.

My mother jolts in the six-inch heels she's wearing,

turning to face me, the extra long, light brown and black curly hair she's wearing flowing wildly.

"Oh," she says, looking back at my door—the very one she was just knocking on. "I thought you said three twenty-one was your apartment." She walks toward me, nearly pushing me out of the way to gain entry. She stops short, blinking when I don't move, continuing to hold firmly to the door.

"What are you doing here?" I question between clenched teeth.

"What do you mean, what am I doing here? I told you I was coming for a visit."

I shake my head. "No ... you didn't."

"Janine, we just talked about this. And what are you doing? Let me in." She pries my hand from the door and barges her way in.

I'm too thrown off by the moment to even make it known that this isn't my place.

"Well, hello," my mother suddenly says behind me in that flirtatious purr that I'm all too familiar with.

I spin around from the door to see Emanuel standing there bold as day, in nothing more than a pair of black boxer briefs as he grins down at my mother. Immediately, I move in front of him, blocking her view, but that doesn't stop her from stretching her neck to look around me.

"And you are ..."

"The man who owns this place."

My mother's chocolate eyes widen before her gaze drops to me. She gives me an admiring look. "Janine, you didn't tell me you were living with a man. I see you've done well for yourself since Matthew dumped you."

I wince at my mother's words as she steps around me, continuing to ogle the man behind me.

I spin around. "*I* dumped Matthew," I get out through a clenched jaw.

My mother doesn't even acknowledge my words.

"And what's your name?"

"Emanuel. And you would be?"

"Whoever you want me to be." She lets out an annoying ass giggle.

"Okay, that's enough." I turn to Emanuel. "I'm sorry. I have to go tend to my mother, apparently." Grabbing my purse from the table, I pull out my keys. "Janet, here. This is the key to my apartment. Use it. I'll be over in a second."

She begins stammering, still looking back at Emanuel as I practically push her body out the door. I close Emanuel's door in her face, not giving her the opportunity to respond. I practically sprint to Emanuel's bedroom and put the clothes I was wearing the day before on and head for the door.

It's that moment when I find Emanuel casually leaning against the doorframe, his big body blocking my exit.

"So that's your mother?"

My shoulders slump. "That's her. Speaking of the devil really does make it appear, apparently."

"You should invite her over for breakfast. You, me, and her. The three of us."

I'm shaking my head before the proposal is fully out of his mouth. "That would be a bad idea."

"Why?" Folding his arms over his chest, he lifts a dark eyebrow. "Ashamed of me?"

"What? No, of course not."

"Ashamed of her?"

"Hell yes."

He chuckles and then drops a kiss to my forehead before pulling me into his arms. My body melts into his. The unease my mother's presence always seems to fill me with begins to subside a little.

"I don't judge you based on your mother, butterfly," he says in my ear. He looks down at me, palming my face before dropping a kiss to my lips. When we separate, he touches my forehead with his own and adds, "And you're the only woman I kiss on the lips before they've brushed their damn teeth in the morning."

I push him away, giggling while lightly punching his arm.

"I'm serious."

"My breath doesn't smell bad." I cover my mouth with my hand and blow into it, trying to smell my own breath.

"I was talking about breakfast. Take a shower at your place. I'll shower here and change, and we can have breakfast here or go out. The three of us."

"I think going out would be the safer choice."

He gives a one shoulder shrug. "I'll just save the eggs in my fridge for another time to cook you breakfast." He drops one more kiss to my lips. "Go get dressed," he orders just before smacking me on the backside.

I laugh, moving past him, but then stop and turn in his direction. "Are you sure about this? My mother can ... uh, she can be a lot to handle."

"You ask me one more time and I'm tossing you over my shoulder and taking you in the shower myself. I don't give a care who's waiting."

When he begins stalking toward me as if he's about to follow through on his threat, I jump and make a beeline for the door.

Chapter Seventeen

Emanuel

"I need to speak with you," Don says in a low voice as he comes up from behind me while I'm at the stove in the kitchen.

I turn to face him, and by the expression on his face I can tell it's something serious. "Hey, rookie?" I call to the rookie sitting at the table watching something on his phone. "Keep an eye on this beef stew. Make sure it doesn't burn," I order before moving away from the stove.

I follow Don into the garage, past the fire truck that's parked inside the parking lot of the fire station. He obviously intends for this to be a private conversation.

"I've been looking into that fire. The one involving the little boy."

I nod as my chest tightens. Those ugly feelings I often try to avoid whenever I think of that night arise.

"But I can't find much information on it."

"Like what?"

"Like, how it really started. What type of investigation was done around it. Nothing is on record at the department except for a report that was written up by your former captain. It was based on that and the accounts of your team that earned you that medal. But as far as anything from the investigator's perspective, there's nothing."

Lifting an eyebrow, I fold my arms over my chest. That's

more than strange. Every fire—especially one involving a person that dies—is supposed to have an investigative report accompanying it.

"I'd like to speak to someone at your old station house about it."

"And you thought having me along would help jog some memories or get them to open up more?" I question, already knowing where this was going.

He nods. "Makes sense, right?"

"It does," I confirm. "My shift ends in an hour."

"I'll be waiting."

An hour later, I'm walking out of Rescue Four and climbing behind the wheel of my Camaro as Don gets in the passenger seat. Moments later, we're heading across town in the direction of my old station house.

"What are you expecting to get out of this questioning?"

I watch out of the corner of my eye as Don runs a hand down his face, sighing. "Some answers as to what happened that night. I know from your perspective what happened. But I need to know more about what started the fire. Was it really an accident or were there signs that this was done on purpose? The other fires—"

"The ones you're sure were arsons?" I ask.

"Yeah, they were ruled arsons, especially the one that injured Corey, but most of those investigations are still open.

No one has been charged."

I briefly look over to see his hands balled into tight fists. I'm reminded of Corey, and the anger I saw on his face the first night he came to group. I've seen him a few more times since then. I consider telling Don that I'd seen him but think better of it. Corey still refuses to see any of his teammates or even show his face anywhere near Rescue Four. If he wanted them to know he was going to group, or struggling, he'd let it be known.

"So there's a fucking murderer walking around, using fire as their weapon of choice?" I growl, growing pissed off at the thought.

"Son of a bitch." Don's words are just as angry and pissed off as my own, if not more so.

We arrive at station two in just under fifteen minutes. I park in the lot across the street facing the firehouse and hop out of the car.

"I must be dreaming," a familiar voice sounds as soon as I pass through the doors.

Grinning, I hold up my hand for Larry. His hand immediately cups mine and he pulls me into a half hug, pounding my back with his fist.

"How the hell are you doing?"

"Couldn't be better."

"Rescue must be treating you good."

I shrug. "I don't have any complaints. This is Don," I

introduce to Larry.

They both shake hands.

"Don wanted to ask some questions about the fire over on Jefferson. The ..." I pause, clearing my throat before continuing. "The one involving the woman and her two young kids."

Larry blinks as he gives me a look. He nods, solemnly, and I'm glad he takes my cue and doesn't let on about my attending group over that very call. "The one with the mother and two kids. Of course."

I nod because my words are caught in my throat.

Larry turns his attention to Don. "What is it you want to know?"

Don goes on to explain what it is he's looking for. He doesn't tell Larry that he suspects the fire was arson or that there actually might be a serial arsonist running around in our city.

Once Don finishes speaking with Larry, I introduce him to Arnold, who was also there that night, and happens to be on shift. Arnold is cooperative as well, actually passing along information that I didn't know about.

"I always felt strange about that night," he says. "I suspected the fire was intentional for some reason. I didn't think it was electrical when we first got there. But after we all stomped around there and our hoses got a hold of it, I couldn't tell which part of the building was which, ya know? Then it was deemed unsafe to enter so no real investigation could be done. A few months later the entire building was torn down," Arnold finishes.

"Torn down before a thorough investigation could be done?" Don questions.

Arnold and I both nod in unison, as I remember that the building had indeed been deemed an eyesore in the neighborhood it sat in so it was torn down.

"They're already constructing a new home in its place," Arnold informs.

"Thanks for your time," Don says.

"Hey, Arnold, is Captain Rogers still in?"

I'm surprised when he nods. "I haven't seen him leave just yet."

Captain Rogers is usually the first one out the door once his shift is over.

"I'll introduce you," I tell Don.

He follows me as we head up the stairs to the captain's office. Per usual, his door is closed. I knock on the door a few times and wait.

Don gives me a look, lifting an eyebrow.

"Just wait for it. He's here," I reply to his unasked question.

About thirty seconds later I hear feet shuffling across the linoleum floor just before the door is pulled open.

Captain Rogers' dark blond eyebrows lift in surprise.

"Captain, how are you?" I force a pleasant smile on my face.

He frowns. "Allende. They kicked you out of Rescue already, huh?"

My smile turns cocky. "Not yet, Cap. But if that happens you'll be the first to know."

His frown deepens as he catches the sarcastic nature in my tone.

"In fact, this is one of my new squad members. Don. He has a few questions about the fire on Jefferson."

Captain Rogers' gaze moves from me to Don, who holds out his hand.

"Captain," Don greets. "Pleasure to meet you. Emanuel has told us so much about you … all good things," he adds.

Captain Rogers looks back to me, knowing Don's words are full of shit. Rogers and I never had any affinity for one another. And while affinity isn't a prerequisite for either one of us to do our jobs well, respect is and … well, I for one, didn't respect Rogers as a captain all that much.

"What's this about?" Rogers demands, folding his arms over his chest.

Don drops his hand. "I see you're a busy man so I'll get right to the point. I suspect the fire on Jefferson was arson but it was ruled an electrical fire."

"It was ruled that way because that's what it was."

"Right, but—"

"Why are you both here wasting my time with this? Does your new captain know you're here?" he questions, looking at me.

"That has nothing to do with why we're here," I assert, feeling defensive.

"It has everything to do with why you're in my station house right now. In fact, maybe I should give Captain Waverly a call—"

"That won't be necessary," Don informs him. "We just wanted to talk, but I see right now isn't a great time for you."

I'm grilling Rogers in his face when I feel Don grab my arm and begin pulling me away from the door. As soon as I turn my back, I hear the door slam shut.

"Asshole," I grit as we turn and head back down the stairs to the exit.

"He was a real pleasure. No wonder you enjoyed working for him so much," Don quips.

"He's a fucking louse. He got to this point by ass kissing and using his connections."

Don grunts as he pulls open the passenger door of my car. "I bet," he says before getting in and shutting the door.

Just as I'm about to climb in my car, I peer up, and standing in front of his window glaring down on the two of us is Captain Rogers. The expression on his face it tight with anger and something else. There's an almost eerie look on his face.

Something strange comes over me and the feeling I used to have sometimes while under his command overtakes me.

I shake it off and climb in, silently thanking the fact that I no longer work at Station Two.

"Hey, I'm fucking starving. You want pizza?" Don asks.

I nod. He's been much more pleasant since he laid everything on the table a few weeks back. And since I know Janine is having dinner with her mother tonight, I'm down to go grab a slice before heading home.

****

Janine

"You're not actually wearing that to work, are you?" Janet didn't bother hiding the disgust in her tone.

I glance down at the black three-quarter length blouse and black slacks I'm wearing. I paired them with cream suede loafers.

"What's wrong with this?" I question. Every day since she's here for the past two weeks my mother made some comment or quip about my boring work attire. I hated to admit that maybe she had a point.

"It's all black."

"All black is classic," I defend.

"Yeah, if you're going to a funeral." She pushes off the couch and swings her long tresses over her shoulder, sauntering toward me in the silk negligee she opted to sleep in the night before. "Where's the color? Where's the pomp? The feeling of the outfit?"

"Work attire doesn't need *pomp*." I frown at the silliness of her suggestion and turn toward the coffee tin to prepare myself a cup of coffee to take with me to work. When I open the lid to find my coffee tin completely empty, I hold it up for her to see.

"Sorry about that." She shrugs. "I guess I used the rest of it last night."

"When did you make coffee last night?"

"When you were on the phone with your boy toy in your bedroom before going to bed."

"He's not my boy toy," I mumble. "And who drinks coffee before going to bed?"

"Some people do, I suppose," my mother answers. "But I made a cup and then went out last night."

I frown, not knowing any of this. "When did you get back in? *How* did you get back in?"

"A few hours ago with the spare key that I made?" Moving to the gold and glass coffee table, she picks up the key to show me.

I had no idea she even made a spare key. It was on the tip of my tongue to ask her when she was leaving but she beat me to the punch.

"So, I'm thinking we should do a shopping spree. You know, get you some nice clothes that actually look good on you."

"My clothes look fine on me," I insist.

"Janine, don't be so touchy. You were always like this as a little girl. I'm not saying this to be mean, I'm just telling you the truth. Maybe it's the reason you aren't married by now. No man wants to look at a woman in drab clothing all day."

She eyes my outfit up and down.

"And everybody knows how desperate you were to have that Matthew marry you. I probably should've told you much sooner. But I see you've moved on. Good for you, but you don't want to repeat the same mistakes as before do you?"

I blink away the tears that try to form in my eyes. "I'm going to work." I snatch my over the shoulder bag off the counter, grab my empty coffee tumbler, keys off the wall, and slam the door behind me.

Nothing like being embarrassed, chastised, and called dull and boring by your mother before you've even started the work day.

****

Things just went from bad to worse today. I wasn't in the office twenty minutes when Zeke comes hustling in, placing his stuff on the desk and telling me that we had to present our campaign idea to Digita in five minutes.

I don't have time to gather my thoughts before I peer up and see Danny walking in with two men from Digita, heading toward his office.

I turn to Zeke. "We're doing it now?" I question.

He gives me his usual impatient look. "That's what I just said. Are you slow or something?" He mumbles something else that I can't quite make out.

It's on the tip of my tongue to ask him who the hell he thinks he's talking to, but he's already leaving me behind to catch up as he gathers the posters he's created and heading to Danny's office.

"Janine?" Danny calls.

I turn to see an impatient expression on his face. Gathering my tablet, I head in his direction behind Zeke. My body begins to quake with nervousness upon realizing I don't even know what campaign Zeke has decided to present in this meeting. We went over it at least four different ways to present this app to the public—none of which were the ideas that I had originally come up with. Whenever I'd thought to reintroduce my campaign, Zeke's words on the true reason why I was hired played out in my head. That, coupled with Danny's confidence in Zeke when he first introduced me to him, stopped me from speaking up. *I am supposed to be in a position of learning from Zeke, not speaking over him*, my mind would remind me whenever I thought something he said didn't sound quite right.

"Gentlemen," Danny begins as he shuts the door behind the five of us. "I appreciate you coming in so early. I'd like to introduce you to one of my top employees. Zeke has been with the company for a number of years and is especially talented."

I watch as Zeke confidently shakes their hands, giving them a look of esteem I didn't even know he was capable of. Hell, I barely realized he was capable of more than sneering since that is about the totality of my experience working with him.

"And this," Danny continues, moving next to me, "is our newest member, Janine. She comes all of the way from Boston and is eager and anxious to get to work supporting the new campaign we've put together."

"Gentlemen," I say, extending my hand.

Both give me polite smiles while firmly shaking my hand.

I'm proud of myself for not displaying the nervousness in my voice.

"Let's have a seat?" Danny offers, pointing the two men from Digita toward the couch, while Zeke takes a seat to their left in one of Danny's chairs and I sit to the right.

Danny pulls out an easel, setting up the posters that Zeke brought into the office on it, turning them backwards so we can't see their contents.

"As I've stated, Zeke is one of my most trusted employees, and as a result, I have given him the utmost trust in taking the lead on this project. So without further ado, I'm going to let Zeke take it away. Zeke."

I carefully watch as Zeke rises and looks between the two men. He immediately opens up with his knowledge of Digita's past projects and how this new app is a natural extension of the company.

"However, given the oversaturation of your current market, I thought it would not be a wise choice to market this product to the same users that you're used to ..."

I wrinkle my forehead, wondering where this is going. All of the campaigns that Zeke and I have discussed focus primarily on Digita's current market base.

"Therefore, I have come up with a campaign that speaks to the new *momprenuer*," he proudly states as he turns the first posterboard around.

I feel like I've been punched in the gut as the air rushes from my lungs. I clamp down on my lips to keep the incredulity from spilling out of my mouth. Silently, I watch as Zeke discusses the market base of working millennial parents, many of whom are opting to use the internet and technology to their advantage to work from home while raising a family. I grow livid as the idea I showed him weeks ago, the very same one he said was ridiculous, is being presented for Digita as his own.

And not only that, but they're eating it up.

My chest aches with the anger that I'm holding in.

"I told you he was a star, didn't I, gentlemen?" Danny says proudly as he stands next to Zeke once the presentation is complete.

"Oh, and Janine assisted as well, I'm sure," Danny adds.

I barely hear my own name as I glare at Zeke. His eyes narrow at me, but when he turns to Danny and the men from Digita, that smile returns.

"I need to speak with you," I say, folding my arms across my chest as soon as Zeke and I are back at our respective desks.

"I'm busy, I—"

"Right now before I march in that office and tell Danny the truth," I seethe.

Danny is still in the office with the men from Digita. They loved the campaign idea and are now discussing the paperwork and contracts that will be issued for this project.

"Fine," Zeke huffs as if I am inconveniencing *him*.

The fucking nerve.

I follow him out into the hallway by the elevators where our coworkers won't overhear us.

"What the hell was that?"

"*That* was me doing my job." His voice is just an angry as mine. You would think I was the one who stole something from him instead of the other way around.

"Your job is to steal ideas?"

"Oh grow up! Your idea didn't have a name on it."

My head snaps backwards in surprise at the viciousness behind his tone.

"My idea didn't have a name on it, yet just weeks ago you were telling me how ridiculous and stupid it was. Now you're presenting it as your own. You're a backstabbing, s—"

"Don't be a sore loser."

"Loser? I had no idea we were in competition with one another. We were supposed to be working on this together."

"You really are this fucking naïve. We're all in competition in this place. For the next promotion, the next raise, the next big campaign that could take us out of here to a bigger firm. I told you, you weren't meant for this job." He gives me another up and down look of disgust before turning, holding his head up high and heading back through the doors of the main office.

Defeated doesn't even begin to describe how I feel in this moment. I try to force myself to go back into the office but I can't. Instead, I make a beeline for the only place where I know I can get some privacy.

The bathroom.

I push through the door angrily and kick the first wall I see. It's not the smartest move but the only one I can think of at the time. I'm so pissed off and have no idea what to do. Thankfully, no one else is in here and I pace back and forth, my anger building as I continue to stew over how Zeke just undercut me. I grow so enraged that I feel the first hot tear of anger escape my eye, falling to my cheek. I've heard over and over again to never cry at work but right now I feel too unsettled to do anything else.

I can't go to Danny and tell him what Zeke has done. That would make me look like an immature child. I used to tell my first graders how constantly tattle-tailing wasn't a good thing. Now, here I am, an adult, wanting to run and tell on a co-worker. *But he freaking stole my idea!* And like so many other times in my life—with my mother, my ex, former job—I felt like my voice had been stripped from me yet again.

Chapter Eighteen

Emanuel

"Allende!" a loud yell comes from the garage right after I hear the doors of the fire truck slamming shut.

I begin laughing before I ever see their faces.

Seconds later, Carter and Sean burst through the kitchen doors, their faces looking pissed as they're covered in sparkly, colorful glitter.

"What? Did a fucking unicorn take a dump on you two?" Roger, one of our part-time guys, questions.

This only forces me to laugh even harder.

"Fuck off!" Carter growls as he lunges in my direction.

I side step him and lead behind the table, but Sean begins approaching me from the other side.

"I, for one, think the glitter glam look is great on you two."

"I'm going to kill you!" Sean blurts out.

I howl even louder because the combination of glitter all over his face and shirt, along with the outraged expression, makes for comedy. I pull out my phone and snap a picture just as he lunges.

"This is definitely going on the Wall of Fame!" I shout.

"I'll break that fucking phone!" Carter yells as he tries to reach me, but I pull out a chair from the table, causing him to stumble.

"The ol' glitter in the AC trick works every time,

gentlemen," I manage to get out between laughs. Both of these guys are trying hard to get to me and I know once they do I'll have to fight for my life.

Earlier in the day—once assignments were given out and I knew I wouldn't be driving the truck today—I decided it was time to implement one of the tricks I've been thinking up for some time. I purchased a huge bag of glitter a week ago and stashed it in my locker. Earlier, when no one had been paying attention in the garage, I eased my way into the truck and poured the glitter in the vents of the AC. As soon as the AC was turned on, Carter, who was driving, and Sean, who was in the passenger seat, were punched in the face by a whole bundle's worth of glitter.

"I'm supposed to pick up my son. Now I have to go looking like a fucking fairy," Sean growls as he finally reaches me, wrapping his massive arms around my waist.

I'm laughing too hard to retaliate too much which is how Carter gets the drop on me as well. We wrestle for I don't know how long.

"I may not be the Chaos I once was but don't fuck with me," I threaten Sean and Carter as I put one of them in a headlock, which one, I don't know because the other one is busy putting me in a headlock.

"Fucking school children," we hear a deep growl.

All three of us pause to see Captain Waverly standing at

the door a grim expression on his face. He merely watches us for a few seconds, grabs a cup of coffee, and heads back out. The three of us pick up exactly where we left off.

****

"What time is it?" I question Carter sometime later, as he passes me on his way to the kitchen. I smirk at his wet hair. He's showered and tried to get the glitter off of him.

He peers at the watch on his wrist. "Uh, quarter after nine."

"Thanks ... Oh, and you still have some glitter in your hair." I laugh as I exit the kitchen while he's tossing me the middle finger. I head to my locker and pull out my cell phone. I frown when I don't see any missed calls. Usually, Janine and I talk on the phone during the evenings when I'm on shift. If I don't answer, she knows it's because I'm on a call and I always call back as soon as I can.

Since I'd forgotten my phone in my locker while we were out, I figured I missed her call but there are no missed calls, voicemails, or texts. A fact which has me immediately pulling up her name in my contacts and calling.

"Hey."

Her voice instantly alerts me that something isn't right.

"What happened?"

There's a pause at the other end of the phone. "Nothing happened, just not a good day."

"Come see me." It's the first thought I have and I go with it. I want to see her face, to kiss her lips, and wipe away whatever it is that's bothering her.

"Emanuel, it's late. And you're working. I—"

"Either you come see me now or I'll pull this big ass fire truck to the front of our building, blocking everyone in, and pissing them off when they find out there's no fire."

"You wouldn't do that." I hear the small grin in her voice.

"Try me." I mean it with every fiber of my being.

"Don't they need the fire truck for actual fires?"

"We have a second one here. So what's it going to be?"

She pushes out a heavy breath. "I'm on my way."

"It should take you fifteen minutes to get down to the station. I'll be generous since you drive slow, and give you twenty."

"I don't drive slow. I just don't drive like a bat out of hell like you do. Plus, I need to put on my shoes."

"Fine, twenty-one minutes. A minute over and I'm coming looking for you."

As I hang up the phone, I hear her mumbling something.

I head down the stairs and wait outside, despite the fact that it's early December and the weather has dipped into the high forties. Watching as a few guys from the station head out, I wave, partially wishing that I was heading out for the night also. I'm working an overnight which is the only reason I was waiting on Janine to come to me instead of going to her.

It still amazes me that she has me wishing to be somewhere other than the firehouse. I've *never* had that feeling before. The fire station has become my home over the past seven years. Even when I couldn't stand the captain I worked for, or I wasn't getting along with a member of my squad, there was no place I'd rather be. Until Janine.

After idling around for a while, I pull my phone from my pocket and frown when I realize it's been twenty-two minutes since we hung up the phone. Just when I turn to head to the garage to climb in the fire truck, her grey Kia pulls into the driveway.

I barely give her enough time to put the car in park, before I'm pulling the driver's side door open, and pulling her into my body. Her arms tighten around my neck.

"You took too long," I growl into her neck and then nip her earlobe.

She sighs. "Sorry. I can't seem to do anything right today."

The dejected tone in her voice tugs at my very soul. I don't like that voice coming from my woman.

I pull back and stare down at her, lifting her face by the chin so she has to look up at me. "Why didn't you call me tonight?"

"I figured you were busy."

The frown I'm wearing deepens. "Lie to me again and I'll show you why that's not a good idea, butterfly."

Her lips pull into a thin line. "My day sucked and I didn't want to bring you down."

"That's closer to the truth. Tell me what happened."

"My mother was on my case first thing this morning." She looks at me and her mouth opens but shuts before whatever she was going to say has a chance to come out. "And then I got to work and it went downhill from there."

"Work still giving you trouble?"

Shaking her head, she gazes out into the distance. "Have you ever felt like you got something that you didn't really earn? Like, it should be a celebration that you got this reward or thing you wanted, but then you find out it's a lie. That you obtained it under false pretenses." She looks back to me.

The overhead lighting from the station behind us illuminates her face, and I'm able to see the uncertainty in her eyes. It pulls at my chest because I know exactly the feeling she's describing. It's like you're walking around living a lie.

"Is that how you feel at work? You earned that job."

"But what if I didn't? What if I'm just a lie?"

"Why the hell would you even think that?"

"Because I was told. Zeke—"

"The asshole?" I grunt, angrily. She's mentioned his

name once or twice before, and I could tell from those few times that he was the one giving her a hard time.

She gives me a small smile. "Yeah, him. He told me the reason I was hired was basically because I'm black and Danny thought he needed some diversity in the office."

"That doesn't even make sense. You have a degree—"

"Yeah, but no experience. I worked as an elementary school teacher for seven years. Not in the field of my degree."

"So what?"

She looks at me in confusion. "What do you mean so what?"

"I mean exactly that. What if you were just hired because of your race ... which is a load of bullshit, by the way. But let's say that's the case. Big fucking deal."

"It *is* a big deal."

"Not if you don't make it one. You have the job now. Look at me," I say, turning her head to face me again. "You know why I'm standing here right now, at this station house as a member of Rescue Four?"

"Because you're a firefighter. You earned your way through the academy."

"Right, but I wasn't assigned at this station until recently. And that was only because a former squad member was injured. So severely he lost his career. There was an opening and I finally got the transfer I'd been aiming for over a year."

"Yeah, but—"

"But nothing. Corey got injured and it fucking sucks for him. And as a result, I got the position I've wanted for a long time. Do you think that makes me any less capable of doing my job? You think the guy I pulled out of a fire earlier today gives a shit how I got this job? He cares that he's still alive because I was there. Plain and simple. He's not looking up my record and asking how many years of experience I do or don't have. None of that shit matters when you're in the middle of a fire."

"But I don't save lives for a living. In my job, people care about my experience—"

"No." I shake my head. "They care about what you bring to the table. They give a shit about what you have of value to offer. You didn't get this job solely because of your race. And Zack is a fucking jackass for even opening his mouth and saying that garbage. But so what if he and everyone else in the office believes it? It's not your job to defend the hiring practices of your boss. It's your job to do what the fuck you were hired to do. Stop letting all of the bullshit get into your head. I see how much you enjoy advertising and learning about it. Show them."

She blinks and lowers her forehead to my chest, wrapping her arms around my waist.

"You know that's not his name, right?"

"I don't give a fuck."

She giggles.

"He stole my campaign idea."

Her words are muffled.

I pull back. "What was that?"

"Zeke. That's what had me so pissed off today. He stole my campaign idea. Presented it as if it was his own."

Anger courses through my veins. My hand cups her chin, raising her face to meet mine. "And that's the son of a bitch you're believing when he says you were just hired to fill some fucking quota?" My voice booms louder than I expected but I can't help the ire I feel for a person I've never even met. "He's trying to get into your head. He wants you to doubt yourself because it makes him feel better about himself. Don't let him, butterfly."

She pushes out a big breath. "But what am I supposed to do? I can't exactly go to Danny and say Zeke stole my idea. That would look totally childish."

I nod. "So do what you can do. You've already proven yourself to be smarter and more creative than that piece of shit. You came up with one idea that was obviously great, which leads me to believe there are just tons more waiting for you to express them."

She looks up at me again. "You're right. First, he says I was hired for false reasons, then goes and steals my idea—an idea the company loved by the way. It's time I play the game the way he's playing it."

"Fuck him," I growl.

She giggles and lays her head against my chest.

I tuck her body against mine, wrapping her with my arms. "You know why I call you butterfly?" I ask as I stare into the distance.

"You won't tell me."

I chuckle. She's right. Every time she asks about the term of endearment, I refuse to give a straight answer. Until now.

"Butterflies start off as caterpillars, a completely different looking entity. They're slow, not always so pretty to look at. But through a whole series of transformations they emerge from their cocoons as some of the most breathtaking creatures to fly. That's how I see you."

Janine pulls back, peering up into my eyes. The wetness that covers her pupils is evident. She doesn't say anything. Instead, she takes my face into her hands and pulls me down so that our lips meet somewhere in the middle. She pours everything into the kiss.

My cock begins stirring in my pants at the small moans she's making in between kisses.

She breaks the kiss, her hands still holding my face. Her eyes penetrate mine as she appears to be searching for something.

"I'm probably going to regret this because it might scare you off but I love you." Her voice is nothing more than a whisper.

I lower my face until we're only about an inch apart. "Only a pussy ass motherfucker would be scared off to hear the woman he loves tell him she loves him."

Janine's eyes double in size but I don't have time to take it because I cover her lips with mine again, needing to touch her. The kiss, albeit excellent, isn't enough. I need more.

"Where are we going?" Janine gasps, looking around.

I'm practically dragging her by the arm around the back of the building. "You ever fucked in a fire station?"

She gasps. "What? Of course not."

I chuckle loudly. I knew she hadn't. I knew that before I even asked the question. "I'm popping that cherry tonight." I lead us behind the station where there is a back entrance that extends down a hallway that's rarely used.

"No, we're not!" she insists.

"Too late."

"Em—" Her protests are cut off when I pull her face to mine, capturing those juicy lips of hers.

And just as I knew would happen, her resistance soon melts to surrender. I let my lips move from hers and create a trail from her jawline down the soft skin of her long neck.

"Wh-What if someone comes in?" she murmurs.

"No one uses this room." My hands move to the skin underneath her shirt. I squeeze her waist, pulling her body into mine and thrusting my hips forward so she can feel how much I want her.

She moans against my lips again.

"Butterfly, I know it's my fault you're so open now with the sounds you make when we're together, but to keep us from getting caught, you're going to have to keep this one quiet."

"It's your fault if we get caught," she whispers, angrily. But I can hear the lust in her voice.

After removing a condom from my wallet, which was in my back pocket, I toss the wallet aside and move to unbutton the black pants Janine is wearing.

"You better not get fired because of this," she says as her hands go to the button of my work pants, beginning to pull them down.

"I won't." I cover her mouth with mine.

Our hands and arms busy themselves, undressing one another, until I have her right where I want her. I lift her legs to wrap my waist, and begin to enter her with my sheathed cock. When she starts to moan in pleasure, I crush our lips together, forcing her to moan into my mouth. My hips move angrily, pounding into her as I press her back against the wall.

Janine secures her legs around my waist even tighter and lowers her face into the crook of my neck, biting down on my shoulder, presumably to keep herself from yelling out loud. Her hands claw at my back in an attempt to relieve the pressure from being unable to yell.

Her release is quick and frenzied just like this fuck, but it leaves her legs trembling and her breathing altered. Once her walls tighten around my cock, my orgasm rushes me, nearly sending me to my knees. I press her deeply against the wall as ripple after ripple of pleasure invades my body.

When I'm able to catch my breath, I pull back from Janine, giving her one last deep kiss before I separate our bodies. The feeling of missing being wrapped up in her warmth is immediate. I want desperately to pound into her again and make her know she's mine but I can't. I'm still at work, and I can tell by her facial expression she's not letting me get in a second round.

"I can't believe we just did that," she whispers while fumbling back into her clothing.

"Believe it, babe."

"Stop that!" she whispers angrily, swatting my hand, which is squeezing her ass, away.

I chuckle. "If it's any consolation you popped my cherry, too."

She finishes buttoning her pants and looks up at me with a curious expression. "This was your first time screwing at the station?"

I plant a kiss on her lips. "Of course. I wouldn't risk losing my job for just *any* woman."

She gives me the cutest fucking smile imaginable. "Somehow that does make me feel better. I should go."

I push out a breath, knowing she's right. It's late and she has to work the next morning. And I still have almost twelve more hours of my shift.

I stick my head out of the door of the closet we were in just to make sure no one is out in the hallway. When the coast is clear, I pull Janine's hand in mine and retrace the steps we took in, going out the back entrance of the station house and around the side to the front parking lot where her car is.

I place my forehead against hers, cupping her face as a wave of guilt takes hold in my gut. "Next time you come, I'll pretend I have actual manners and introduce you to the rest of the squad."

She gives me a brilliant smile. "I'd like that ... but this was fun, too. Thank you." Lifting up on to her tiptoes, she presses a kiss to my lips.

I reluctantly take a step backwards, making room for her to open and climb into the driver's seat of her car.

I rap my knuckles against the window. "Call me when you get home so I know you made it," I say once she rolls the window down.

She nods and blows me a kiss.

I know I'm completely fucked up and in deep with this woman when I actually use my hand and grab the imaginary kiss out of the air. The lame shit I've seen in movies. But I don't even chide myself for long because the giddy expression that crosses Janine's face is all the reassurance I need.

Yeah, I'm in deep.

Chapter Nineteen

Janine

"I need to go shopping," I tell Angela as I stare down at the pile of clothing lying on my bed, frowning.

"Okay, shopping for what? Are you looking for winter clothing, a new coat, boots?" Angela questions as she stands beside me.

"Everything," I respond, turning toward her.

Her face wrinkles up curiously. "Everything," she repeats as if to make sure she heard me correctly.

"Yes. I need a whole new wardrobe."

"And you want to get that all in one day?"

"Well, it's Saturday and both of our guys are working doubles this weekend. What else do you have to do? And I love your fashion sense. I'll let you leave early if you have to go into the bar tonight. Please!" I practically beg, tugging on Angela's hand.

A smile opens up on her face. "Where is this coming from?"

I shrug. "I just think I need a change. My wardrobe is ... boring. Everything is either black or grey with some white mixed in there. It's dull. Even all of my panties are all black."

"Okay, *that* was a little TMI," she giggles.

"Sorry. But I'm serious. I need your help. Your style is cute and a little on edge, but not too much." I look over the waist high jeans and the crop top she's wearing that shows just a touch of her honey brown abdomen. Her curly hair rests against her shoulders, and the streak of purple she had months ago is now a rose pink.

"And this is your decision, right?"

"Who else's decision would it be?" I ask defensively, having an inkling of where this conversation is going.

"Don't get upset. I just remember how you started changing your wardrobe in college because Matthew didn't like when you wore too much color, or hated a particular hairstyle. I don't want the same thing to happen."

"It's not." Pausing to stare at my clothing on the bed again, I and plop down on the bed. "You're right. I made so many concessions in my life for Matthew. I stopped wearing color because he'd told me his mother said that it was unbecoming. Whatever the hell that means. I longed to be exactly who he wanted me to in hopes that one day he'd finally see I was worthy of him and his last name. But I lost myself in all of that. This isn't the same.

"I don't feel like I have to conform or be perfect with Emanuel. I can just be. Now, I get to figure out who that is. And part of that starts with new clothes. So will you take me shopping or not? I'll be a total mess in the stores if left alone."

Angela holds up two very bland looking black shirts that I often wear to work. "Yes, you obviously need some help."

My eyes balloon and I toss a balled up T-shirt at her. "You could've said something before."

"Girl, I tried but you had your head so far up Matthew's—"

"Okay, you don't need to finish the rest of that sentence."

"Great, let's go!" Giggling, Angela wraps her arm around mine, pulling me up from the bed. "First, we need to get something to eat because I'm starving."

"You just had breakfast not too long ago."

"I know, and I'm hungry again."

I give her a side-eye but don't say anything. I grab my brown leather shoulder bag, slip into a pair of black ballet flats, and follow Angela out of my bedroom toward my front door.

"Hey, where's your m—"

Angela's question is cut off as soon as Janet comes barging through the door.

"Hey, Janine. Angela, right?" she questions looking between Angela and I.

"Yes." Angela nods. "Hi, Ms. Thompson."

"Where're you two headed off to?"

"Shopping," I murmur and turn toward the door.

"Where?" my mothers asks.

"We have a long list. Janine wants to do an overhaul on her wardrobe," Angela answers.

I wince, knowing my mother is going to seize this opportunity ... and she does.

"Oh my god! Finally. It's about time you let someone talk some sense into you about those clothes. All that black and grey." She shivers.

I take in the metallic leggings and lime green, long-sleeved top my mother is adorning, coupled with the six-inch black stilettos. The long weave she wears is styled in barrel curls that reach all of the way down to her waist.

"Would you like to come?" Angela offers.

"Yes!"

"No!"

My mother and I say at the same time. Angela gives me a look.

"You're going to need some help with this one, Angela. She can be so stubborn when it comes to how she dresses ... about anything really. You would think she'd learn to take advice from someone who knows better," my mother begins.

Angela laughs. "My mother used to call me stubborn sometimes, too."

I roll my eyes. I can guarantee my mother and Angela's mother were not one in the same.

"Right? I guess it's a mother-daughter thing. I tried giving her advice on that boy Matthew but she wouldn't listen. And you see how that turned out, right, Janine? I told you that boy was never going to marry you. You gave him too much of what he wanted. Were always at his beck and call. Men don't like that. Tell her, Angela. You're married," my mother continues.

Angela gives me a wide-eyed expression.

"Though, your husband is Asian so he might be different. Never been with an Asian man before. Well, there was that one time—"

"Janet!" I yell, feeling embarrassed.

She gives me an innocent look.

Rolling my eyes, I turn to Angela. "I'm sorry. She says whatever's on her mind most of the time."

"Damn right I do. Let's go," Janet insists, pulling on the long jacket she's just taken off.

"You're wearing that?" I don't know why I ask. Of course, she has no problem going out in the middle of the day in the same clothes she wore to stay out the entire night before.

"Why not?"

Not bothering to respond, I wait for Angela to pass over the threshold of the door to close and lock it behind me. I had been so looking forward to going shopping with Angela and sprucing up my wardrobe. Now that my mother is tagging along, I'm so sure I even want to go anymore. At least, not with her in tow.

****

Emanuel

"What are you up to?" I question into the phone as I step into the kitchen which is unusually empty at the moment.

"Shopping."

"You don't sound to happy about it."

"I was ... I am. It was supposed to be just Angela and I, and then Janet decided to tag along."

"What's wrong with that?"

"Emanuel, you've met my mother, right?"

I chuckle into the phone. Janet is definitely eccentric and probably thinks she's fifteen years younger than her actual age, but I don't see why that has to ruin Janine's time.

"Tell me what you've gotten so far."

She runs off a list of clothing items she purchased for work and for going out.

I check over my shoulder to make sure no one is around.

"What color are the new panties?"

"I never said anything about buying new panties."

"Yeah, but you can't get a new wardrobe without new undergarments. What color are they?" I growl into the phone.

"I'm not telling. You're going to have to find out for yourself."

"That won't be a problem."

Janine giggles into the phone, and it reaches through and massages the ache in my chest. The one that is almost always present now when I'm not with her.

"I have to go," I tell her reluctantly.

"Okay. Love you," she says casually as if we've been saying it for years to one another, instead of just a couple of weeks.

"Love you, too," comes my response, just as casually.

I hang up the phone and stare at it, marveling at the depth of my feelings for this woman.

"Oooh, love you, muah," comes a deep, mocking voice behind me.

Turning, I find Don continuing to make dumbass kissy face sounds. Sean and Carter stand behind him laughing.

"Fuck all of you," I grunt.

Their laughter grows louder.

"What the hell are you laughing at? You're worse than I am." I point at Carter.

"I know. They gave me shit for it, too. Comes with the territory."

"Bet your ass it does," Don says, slapping me on the back.

Chuckling, I shake my head. Ever since we had it out over two months ago, Don has been much more relaxed with me. I've gotten to see the funny, shit-talking, wise ass that everyone refers to when they talk about him. But I've also gotten to see the kickass, take no prisoners firefighter that holds nothing back while on the job. It's evident that he still misses his friend. Not to mention he's still working hard to figure out who the hell is behind these fires, and if there's a cover up or not. So far, there haven't been any incidents.

"Allende, there're some people here to see you," Captain Waverly barges into the kitchen and calls out.

Frowning, I wonder who would be here to see me. I just got off the phone with Janine, who said she was all the way across town with her mother and Angela shopping.

"I hope you get to tell them you love 'em," Don calls behind me.

I can hear Carter and Sean laughing as I pass through the door. I head toward the front of the station house by the front entrance. There's a woman, about five-five in height, slender with medium-length brown hair. She seems familiar but I can't quite put my finger on it. The man next to her doesn't look familiar at all.

She looks nervous when she sees me. She switches the squirming baby in her arms from one hip to the other, and then it hits me.

I stop, freezing in place, about three feet away from her.

"Mrs. Powell," I say just above a whisper. My heart begins beating wildly in my chest. It's the first time I've seen her since that awful night. This is Jackson's mother.

"Are you Emanuel Allende?" she asks hesitantly.

I nod.

Her smile is shaky at first, until it grows and tears spill over onto her cheeks. Before I know what's happening, she's thrown her free arm around my shoulders, hugging me tightly.

I remain frozen, not knowing what to do. Lifting my gaze to the man who is with her, I see he has tears in his eyes as well as her gives me a cautious smile.

The baby in Mrs. Powell's arms is what eventually forces her to pull back.

"I'm sorry," she says, wiping her tears and trying to gather herself. "I didn't mean to be a mess. I thought I got all of my tears out." Releasing a small laugh, she takes the offered tissue from the man I suspect is her husband.

"What my wife means to say is thank you."

Mrs. Powell nods her head vigorously, agreeing with her husband.

"This," he says, taking the baby girl from his wife, "is our baby girl, Sabrina. She was only three weeks old when you pulled them both out. Now she's almost ten months."

I swallow the lump in my throat as I stare down at the little girl. I remember that night as if it just happened the day before. She was so tiny back then. She had no idea of the danger she was in. Just the terror she felt from her mom. Now, as her big, brown eyes look at me with curiosity, I find myself reaching for her.

"Can I?" I ask Mr. Powell.

He nods. "Of course."

I take ahold of Sabrina, who willingly comes to me. "Hi," I whisper.

She makes a sound, almost as if saying hi back. Her little hand reaches out and grabs my bottom lip. All three of us laugh.

"You're a lot bigger now than when I first met you." Staring at her, all of a sudden a sadness overcomes me. "She looks like him," I blurt out. I vividly recall the picture from Jackson's obituary. I still keep the newspaper cutout with the image in my locker.

A second later, I realize what I've just said and my gaze shoots over to her parents.

"I'm sorry." I shake my head, trying to keep the tears from welling up in my eyes. "I'm so sorry I couldn't save—"

"Don't," Mrs. Powell says forcefully. She moves to my side, placing a hand on my back and the other on her daughter's. "Jackson was such a restless sleeper. That night he'd fallen asleep in bed with me, but somehow ended up in his closet. He did that often. I blamed myself for so long not realizing he had gone back to his room in the middle of the night. We've been through all of that." She glances at her husband. "All of the would haves, should haves, and could haves. Michael blamed himself for not being there that night. For working. I blamed myself for not being able to get to Jackson. None of that is going to bring him back. The man who saved our Sabrina and me, doesn't get to blame himself either."

I really am at a loss for words. I can't do anything but nod as Mr. Powell moves closer, and soon his arms are wrapped around my shoulders. Again, Sabrina only stands to be squeezed in between her parents and I for so long before she let it be known she is over all of it.

I hand the baby over to her mother as we laugh at her tiny squeals.

"Thank you." Mrs. Powell looks up at her husband, then back to me. "We wanted to come sooner but ..."

I shake my head. "Your timing is perfect."

"Thank you doesn't seem like enough for saving my wife and daughter ... and for pulling Jackson out. We got to say good-bye to our little boy." Mr. Powell takes something out of his pocket. It's a charred baseball.

"Jackson had his first T-ball game a few days earlier. He wanted to be a baseball player when ..." he pauses, his voice cracking, "when he grew up." He extends his hand with the ball in it to me.

"We want you to have it," Mrs. Powell finishes.

"I can't." I shake my head. "You should keep it."

"We'd like for you to."

My gaze rises from the ball to Mrs. Powell.

"Please."

Taking the ball from her husband, I turn it over and over in my hands as I stare at it.

I don't recall the exchanges of good-byes. I only take my next breath when I hear the door close behind them as they exit, remembering the sound of Sabrina's giggle as her mother tickles her belly on the way out.

I turn to see Carter standing there.

The expression on his face says it all.

I use the pointer finger and thumb of my free hand to wipe the tears out of my eyes. "Who the fuck is cutting onions in this place?" I say.

Carter pats me on the back. "I sure fucking hope it isn't Don. He can't cook for shit."

A snort pushes through my lips.

"Pizza's on its way. I'm headed to the kitchen. You coming?"

I stare at the ball in my hand. "Yeah, in a minute. I'm gonna put this in my locker." I hold the ball up for him to see.

He nods.

When I reach my locker, I place the ball on the top shelf, next to the photos I have of me with some guys from Station Two, and from the day I graduated from the academy, and of course, Jackson's obituary. The most prominent picture in my possession isn't in my locker. It's taped to the inside of my helmet. It's one of Janine and I on our final day in Mexico. My favorite picture of us.

After shutting my locker, I head down the stairs toward the kitchen, following the smell of the just delivered pizza.

Chapter Twenty

Janine

I step off the elevator with my head held high and the high heels I wear creating a rhythm against the floor as I stroll toward the door of Lux Advertising.

As soon as the door swings open, Shelah's eyes widen. "Good morning. Loving the pink on you."

I smile. "Thank you."

"The outfits your friend helped you pick out are really working for you."

I give her a little spin and dip to show off the entirety of my outfit. It's simple, yet the soft pink, high-rise pants paired with the tucked in cream-colored turtleneck really does look great on me. I found myself staring in my full length mirror for some time this morning, marveling at it.

"The things a personal stylist can do for you." The day Angela and I went shopping, we stopped at one of Angela's favorite thrift stores. The stylist who works there part-time gave me some great tips on how to dress right for my body type. She also convinced me that color could be professional, and that the no white after Labor Day thing is outdated.

"I loved those leopard print heels you wore last week," Shelah adds.

"Those are one of my faves." It took me four full days to muster up the courage to wear those shoes and when I did, I never wanted to take them off.

I spend a few more minutes talking with Shelah before I hear the door open behind me. Glancing over my shoulder, I see Zeke walk in—he looks just as displeased to see me as I am to see him. I don't hide the eyeroll I toss him.

I turn back to Shelah. "Time to get the day started. Let's have lunch together."

"Sure thing. That little shop across the street has some good sandwiches."

"Sounds good."

I head back to my desk feeling more confident than I ever remember feeling. The new clothes are part of it, along with the fact that Danny has given me a couple of compliments over the last couple of weeks on some small projects he has me working on by myself. Zeke and I still aren't getting on great, but to hell with him. After my talk with Emanuel, that night at his station, I feel like I can walk on water. He reminded me that I did have the talent and intelligence to make it in this career. Obviously, my idea had been a good one, otherwise Zeke wouldn't have felt the need to steal it, and Danny wouldn't have loved it. I can come up with more ideas. That wasn't a one off. Zeke could steal one and claim it as his, but he didn't have my intellect, creativity, or savvy. Those, he could never take from me.

"Good morning, Zeke," I greet him as I arrive at my desk

and place my purse inside of the bottom drawer. I ignore the fact that he doesn't respond. "I hear we're meeting with Digita again today. That's great news because there are some issues that we need to go over."

"The campaign's fine."

I lift an eyebrow. "Are you sure about that?" I feel a sense of superiority when that haughty know-it-all look of his falters for one second. I know that look well. I remember seeing it on the faces of my ex and his family, and high-society friends often while we were dating.

"I know what I'm doing."

I give him a smile. "You and I both know if you were that confident in knowing what you were doing, you wouldn't need to steal, would you?"

"Will you come off it?" he whispers across the desk so our other colleagues don't overhear.

"I sure will." I sit down to finally turn on my computer, without another word. I can feel his eyes on me as I check my emails. He's definitely grown more and more uneasy around me over the past couple of weeks.

Good.

An hour and a half later, Zeke and I are entering Danny's office behind the two men from Digita who were here for the last meeting with the company.

"Gentlemen, it's come to my attention that you've taken

issue with an aspect of our campaign," Danny says, a chagrined expression covering his face.

"We thought there'd be much more social media adverts than there currently are," one of the men, Anthony Lomax, explains.

I want to roll my eyes so bad. I made it a point to tell Zeke that this campaign needed a bigger push on social media. That's where our target market for this campaign is. But he insisted that the bigger push needed to be on traditional media outlets. Again, his cocky attitude that he knew better won out.

"I'm certain Zeke has a reason as to why he chose to stick more closely to the traditional media route."

Zeke stands in front of everyone in the room. "Gentlemen, yes, it's true that social media adverts are not as prominent in this campaign. I believe that traditional is more the way to go with this campaign simply because of the reach we can have. Millions of people—"

"But are they in our market? Because the data says if we want deeper market penetration, social media is the way to go," Benjamin Walker, the other Digita employee, states.

"Yes, well, with the pushback many social media outlets are receiving—"

"What pushback?"

I lift an eyebrow, wanting to understand what Zeke is saying as well.

"There's been a lot of backlash on social media, and from a business perspective ... we just think it's better to stick with what we know."

I look to the two Digita men and they are not buying what Zeke is trying to sell.

"If I may," I finally interject. I shift my gaze between Danny, Benjamin, Anthony, and lastly, Zeke. "What I believe Zeke is trying to get at is the fact that advertising on social media can be a tricky business." Standing, I move over to the easel that Danny had set up with an image of Digita's logo. "We have to be cautious about our approach to social media advertising because users are finicky. I'm sure you gentlemen, at some point, have found yourselves scrolling through your social media timeline only to be turned off by the number of advertisements and sponsored posts that keep popping up."

"Yes, and—"

"However," I say, cutting Zeke off, "that doesn't mean we ignore social media. Of course not. All indicators point to the fact that social media is where your target is for this product. Therefore, I would propose a sixty-forty split when it comes to social media and traditional advertising. The great thing about posting on social media is that it is financially beneficial. The benefits greatly outweigh the costs. And once your current product gains some steam online, which it will because it's a great product, by the way, then we can shift into giving more attention to traditional media outlets."

Pausing, take in the room. Danny is cautiously watching the men from Digita, who are looking between one another, silently communicating. Out of the corner of my eye, I see Zeke giving me the stink eye. Of course, I ignore him.

"That sounds like a great approach. What was your name again?"

My smile grows. "Janine."

"Janine, can you give us some specifics of what you were thinking?" Anthony asks.

"I'd like to hear as well," Danny adds.

"Yes, well, I've already done some mockups on my tablet. Let me pull them up." For the next twenty minutes we go over the social media campaign that I've designed for Digita. The two men point out some things for consideration but overall they are very happy with what I've come up with. By the time we are exiting Danny's office, the two men's demeanors have totally changed, Danny appears to be content, Zeke seems pissed, and I am on top of the world.

Today is one of the best days I've had at work in ... ever.

****

Emanuel

"Whoa!" I blurt out, surprised when my woman suddenly pushes me down on the couch. We're in my place, the lights down low, after having just finished a delicious Thai dinner.

My hands go to Janine's waist as she climbs on top of me, straddling my legs.

"You're lucky I happen to appreciate this position."

Her eyebrows wiggle and her lips widen with mischievousness. "You're really handsome, you know that?" Her voice is sultry.

My hands tighten around her hips as I frown. "Just handsome?"

"And sexy as fuck."

"That's more like it. Come here."

"No, wait!" She presses her hand against my chest as she pushes back to stand in front of me. "I wanted to show you something."

I lift an eyebrow.

"I thought you wanted to see what color panties I bought on my shopping spree."

"There's more?" So far she'd shown me at least four new pairs of panties she'd bought. They had ended up on my bedroom floor, or dresser, or kitchen countertop. I recall one ended up *inside* of the refrigerator. That was a great night.

"Let me see."

"Wait! Patience ... learn to practice it, Emanuel," she protests, pushing my hands out of the way as I go to reach for her again.

"I don't have much patience when it comes to you, butterfly."

I watch as her eyelids flutter and that little vein at the side of her neck quickens. She fucking loves that nickname.

"Don't you want to know what has me in such a good mood?"

I frown. "You mean it isn't the fact that I'm about to make you scream my name so loudly you'll lose your voice?"

"That too ... but there's more."

I rise from the couch and move closer to her, slowly. "You better make it quick." I follow her all of the way to the far end of my living room, trapping her body in with my arms against the wall directly next to the door.

"I had a great day at work. I showed Digita the social media campaign I'd come up with and they loved it!" Her excitement is contagious.

"That's great, babe," I say before dropping a kiss to the side of her neck.

She shivers. "It's because of you. I took your advice and said screw the whole being timid thing." She wraps her arms around my neck. "I saw where Zeke was being weak in the campaign and proposed my idea to our clients and they ate it up."

Those golden eyes of hers sparkle with pride.

I'm certain the same level of pride echoes in my

reflection. "You are amazing."

"Thank you for pushing me to believe in myself. For a while there I really believed I'd gotten a job I hadn't earned. It made me doubt every decision I made at work."

I snort. "I know that feeling."

"Do you? How? You're so confident," she declares.

"I put on a good show."

Grinning, she shakes her head. "No you don't. It's who you are. How could you doubt yourself?"

My hands moves to her waist and I stare her in the eyes. I drop a kiss to her lightly glossed lips simply because they're there and I can't resist.

"Remember I told you I received a Thomas Webster Award?"

Her forehead wrinkles as she thinks back to the conversation we had in Mexico. "Oh, yeah. You said it was like the bronze medal of the department or something, right? You earned it for saving that little boy."

"I didn't save him."

"Yeah, but—"

"He still died," I say gloomily. "I pulled out his mother and baby sister first, and had to go back in to search for him. By the time we got out, it was too late for Jackson. I received the Thomas Webster for *acts of bravery* as they call it. It was supposed to be a symbol of excellence on the job but it didn't feel that way."

Her hand moves up to cup my face. "But you saved that family."

Turning, I kiss the inside of her palm. "Still. It felt like a loss. Jackson is my one."

"Your one?"

I explain to her what that means and she raises up on her tiptoes, planting a soft kiss to my lips.

"His family came by earlier this week. To thank me, of all things."

"Of course they did. They lost their little boy but that father would've lost his wife and both of his children if it hadn't of been for you. As hard as it sounds to hear, you can't save everybody."

My lips pinch. Logically, I know what she says is true but I hate hearing it. "I didn't get into this career not to save people."

This time she cups my face with both of her hands, and gives me a small smile as she reaches up, kissing my lips again.

"If I'm ever in a fire I'd let you save me," she grins.

"Don't joke like that," I insist, my hands covering her wrist.

Her smile fades. "I was just ki—"

"I know, but you're too important to me to even imagine something like that happening to you and I can't get to you."

"I'm sorry."

Our lips meet somewhere in the middle. I pour all of my emotions into the kiss, telling her without words how important she is to me. My base instincts take over as I pull back.

"You still haven't shown me the color of the panties that'll be laying on the floor in a minute." I don't wait for her to move. My hands go to the waistband of the pink pants she's wearing, undoing the bow that holds the belt in place. I get a glimpse of the yellow lace panties she's wearing underneath.

"Yellow looks damn good on you."

"You haven't even seen the bra yet." Her eyebrows wiggle.

"They're matching?"

She nods and my lips form a frown.

"You wore these to work?" The jealousy bubbles up in my chest just thinking of her wearing a matching lace bra and panty set all day while away from me.

"I put them on this morning with you in mind," she whispers.

"You better have." I fuse our lips together and move to push her pants the hell out of the way when—

"Janine! Are you in there?" The yelling is followed by a loud pounding on my door. "Girl, I know you're there!"

"You've got to be kidding me," Janine sighs. She looks to

me with wide eyes. "I'm sorry."

Reluctantly, I let her pull away and quickly redo her clothing so she can open the door for her mother, who's still banging on the door.

"Janet, what are you doing here?" she questions as she yanks the door open.

Janet is so intent on knocking she nearly falls over when the door is pulled open.

"Hey, Janine. Hi, Emanuel," she purrs.

Janine rolls her eyes. "What do you need?"

"Oh." Janet blinks. "I, uh, keys! I forgot my set of keys and the door is locked. Can I get yours?"

I move behind Janine, placing my hand at the small of her back. I can feel the tension as it builds in her body. Not an unusual thing to happen whenever she is in the presence of her mother.

"I never gave you a set of keys to begin with," Janine mumbles. "Hang on a sec. My purse is in the bedroom," she turns to tell me.

I nod. "I can get—"

"No, it's fine. I'll grab them real quick." She hurries off in the direction of my bedroom, down the hall, leaving me standing at the door with her mother.

Janet turns to me, lowering and raising her eyelids in a way that I'm pretty sure is meant to be seductive. Stepping closer, she raises a hand to my chest, lightly running her pointer finger over my shirt.

I grab her hand by the wrist and tilt my head, giving her a look.

"You know, I'd be a lot more fun than my daughter." Her voice is low, just above a whisper as she gazes into my eyes.

Releasing her wrist, I take a move back. "I have enough fun in my life."

"You sure about that?" she questions in a coquettish voice, stepping closer, allowing her breasts to softly graze my chest.

"I'll send Janine over with the key." I begin shutting the door in this woman's face, feeling completely disgusted.

Just before the door closes, Janine emerges from the bedroom. "I've got it. Let me go unlock the door for her. I don't trust her with my key," she murmurs the last part so only I can hear it.

Janine certainly has good reason not to trust her mother with anything.

"Make it quick," I growl, as I pull her to me and kiss her lips possessively, while holding the door open with one hand so Janet can see.

Janine quickly crosses the hall and unlocks the door for her mother before returning to where I'm still watching. Just before I shut the door behind us, I see Janet peek her head out of the door and toss me a wink.

My response is to slam my door shut. "When is she leaving?"

Janine giggles. "She's a nuisance, right? Soon, I think. She mentioned something about a job in D.C. Or was it a guy? I don't know. My mother's a mess." She waves her hand in the air dismissively. "Where were we?" She wraps her arms around my waist.

"Right here," I growl, pulling her to me, and kissing the life out of her.

Chapter Twenty-One

Janine

"I cannot believe her," I groan while leaning against the bar, but staring out into the crowd as my mother grinds her body in the middle of two firefighters.

"She's not that bad," Angela tries to reassure.

I peer at my best friend who is behind the bar, wiping it down but curiously watching the woman who gave birth to me.

"Even your face can't hold onto that lie. She's embarrassing." I slouch down lower, rethinking my decision to even come to the bar that night. Luckily, I'm reminded why, seconds later when in walks the finest man in Rescue Four.

Emanuel's face immediately brightens when he catches my eye.

I rise from the wooden stool and move to the door, barely giving him a chance to fully enter before I wrap my arms around his shoulders. He's just as anxious because his lips cover mine without so much as a *hello.* The kiss steals my breath and sends a chill down my spine.

"Thanks for coming," he says after ending the kiss and placing his forehead against mine.

"Hey, Janine, you think you could give this guy a break? He's falling asleep on the job," Don's voice bellows from behind Emanuel.

"Fuck off, Don," Emanuel growls, causing Don and Sean to

crack up laughing.

I smile as Don and Sean walk past us, smirking. I'm happy to see Emanuel and Don getting along so well. He'd mentioned before that Don was the one holding out at the station when he first arrived.

"I missed you today," I say.

"Yeah, how much?"

"This much." Pulling his head down, I kiss him again.

Emanuel takes over the kiss, possessing my entire body. I only move back when a loud round of laughter behind us forces me to remember we're in a public place.

Emanuel's head rises to look over my head. "Your mother's here."

I roll my eyes. "Don't remind me. She was actually waiting for me in front of my job when I got off. She must've overheard me yesterday when I told you I'd meet you here after work. She insisted on coming. Let's pretend she's not here."

His eyes lower to meet mine. "Suits me."

I take him by the hand and lead him to the bar, ordering two beers. "They're on me," I insist, smacking his hand away when he tries to pay.

"I'll pay you back later," he growls in my ear.

"How was your day?" I question as he moves around one of the circle tables, to sit across from me.

"Long. We had more calls than I can count over the last

twenty-four hours."

Reaching across the table, I take his free hand into mine. "Did you get any sleep? Do you want to head home?" I try not to baby my big, strong firefighter, but he works his ass off and a part of me feels guilty for keeping him out after a long shift.

"Not on your life. Because first you're going to dance for me in this bar, and then we're going home so you can dance for me again, before you tuck me into bed." He wiggles his eyebrows.

Tossing my head back, I laugh.

"You think I'm joking. Let's go." He stands, grasps my hand, and pulls me up.

I can already see the movement of his hips. "Emanuel," I whisper loudly, looking around.

"Nope. Don't even try to play shy with me anymore. Especially not in those fucking heels." He tilts his head downward toward the leopard-print shoes I've paired with black skinny jeans and a light pink sweater, since it was casual Friday at work.

Emanuel moves closer, lowering to my ear. "I can't wait to have those fucking heels over my shoulders again as I thrust my cock into you. But first, you're going to dance for me."

I'm not given time for my embarrassment to rise before he's whipping me around into a spin.

"Oh, sorry."

I turn to acknowledge the familiar voice that just apologized for nearly knocking me over. Of course, it's none other than my mother.

"Janine, you know you've always had two left feet. Why don't you let me show Emanuel how a real—"

"She moves just fine, Janet."

I look over my shoulder at Emanuel whose face is set in stone as he glares at my mother.

"Excuse us," he says, leaving no room for argument.

I turn back to him.

"When is she leaving again?" I can hear the irritation in his voice.

It mirrors my own sentiments regarding my mother. "Soon."

The sounds of Celia Cruz's "Quimbara" begins to play loudly.

"I hope you've been practicing your salsa," Emanuel says, his countenance changing as he peers down at me.

I don't miss a beat as I begin swaying in time with the rhythm of the song. Emanuel falls in line and we dance together, our bodies not falling in time with the music and each other, to the queen of salsa herself.

The song quickly moves into another pop song, and Emanuel and I don't stop dancing to that one either. I can hear a few cheers around the bar, urging us on, but it's the gleam in

Emanuel's eyes that keeps me going. When I stare into those pupils of his, I can't even fathom what it's like to doubt myself. The world around us stops being important. All that makes sense is the feeling of our bodies as we move. Not until I danced with Emanuel, had I ever known why people often refer to it as making love on the dance floor.

"I love you," I say against his lips after he pulls me into his arms.

"You better, 'cause you're sure as fuck stuck with me."

"For how long?"

"As long as you'll have me, baby."

My heart practically starts beating out of my chest. "I'm starting to think forever sounds like long enough."

His grin is so wide that I can see just about all of his teeth. "Now you're catching up, butterfly."

Any retort I might have is caught in my throat at the promise I see in his eyes.

"Janine?"

I blink, realizing it wasn't Emanuel who just called my name.

"What the hell are you doing?"

My heart beats faster for an entirely different reason as I glance over my shoulder to see Matthew standing in the middle of Angela's bar. There's a flash of anger in his blue eyes.

"Matthew?" I ask, confused, as if seeing him for the first

time. I pull away from Emanuel. "What are you doing here?"

"Trying to find you. And I see you've been busy." He looks behind me, and I don't need to turn to see what he's staring at. I can feel the heat radiating off of Emanuel's body from behind me.

"We need to ta—" He started reaching for my arm, I assume to pull me away, but Emanuel's larger hand covers his first.

"You're going to have to keep your hands to your fucking self," Emanuel barks.

I glance around to see a few patrons staring. My stomach drops. The last thing I want to do is cause a scene.

"Don't touch me," Matthew insists, snatching his hand away from Emanuel.

"Don't touch my woman."

"Your *woman*? She's m—"

"Matthew, what are you doing here?" I ask again, stepping in between both men, trying to calm the situation down before it escalates to something uglier.

"I came to talk to you. To talk some sense *into* you."

My shoulders slump. I see the fact that I've had his number blocked for the last two months, thereby not taking any of his calls, hasn't resonated with my ex just yet. I turn back to Emanuel who appears as if he's ready to knock his head off. That would not be good.

"I just need to talk to him," I say.

Emanuel starts shaking his head.

Reaching up, I cup his face, shaking it so he looks at me instead of the guy behind me. "Just for a minute. Outside. This doesn't have to be a scene."

Emanuel's jaw tightens. "One minute."

I kiss his lips and then quickly turn, striding past Matthew. "Follow me."

****

"I really cannot believe you'd just show up out of the blue like this. How did you even know where I'd be tonight?"

"Your mother."

I blink, shaking my head in confusion. "My *who*?"

"Your mother." He rolls his eyes as if that makes total sense. "Look. I came here to discuss your moving back to Boston and us finally getting married. Isn't that what this whole charade of yours is about? Then I come and find you dancing all over some guy, like a—"

"Like a what?" I angrily question with my hands on my hips.

Matthew blinks, obviously shocked by my attitude. I can't remember a time in our relationship when I actually stood up to him.

He shakes his head. "We'll discuss this later. Back in

Boston. Right now it's time for you to pack up your stuff and—"

"You're obviously not getting this. I'm. Not. Going. Back. To. Boston. *Ever.* You and I ... There is no *you and I.* We're over. Done. Past. Expired. Finito. Got it? I have no idea why you even bothered to come down here to Williamsport, but you can catch whatever airline you took back to the northeast."

I shake my head, still unable to believe that Matthew is actually standing in front of me. Most of the time we were together he hadn't put in this much effort. It took me way too long to figure out that he just wasn't the one for me. But being separated from him for months, and more importantly, falling in love with a man who showed me in word and in deed how much he cared for me and wanted to be with me, made it all crystal clear.

"What the hell are you saying?" Matthew spat as he moves closer, invading my personal space.

When I try to take a step back, his hand curls around my arm, tightly. "Let go of me."

"I took time off of work to show up here, and you continue to behave like a petulant child who can't get her way. You ungrateful—"

"Matthew, get off—"

"I treated you well. I gave you what you wanted, didn't I? In spite of what my parents told me about you ..."

"And what did your lovely parents have to say about

me?" I question angrily, while still trying to yank my arm from his hold.

"Doesn't matter. I should've listened and treated you like the whore you are instead of a—"

Gasping, I cover my mouth in shock when Matthew's hostile tirade is brutally cut off by a blow to the side of his face. Something or someone pulls me from behind, moving me out of the way. I have to blink a few times before I realize that I'm seeing Emanuel pummel Matthew right in front of me.

"Say some more disrespectful shit to her again!" Emanuel charges once more, sending a punch to Matthew's ribs.

"Emanuel, stop!" I yell, trying to get to him, but whoever is holding me back has a tight grip. I'm not yelling out of fear that he might do serious damage to Matthew. My panic is for Emanuel.

"Okay, okay, that's enough," someone says.

I look around and realize it's Sean, Angela's brother, who, along with Don, moves to get in between Emanuel and Matthew who is now stumbling to get up off of the sidewalk as he holds his ribs. I inhale sharply when I notice blood spilling out of the hand covering his nose.

"I'm calling the fucking cops!" Matthew's yells are muffled due to his hand over his bloody face.

"That's not necessary," Sean states, trying to calm the

situation down.

Emanuel isn't saying anything as he drills into Matthew with a dark gaze, and looking like he could break the hold Don has on him at any moment to pick up where he left off.

"This is who you're with now?" Matthew turns to me, yelling. "I always knew you weren't worth the fucking trouble. I should've listened to—"

"Oops!" Don declares as he lifts his arms, releasing Emanuel, who does exactly what I knew he was going to.

"Emanuel, stop! Please." I get free of whoever is holding me and run to Emanuel, pulling him by the arm. Eventually, I get his attention just before he lands another blow to Matthew's ribcage.

"Please, he's not worth it," I plead.

The far off look in his eyes tells me he's not truly comprehending my words. When he takes another angry glare over my shoulder, I begin pulling him back toward Charlie's. Thankfully, he doesn't resist too much. At least three of his squad members have put themselves in between his body and Matthew's.

"Angela, can we have some ice?" I question my stunned friend who is still behind the bar.

"The fuck are you getting him ice for?"

I blink. "It's for you, moron!" I tell Emanuel. "Sit your butt on that stool and don't move!" I glare at him so he knows

I'm not kidding around. When he sits, I move around the bar and grab one of the clean towels the bartenders use to wipe down the tables.

Angela hands me a cup of ice.

I pour the ice into the towel and ball it up, taking it over to Emanuel.

"Give me your hand."

Reluctantly, he holds out his hand and I slap the ice pack on top to prevent the inevitable swelling of his knuckles.

"I can't believe you did that." I shake my head.

"I can't believe you actually thought I'd stand there and let that motherfucker speak to you like that."

I didn't say anything. I'd gotten so used to the way my ex used to speak to me, I didn't even think twice of it. Hell, it was similar to how my own mother talked to me as a child and as an adult.

"You shouldn't have done that," I say, staring into Emanuel's eyes.

"Why the hell not?"

Sighing, I glance out the window, seeing a few of Emanuel's squad members getting a dazed and confused Matthew into a taxi.

"He can be cruel when he wants to be. He has a vindictive streak." I remember many conversations Matthew and I had when he would discuss a business deal or someone he thought had crossed him and the ways in which he talked about getting revenge. I know of more than one person whose reputations he completely destroyed because he believed they betrayed or disrespected him. His family had the means and power to ruin people. I did not want to see that happen to Emanuel.

"Don't worry about it."

"I am worried," I protest. "Because—"

"That was funny as hell to watch!"

I roll my eyes heavenward at the sound of my mother's voice. I forgot she was still here.

"Your hand hurt already, Emanuel? I would think so with—"

"He's fine." I glare at my mother. "We're leaving," I tell Emanuel.

He shrugs. "Fine with me." Standing, he wraps his arm around my shoulders possessively as we stride toward the door.

"Hey, don't kill anyone on your way out, all right?" Don chuckles as he passes us. Sean chuckles, too, shaking his head and patting Emanuel on the back as we walk by.

"You pissed at me?" he questions, grasping my chin as we wait for the Uber we ordered.

"Yes." I swat his hand away.

"Good." He lowers his face to the crook of my neck,

burying it there. "You can show me how pissed you are once I get you behind closed doors."

I shiver from the feel of his warm breath as it moves over my sensitized skin.

I have to say, I was never a woman to go after the bad boy types. I always wanted the clean cut, stick to the rules guys. I'm pretty sure it was a side-effect of the way I grew up. But as Emanuel wraps his arms around me and begins whispering in my ear all of the things he plans on doing to my body, once we get home, coupled with the memory of him beating the hell out of Matthew ... Let's just say I might be a convert.

But only for him.

****

Emanuel

"Well, well, well, if it isn't the dancing king himself."

"Fuck off, Don," I respond as he and two other squad members laugh as they sit around the table in the kitchen.

"What?" Don questions in a way that lets me know he knows *exactly* what he did. "I could've called you the dancing *queen.* That would've been a real insult, would it not?" He laughs as if his jokes are the funniest fucking thing in the world.

"Asshole," I grunt.

"Yeah, he can't help himself," Eric adds as he enters the

kitchen from the side hallway entrance.

"No, I really could've called him hitter or killer or some other shit for beating the hell out of that guy two nights ago."

I roll my eyes.

"Your knuckles still swollen?"

I hold my fist up. "Bring your ass over here and find out," I threaten.

Another round of laughs.

"Anyway, who was that asshole?" Don questions.

"A piece of shit not worth mentioning."

Eric grunts in agreeance.

"So, Janine's ex, huh?"

"You really talk too fucking much. Go back to not speaking to me," I growl at Don, who of course, just laughs it off. I know he's only joking but the idea of that shitbag, or anyone for that matter, being with Janine, pisses me off.

"This is how it starts." Don shakes his head.

"What starts?"

His eyebrows go up.

"Here we fucking go," Eric mumbles, looking exasperated.

"You, this, them." Don gestures his hand in the direction of Eric. "Where's Carter?" Don asks.

"Garage," I respond.

"Follow me."

Eric and I follow Don out to the garage where Carter is

there finishing up the count on equipment after the last run we just got back from.

"These two guys ..." Don starts as he pats both Carter and Eric's backs, "are two of the finest individuals in this station. Everyone fucking new when they were falling. This guy," he points to Eric, who's now giving him a sideways glare, "had me accompany him in the fucking truck to a community center to threaten Angela's ex."

"That was supposed to be between the two of us," Eric's voice is low but cautioning.

Don ignores him and proceeds, "And this fucker here ..." he taps Carter on the shoulder, "nearly decapitated anyone who got in the way of pulling Michelle out of that car. The crazy bastard nearly fell for her right there on the spot at that accident. We *still* don't even know what really happened to her son's father."

"*I'm* Diego's father," Carter growls, startling even Don.

Don gives a half grin. "See what I mean? Touchy as hell over their women. Anyway, you, my friend ..." He points at me, moving closer. "Are lost just like those two. I wouldn't be surprised if wedding bells are in your future. Another fucker lost."

"Lost?" I question with a lifted eyebrow.

"To the bullshit. Family. Love. Whatever. Janine has your head completely up her ass. And hell, I can't blame you too much, I guess. I saw those leopard print—"

"Shit!" Carter curses just as I take a swing at Don.

He's quick enough to duck in time, my fist missing his face by mere inches.

"Don't talk about her," I warn.

Don laughs it off. "What the hell did I tell you?"

My jaw tightens at the knowledge that he might be right. No. What the hell am I saying? He *is* one hundred percent correct. The mention of wedding bells a minute ago didn't frighten me but it intrigued me. I've already admitted out loud that I am in love with Janine. And in the many nights that we've spent together, I'd stayed up during the night with her in my arms, picturing doing this every night for the rest of my life, and instead of running from that thought, I embrace it. I want it. With her I've finally found my home. The same home I would do anything to protect.

I glance up into the dark of eyes of Eric's and see he knows exactly what I was feeling at that moment. Eric doesn't talk much, at least not as much as the other guys at the station, but he has an uncanny way of making his feelings very clear. He gives me a small nod.

"On a more serious note," Don says, pulling my attention from Janine and our life together, back to him, "I talked to more guys at your old station."

That piques my curiosity. It must gain the interest of the

other guys as well because Eric and Carter move in closer to hear what Don has to say.

"Turns out, after we left, your old captain made it clear to his squad that no one is to talk to me about that night. They said Captain Rogers directed them not to speak with you about that night either."

"Really?" I question, folding my arms across my chest. That didn't settle well with me. "Why the hell would a captain direct the guys not to speak of a fire that happened nearly a year go?"

"Good fucking question. One that has me definitely planning to ask more questions."

"Did you find out anything else?" Carter asks.

Don shakes his head. "They clammed up. All except for Larry ... He told me he has more to say but asked that I give him a month. He's retiring from the department soon. Going to go work for the family business. Says he'll be comfortable opening up then."

I nod, remembering that Larry's brother owned a very successful home renovation company. He was always trying to get Larry to work full-time for the business their father had started when they were young.

"Larry's a hell of a firefighter," I comment.

"Do you trust him?" Eric asks, looking me squarely in the eye.

I return the stare. "With my life." I never doubted Larry

or any of my other squad members. Captain Rogers, on the other hand ...

"Whoever's been behind this has been quiet for some time," Carter says.

"Or, his fires are just going unreported. Marked down as accidents like the one over at station two."

"Yeah, but we thought he was targeting us, too. We haven't had any incidents. Not since ..." An eerie silence falls over us after Carter's last word.

Everyone is thinking back to the night Corey was injured. The three of them are, at least. Looking at Don, Eric, and Carter's solemn faces it's still obvious how much they care for their missing teammate.

"I saw him," I say.

Three pairs of eyes pin me with their gazes.

"Where?"

"When?"

"How'd he look?"

All three ask.

"At headquarters while I was there to complete some paperwork," I lie. I probably shouldn't have opened up this can of worms. At the very minimum, I wouldn't violate Corey's privacy by telling them where I saw him last. And that it wasn't the only time I've seen him.

"How'd he look?" Don asks again, the anxiousness in his

voice is evident.

"Pissed off. Angry as hell." No need to lie about that. Corey still had the chip on his shoulder over his injury.

"He still won't fucking take physical therapy seriously," Don blurts out.

Eric's forehead wrinkles. "You've seen him? I thought he was still refusing visitors."

Don glances up, looking around as if he divulged something he shouldn't have. "I keep in contact with his ... mother. She lets me know how he's doing."

Carter and Eric both eye Don, knowing he's not telling the whole truth. I suspect they're about to prod him for more information when we're interrupted.

"Excuse us, gentlemen?"

All four of us turn toward the opened garage door to see two police officers entering.

"Officers, how can we help you?" Don questions.

"We're looking for an Emanuel Allende."

I narrow my eyes on the officers. I can tell by their demeanors this isn't a friendly call.

"He's not here," Carter interjects, obviously picking up on what I had as well.

"Are you sure about that?" the second officer questions.

"I'm right here." I nod at Carter as I move past, letting him know it's okay. "What is this about?"

"Emanuel Allende, you are under arrest for the assault and battery of Matthew Adams ..."

My first urge is to punch the officer, who aggressively captures my wrist and spins me around to cuff both of my hands behind my back, in the face. However, I resist that urge and allow myself to be read my Miranda rights, quietly, without letting my anger take over.

"What the hell? That douchebag was assaulting his lady," Don protests.

"Don, it's okay," I say.

"No, this is bullshit. How the hell can you come into a fire station and make an arrest?" Carter challenges.

"Calm down," I tell him. "It's fine." I'd already had this conversation with Janine when we got home two nights prior. She was certain that something would happen. Any noise she heard of someone passing my door that night, she believed it was the police. I assured her I would be fine. I intend to hold that promise now.

"We'll get you a lawyer," Carter says.

I shake my head. "That won't be necessary."

I clench my fists, holding my own anger in as I'm shoved into the back of the police car.

"You think you guys could make these things any tighter," I question as we pull off.

"Shut up," the officer in the passenger seats snaps.

"Fuck you," I retort as we drive past my station house. I only need to make one phone call to fix this shit.

Chapter Twenty-Two

Janine

"I'm so glad we could finally get together for lunch," Shelah says as we sit down at the table in the middle of the Greek restaurant that's not too far from our job. We've been meaning to have lunch together for a while but something always came up. Especially now that I was practically taking lead on the Digita campaign.

"Me too. Work has been so busy."

"That's a good thing, right?"

"It's great," I say, feeling excited. "Digita is loving how the campaign is going so far. There is a lot of interest leading up to the rollout. I'm nervous as hell about it but looking forward to doing my first major campaign."

"I bet. I can't wait to get promoted to associate."

I raise my eyebrows but pause as our waitress delivers my salmon Greek salad and Shelah's gyro salad.

"Promoted?" I question once the waitress leaves.

Shelah nods as she uses her knife and fork to cut her food. "Yes. I've been at Lux for over eighteen months now. I started as a temp but was quickly promoted to full-time receptionist when Danny said he appreciated my work ethic. *I* loved that his offer came with full benefits because most receptionist positions were just the straight hourly rate. He also doesn't mind that I study or do schoolwork in the office, as long as my work in the office is done, of course."

"That's nice of him."

"Absolutely. I only have another two courses to take after this semester to complete my degree, and Danny has already talked about my moving into the main office to become his newest associate."

I grin, feeling excited for her. "That sounds wonderful. Maybe what Zeke said isn't true."

Her perfectly arched eyebrows narrow inward. "What did that fool say?"

I giggle before covering my mouth to wipe it with the cloth napkin while swallowing the forkful of salmon I'd just eaten. "Something about my getting the job only because Danny wanted more diversity for appearances' sake."

Shelah's brown eyes double in size as she pushes back from the table. "Please tell me you didn't believe that load of b—" Catching herself, she glances around the room. "Garbage."

I give a one shoulder shrug. "For a little bit."

She shakes her head. "I knew putting him with you was going to be trouble. Zeke is one of the best associates on the team. When he's on, he's *on*. But ... he's a jerk."

Shelah and I both laugh.

"No, but seriously, he is. Danny's had a hard time pairing him with *anyone*. Which is how you ended up stuck with him. But also ..." She stops talking briefly as her gaze shifts around the dining space of the restaurant. She leans in. "Zeke was eyeing your position for someone else. He approached Danny about hiring his girlfriend's younger sister. Gave him the resume and everything. Danny even gave him the courtesy of interviewing the girl. But she came into the office with the nastiest attitude. She was extremely rude to me."

Her eyes shift around some more before landing on me.

"Don't tell anyone I told you this but Danny always calls me after a candidate's interview to ask how they were when they first entered. If someone is rude or nasty to me, no matter how well the interview went, he disqualifies them. Says he doesn't trust employees who are rude to administrative staff but suck up to him."

"So what happened with Zeke?" I wonder out loud.

"Pretty sure he learned that lesson *after* he hired Zeke."

We giggle together on that.

My conversation with Shelah has me feeling a little better. I realize over the last few weeks how little Zeke's words meant, but hearing that Danny truly didn't hire me just because of whatever bullshit reason Zeke suggested, solidified it for me. Plus, Shelah is a new work ally that I am enjoying getting to know. I look forward to the time when she is promoted and we might get to work more closely together.

After lunch and for the rest of the day, I feel like I'm on cloud nine. So when I get a call from Angela as I'm leaving work, I assume it's because she's telling me she wants to meet at her bar for drinks. I still need to apologize to her face for what happened a few days ago with Matthew and Emanuel. Thankfully, I haven't heard from Matthew since that night.

"Hey, Angela, I'm just leaving—"

"Emanuel was arrested!" she blurts out.

I freeze in place just outside of my office building's doors. "What do you mean he was arrested?"

"I mean police officers went to Rescue Four and put handcuffs on his wrists for—"

"Matthew."

"Yes. He was arrested for assault and battery."

"Oh god. I gotta go," I say hurriedly, hanging up the phone and practically running to my car. I need to get to the nearest police station to figure out what is going on. I'm rushing so quickly that when my phone beeps annoyance springs up. But as I look at my phone I see it's a text from Angela. She's sent me the police precinct that has arrested Emanuel along with its address to put into my GPS.

What would I do without her?

****

Emanuel

"Gentlemen," I say sarcastically as I pass by the two officers who arrested me, as I move down the hallway of the gloomy police station. I massage my wrists that are now free after being in those tight cuffs longer than necessary.

The officers glare at me silently.

"Whatever," I grumble as I step into the lobby. "What the fuck took you so long?" I question, glaring at Christian.

After giving the precinct's receptionist a shit-eating grin, he moves away from the desk. "You're just lucky I was nearby. I'm supposed to be on a flight to Palermo tonight." He holds up his hand, patting me on the shoulder and looking me over.

"They didn't fuck with you did they?" His voice is dark, as he eyes a few people behind me, presumably officers.

"I'm cool," I say.

"Lawyer had all of the charges dropped. As for the other thing ... We're pretty certain he's still here in Williamsport."

"Good." I crack my knuckles as my eyes narrow. "Find him quick because we need to pay him a visit." The fucker thought the last beating I gave him was worth an arrest, he has no idea what the fuck he's just set in motion.

"I need my phone so I can call the guys and tell them not to—"

"Emanuel!"

"Tell Janine," I mumble as she bursts through the second pair of doors of the precinct and runs into my arms.

"I heard you were arrested. I knew he would do this shit. Are you okay?" She pulls back and cups my cheek, her eyes searching my face and body as if she's afraid I've been hurt.

"I'm fine."

"No you're not fine. You're at the police station. What are the charges? He's such an asshole. If he would've just stayed in Boston. Look, I can ask around for a good lawyer. I know—"

"That won't be necessary, doll face."

Janine pauses to look toward the voice that's just spoken.

"Don't give her one of your fucking pet names. Her name's Janine."

"I thought it was Nadine?" Christian says with a grin.

"Fucking wise guy."

"Who's this?" Janine asks, her arms still around my shoulders.

"My cousin, though I'm starting to reconsider." Christian moves closer, extending his hand for her to shake.

"Christian Genovese, pleasure to meet you."

"You look familiar. Have we met before?"

"She's got a good memory," my cousin states before focusing his attention on Janine. "I was in Mexico with Emanuel. Unfortunately, you and I were never formally introduced. I think my cousin was keeping you all to himself."

"I still am." My tone is threatening as I tighten my arm around Janine's waist.

Christian chuckles.

"I don't understand. How are you standing out here, free? With no cuffs or anything? I thought it'd take forever to get you out of here. Did you find a lawyer already?"

"It's a bit of a long story."

"Go, Emanuel. Take the car. I have another one coming for me. Take your lady home and talk. I'll be in touch soon," Christian instructs as his phone begins ringing. "Go, this has to do with another matter."

I nod and redirect Janine toward the exit. "Let's talk at home."

****

Janine

"I still can't believe that son of a bitch," I grumble as I pace back and forth in Emanuel's living room. I'm so livid that even thirty minutes after falling into Emanuel's arms at the police station, I can't manage to calm down. Instead of taking his cousin's chauffeured car, Emanuel had to drive my car home from the station because my hands were shaking with anger so much.

"Calm down, butterfly."

"Calm down? How the hell am I supposed to be calm when my ex had you arrested?" I squeal, raising my hands in the air.

"I forgot saying *calm down* to an upset woman is the last thing any man should do."

"Please remember it from now on," I retort.

"Come here." Emanuel doesn't wait for me to move in his direction, instead coming off the stool he was sitting on and pulling me by the waist to sit down on his lap, on the couch.

"I don't understand how you can be so nonchalant about all of this. This could hurt your reputation. Oh my god! You could get fired from the department over this," I gasp, covering my mouth. "We can't let that happen."

"It's not going to happen."

"How do you know?"

"Because all of the charges were dropped. The arrest will be expunged. It'll be like it never happened."

Feeling totally confused, I study him. "How is that possible? I didn't see your lawyer down there. How did they work so quickly?"

Emanuel briefly averts his gaze away from me to something over my shoulder. "Christian's lawyer was there. He left just before you came. Had a meeting with the commissioner."

"The commissioner? Isn't that someone really high up in the police department?"

He nods. "The highest."

"Oh, so the lawyer knows the head of the department? Now I'm totally confused."

Emanuel inhales deeply, his eyes narrowing a bit as if

preparing to tell me something important. "When I got arrested, I used my call to phone Christian. Thankfully, he was in Williamsport at the time. However, even if he wasn't he would've sent his attorney to get it straightened out."

"And Christian is your cousin?" I ask with furrowed brows, feeling even more confused.

He nods.

"Like, your play cousin or a real cousin?"

"If a *play cousin* is what I think it means, he's my *real* cousin. As in we share some of the same genetic line."

"How is that possible? I thought you were raised in foster care your entire life. That you don't have a family."

"I was and I do."

I wrinkle my forehead, obviously looking perplexed.

"What I told you about being brought up in foster care is true. I was. Ever since I was about one, I was a ward of the state. At seventeen I went off to the military without a second thought. But at about year seven of my eight years of service, I began wondering for the first time where I'd come from. Who made me? So, I hired a PI. The guy was good. He was able to find out information that was supposed to have been sealed up and locked away forever.

"It turns out, my mother was a Spanish immigrant. She was pregnant when she arrived in the U.S., by most accounts. Her name was Lucia Allende. She struggled after she had me, but after a year she thought the best thing to do was to give me up for a while, until she got on her feet. That never happened. She fell into a world of drugs and prostitution, and eventually she was killed by the time I was ten."

"Oh no," I whisper, covering my hand with my mouth.

Emanuel presses a kiss to my temple, as if he's trying to comfort me. As if this isn't the story of his own mother.

"Anyway, Lucia had been born in Spain, and at age sixteen, she'd met and fallen in love with an Italian man who was ten years older than her. His name was Riccardo Genovese."

"Same last name as Christian," I say, starting to put it together.

He nods. "The Allendes and Genoveses were something like sworn enemies. Neither family would've approved of my mother and father being together."

"Like the Montagues and the Capulets."

"The who?"

I blink and stare at his handsome face. He is completely confused. "You really have never read *Romeo and Juliet*?"

"Not on fucking purpose."

I smirk. "Their families were the Montagues and Capulets. They were sworn enemies and the couple fell in love."

"I hope it ended better for them than it did for my mother."

I shake my head. "It didn't."

"Yeah, well, supposedly my maternal grandfather found

out about the relationship once she got pregnant, and demanded she put an end to it. She somehow ran away, hoping that my father would join her in the States and they'd be together. That didn't exactly pan out. He later died from a drug overdose or something. The details of his death are still sketchy."

"So how did you meet Christian?"

"He knocked on my door one day. The P.I. I hired had gotten close to the truth, and the Genoveses found out about me. Christian showed up and introduced himself, filling me in on the rest of the story."

"Which is?"

He shrugged. "The Genoveses are widely known throughout Italy, though they're from Sicily, Palermo to be exact. They're ... important people, I guess you could say."

I watch as his lips form a thin line. Something's not adding up.

Rising, I begin pacing back and forth in front of the couch this time. "So your father's side of the family is from Sicily?"

"Yes."

"And your cousin, Christian, just happens to know an attorney powerful enough to get all of the charges against you dropped in a few hours, and *then* go have a meeting with the commissioner of the police?"

"Apparently."

"Apparently? The charges were *dropped,*" I say with my hands high. "And the arrest wiped clean. That means there will never be a record that this ever happened. You *assaulted* Matthew. In broad daylight, with numerous eyewitnesses around. I mean, yes, you had good reason and I enjoyed seeing every second of it, but Matthew's family has connections. Even here in Williamsport."

Emanuel looks me right in the eye. "Mine has more."

I stop moving in my tracks, my back going straight as I take in his words along with his demeanor. I run everything through my head again. From the time we first met in Mexico. I remember him telling me that he was there for his cousin's wedding.

"Who was your cousin that got married in Mexico?"

"Emilio Genovese. Christian's older brother."

I shake my head because the thoughts running through my mind aren't making much sense but I have to ask the question that keeps coming up.

"Are you in the mafia?"

"No." He adamantly shakes his head.

I push out a relieved breath until he says ...

"But my family is."

My eyes bulge and mouth falls open.

He stands, apparently seeing me freak out, and grabs my face. "Listen. This isn't something to get worked up over. I'm still the same guy you've always known. My family, not even the family I grew up with, but was born into, apparently, is in a line of work some would classify as the mafia, or whatever the fuck. But that's not—"

"Not what? Not a big deal? I beg to differ." Needing some space to gather my thoughts, I pull out of his embrace and move away from him.

"It's not a big deal. I'm not in the family business. I just—"

"Can call on them whenever you need them, however, right?"

"Would you rather I be sitting in a jail cell right now?"

"Of course not. But this isn't—" I shake my head. "What if they, like, call in a favor? Say they come back and say remember that little assault and battery charge we dropped for you, now we want you to off somebody for us."

"Off somebody? Babe, you've been watching too many films from the 70s."

"This isn't funny, Emanuel."

His chuckling ceases, and he pushes out a heavy breath. "I see that. Look, this doesn't have to be an issue between us. I'm not who my cousins are. I'm not in the family business."

"Now. Not right now you're not. But what about tomorrow, or next year, or five years from now? What if you get tired of firefighting and decide the family business is a good option to try? You've got military skills. I'm sure they'd love to hire an already trained assassin."

"I'm not a trained ass—"

"You've been to war! Went on missions with the Army that I couldn't even dream of. I know you've done things I don't even want to think about." My breathing begins to increase. His Army background never had occurred to me before, but now thinking of it in combination with knowing the new information about his family, a heavy dread begins to settle on my chest.

"So don't." Moving closer to me, he cups my face again.

"I didn't. I let those thoughts go because I believed I knew who you are now. My guy that protects people and serves his community by working as a firefighter. The one who loves a good time but is still settled enough to be a one woman man, fall in love, and possibly get married and have a family one day."

"I am. That's exactly who I am."

I shake my head. "No. Maybe ... that's who you want to be or maybe it is who you are. But what about when you get bored? When you want some adventure in your life? Will you pick up and leave the department for a life with your real family? Where does that leave me?"

"With me. That's where you belong."

I shake my head. "No. I need more stability than that. I spent too much of my life being dragged around from one place to another by a parent who couldn't make up her damn mind about where she wanted to live because she was busy chasing the next man or party. And I spent the next ten years of my adult life chasing after a guy who strung me along because he refused to just admit that I wasn't good enough for his family. I'm not going through all of that upheaval again. I need stability. You can't provide that!"

Taking a step back, I blink because I refuse to let the tears welling up in my eyes fall.

"Janine, don't do this. What are you saying?"

"I'm saying—"

"You're not saying we're done. I won't let you."

My mouth clamps shut and I shake my head. I couldn't get the words out even if I tried. "I need some time."

I spin on my heels, grab my large over-the-shoulder bag I'd taken to work with me that morning, and reach Emanuel's door in three steps, pulling it open and quickly slamming it shut behind me.

I root around in my bag for my keys, but just as I find them my door is pulled open by my mother.

"Oh, hey," she says with a bewildered expression.

"Excuse me." I barrel through the door, pushing her aside, not wanting to see or deal with her at the moment.

"Well, hello to you, too," she mutters, closing the door behind me.

I head toward my bedroom, ready to shut the door behind me, but she is hot on my heels.

"What's wrong with you?"

"Nothing. It's been a long day." After tossing my stuff onto my bed, I kick off the heels I'm wearing. "Did you need something?" She's still standing in the doorway looking me over.

"I was gonna invite you to go out with me, but I don't need your attitude getting in the way of me trying to find my next meal ticket."

I roll my eyes. "No thanks."

"I would've thought Matthew coming all of the way down here to try and win you back would've put some pep in your step."

My head pops up at the mentioning of my ex. It reminds me of something he said. "You spoke with him? Gave him my address and told him I was at Charlie's."

Her eyes enlarge but she quickly shrugs it off. "He called your cell phone one day while you were in the shower. I thought it was mine so I answered."

"And you figured it'd be a good idea to tell him where I live and where I'd be?"

"The boy practically begged me for your information. I thought you loved him. Shit, I don't know. You were with him for what, eight, nine years? Had your head all up his ass. Got a new wardrobe for him."

"My new clothes weren't for him."

"Oh, they must've been for Emanuel. I don't know."

"They weren't for him either." Not completely, anyway.

"Then who were they for?"

"For *me*." My answer comes out angrier than I'd intended. "I dress for me now."

My mother looks totally confused and perplexed. "Whatever. I see you're dealing with some shit. I'll let you handle that. I'm going out. Don't expect me back home tonight." She waves a hand in the air and disappears from my doorway.

Seconds later, I hear the front door open and close.

Sighing, I fall to my bed. I'm used to my mother's instability by now. Her nonchalant attitude toward my feelings bothers me less and less as time goes by. But the ache in my chest has nothing to do with my mother. It has everything to do with the man across the hall.

The man that I love.

The man I think I just broke up with.

Chapter Twenty-Three

Emanuel

"What the hell crawled up your ass and died?!" Don growls as I toss the truck's hose down the length of the garage.

"Nothing!" I retort, kicking the kinks out of the hose so I can finish rolling it back up and sticking it into the truck where it belongs.

"Oh shit," Sean sighs. "I know this fucking look. Seen this shit with Carter when Michelle dropped his ass like a bad habit."

"I remember that shit," Don cosigns. "What the hell did you do?"

My gaze bounces between Don and Sean, and I give them both them middle finger. "I said, fuck off."

"Every relationship in this damn station house has to come with some form of drama," Sean sighs. "That's why you fucks will never know whether I'm in a relationship or not. I'll pop up with a whole wife on your asses and you'd never be the wiser. Keeping my business to myself."

Don whistles. "The single life is all I need. No woman can keep up with me anyway," he argues.

"You mean no woman can stand being around you for too long," Eric interjects as he enters the garage.

Everyone in the garage gets a good laugh out of that, except for me. There's a heaviness I've never known that's settled around me ever since Janine walked out of my door almost a week ago. Since then, she's refused to take my calls or answer her door. I only found out once when Janet answered the door that Janine had actually gone over to Angela and Eric's place to stay for a couple of days.

My eyes narrow at the invite Janet gave me right after telling me her daughter wasn't home.

"Whatever spat you and Janine had, I'm sure it'll work itself out." Don wraps his arms around my shoulders. "Either that or you'll find someone else, right? There's plenty of fish in the sea."

"Get the hell off of me," I growl, throwing his arm off me. "There are no other fucking fish. And don't call her a goddamned fish. The hell is wrong with you?" I glare at Don.

His eyebrows slowly raise and he looks over my shoulder, his dark eye glinting with mischievousness. "I fucking told you. He's gone."

"We already knew that," Eric asserts.

"Well you better win her back somehow," Don says.

Just when I'm about to tell him to mind his damn business, Captain Waverly enters the garage.

"Allende! Upstairs. I need to speak with you." And as is his habit, the captain doesn't wait for a response before turning and disappearing back into the station house, presumably heading up the stairs, assuming I'll be in right behind him.

"What'd you do this time?" Carter questions.

I shrug. "Not a damn thing." Turning, I head in the direction of the captain, making my way through the station's entryway and up the stairs to the captain's office.

"Close the door," he says without peering up from his desk.

How the man managed to get up the stairs to his office so quickly and sit down to read over whatever papers are in front of him, looking like he's been in that position all morning, remains baffling to me. But Captain Waverly is one of the sharpest and quickest captains I've seen in all of my years with the Williamsport Fire Department.

"You wanted to see me, sir?"

Slowly, he lifts his head and pulls off his eye glasses. "I don't like cops showing up at my station house."

I move closer to his desk but don't sit down. My shoulders pull downward. "I apologize for that happening. It was an honest mix up."

"A mix up?" His thick, bushy eyebrows lift.

I nod. "Yes, sir. They had the wrong guy. Happens a lot apparently. You'd think in this day and age, cops would be more responsib—"

"Cut the shit, Allende."

I close my mouth trying to hide the grin that wants to escape.

"You're so full of shit. Like the rest of these clowns," he grumbles, shaking his head. He's trying hard to come off as pissed but I can hear the levity in his voice. "Anyway, make sure the *mix up* doesn't happen again."

"Will do, Captain."

"I'd hate to lose a great firefighter over some bullshit."

"It wasn't bullshit."

"What was that?"

"Nothing, sir."

"Good. Now that that's out of the way, let's talk about you and Don going to visit your old station."

"I don't kn—" I stop talking when he holds up his hand.

"Sit down." He waves to the chair in front of his desk.

I move around the chair to sit.

"I know you two went to Station Two, and I know why. Your former captain came to visit me, very pissed off that my guys would come questioning him."

First of all, for my former captain to be thinking that I need to be handled like some kind of child having a temper tantrum annoys the hell out of me. Secondly, it leads me to believe even more that he's hiding something.

"My thoughts exactly."

Lifting my gaze, I see Captain Waverly sitting back in his chair, hands clasped over his abdomen as he watches me.

"I asked myself, why the hell would the captain of

Station Two make it a point to come to me personally and order that I keep my guys in line? And then to discover that their grievous offense was to ask a couple of the squad members there about the circumstances of a fire that killed a little boy and nearly took the life of a firefighter ... well," he sits back farther in his seat, "that not only angered me, it made me curious as well."

"So you're saying?"

"I'm saying I've given Don permission to keep asking questions, investigating, and looking into what happened the night you pulled that family out of that fire."

"You think the fire could be connected to what happened before?"

He shakes his head. "I don't know what the hell is going on." He pitches forward, placing his clasped hands on his desk and looking deep into my eyes. "What I do know is that I lost a hell of a firefighter when that beam fell on Corey. I know that I lie awake at night wondering if with every call I make, I'm sending my guys to their deaths. And I know I could never live with myself if that were the case. So ..." he pauses to stand, as do I, "I gave Don the space he needs to work this privately with the full resources I can provide, until we have enough evidence to take this up with the brass. But for now, he's to do so quietly. That goes for you as well. You are to stay away from Station Two and Captain Rogers. And we never had the second half of this conversation. Understood?"

"Loud and clear." I give him an affirmative nod.

He waves his hand toward the door, dismissing me.

I exit, leaving the door open behind me, and head down to the main floor. I find Don by himself in the kitchen.

"Everything good?" he asks while looking over his shoulder from the refrigerator that he was peering into.

"Yeah. Let me ask you something," I begin.

He stands, closing the door of the fridge and turning to me.

"How do we know this guy, or whoever's behind those fires is still out there? There haven't been any similar instances in months. Since Corey, no one in Rescue Four has been hurt or even targeted, as far as we know. Do you think this person is still active? Maybe they've moved to a different city or stopped altogether … or hell, maybe they're dead."

Folding his arms over his chest, Don begins shaking his head. "No, the fucker is still alive and active. I can feel it."

"Feel it?"

"Yes. So much so. I know he's planning something big. What? I can't put my finger on but I know he's out there."

I don't want to ask my next question but I need to. "Do you think my former captain is behind this?"

Don's face forms into an angry scowl. "I've definitely considered the possibility."

"Me too." Ever since the day we visited my old squad and I caught Captain Rogers peering down at us from his window, after refusing to talk to us about that night, an eerie feeling crawls down my spine every time I think of him. And to know that he came and visited Captain Waverly to warn us to stay off this investigation, well, that spoke volumes.

"What'd you do in the Army?"

I had an inkling of where this line of questioning was headed. "Ranger. Forward observer. Was my job to be the eyes and ears of the team."

He nods. "That's what we need now. This investigation has to go underground and I'm going to need your eyes and ears."

I nod. "We'll get the son of a bitch."

"We damn sure will."

But before I can fully concentrate on helping Don there are a few things in my personal life I needed to clear up. Both of them center around the love of my life.

****

Emanuel

"I can't believe you're eating again," Christian chides, our other cousin, Lorenzo, as we drive toward the private airport.

"I'm fucking hungry. I haven't eaten since ..."

"A full hour," Christian finishes.

"Can you both shut the hell up?" I insist from the backseat of the town car. "I didn't come all of this way to talk about Lorenzo's fucking appetite."

Both men look at me with a narrowed gaze, Lorenzo more so than Christian. He and I aren't as close or on as friendly terms as Christian and I are. Whatever.

"Americans, so impatient," Lorenzo tosses out.

Christian chuckles.

"Are you sure he's going to be here?" I look between the two men.

They both nod.

"His plane is scheduled to leave in forty-five minutes. Matteo has already spotted him waiting at the airport in a pair of dark shades." Lorenzo snickers, as does Christian.

"Almost nine o'clock at night and he's inside wearing sunglasses. You should see his fucking eye, Zo," Christian says, his laughter growing.

Both men look at me and I shrug.

Five minutes later we're pulling up to the front of the private airport that is about twenty minutes outside of the city of Williamsport. Christian and Lorenzo had been at my place waiting for me once I got in from my shift, to help me finish this bullshit with Janine's ex. Apparently, the dumb fuck hadn't quite gotten the message to back off, and was still trying to get law enforcement to press charges against me, even phony charges. He also attempted to meet with the head of the Fire Department to try and get me fired from my job.

Those two issues weren't even the straw that broke the camel's back. According to the information Christian found out on him, Matthew had had the fucking gall to rent out a place in Williamsport in my building, in an attempt to remain close to Janine to win her back. He's flying back to Boston tonight for work purposes, but was scheduled to be back in a few days. That isn't a trip he was going to make. The man obviously needed to learn his time was up.

"Where is he?" I question Matteo, Lorenzo's twin brother, as soon as he approaches us in the lobby of the private airport.

"Bathroom. I've got two guards blocking the door so no one can get in or out."

I nod and head in the direction he points in. Once I arrive, the two men in dark suits, look over my shoulder to Lorenzo. I glance back to see Lorenzo nod. When he does, the men move out of my way to allow me entrance.

I push the door open and make sure to lock it behind me, just so Matthew can't get out too easily. I hear the toilet flush which is then followed by footsteps against the tiled floor, moving toward the sink. I stand back, so he can't see me quite yet. Silently, I watch as Matthew removes his glasses. I snicker to myself at his face. His right eye is still swollen and an ugly purple and yellowish tint are apparent. You would think after such an experience, he would've learned.

I shake my head. *Some people are just hard-headed.*

"Taking a trip?" I finally say, emerging from the shadows.

Matthew is startled as he peers at me through the mirror. When he registers who I am, his mouth drops open and he spins around to face me.

"What the hell are you doing here?"

"I should be asking you the same thing." I move closer, getting in his face. He's only shorter than me by a couple of inches, but the expression on his face makes him seem that much smaller. Though, he tries to recover, plastering on the cocky, confident, know-it-all look I'm sure he's refined over the years.

"You're following me. I will have a restraining order put on you so damned fast—"

"Is that right?" I ask, leaning past him to reach for the sunglasses he's left sitting on the back of the sink. "Cartier's. Nice." I hold up his glasses in front of his face before dropping them to the floor and stepping on them.

"What the he—"

He makes a gagging sound as I wrap my right hand around the side of his neck, using my thumb to press into his lower throat, cutting off his airway.

"Shut up. You've done enough talking and I don't fucking like the sound of your voice. This is what we're going to do. You are going to stop trying to interfere in my fucking life. You're going to leave *my* future wife the fuck alone. You're going to rip up that lease you just signed in my apartment building, delete Janine's phone number, her email address, and throw away any old pictures you may have of her. She's done with you. She has been ever since she first walked into my life in Mexico.

"You are going to go back to Boston, continue working for your daddy's hedge fund, find a woman your parents approve of, and marry her. Have your kids and send them to private school, and live the boring ass life that your parents can approve of. I'm being nice to you by letting you even walk out of this bathroom with your five senses still in place. But don't mistake my kindness for weakness. I can get to you anytime and anywhere. Don't test me on this. My patience only lasts but so long. Got it?"

Releasing his throat, I step back as he bends over, attempting to breathe again. "I didn't hear an answer. Do you understand?"

He nods, still struggling to find his voice again. That's good enough. I step back and proceed to the door, but like motherfuckers who just don't know when to quit, Matthew opens his mouth again.

"Her mother was a better lay anyway."

I turn from the door, and in three large strides am back in Matthew's face, sending a blow to his ribs, and then the left side of his face. The punches are so vicious that he is instantly rendered unconscious by the second one.

"That was for Janine. Dumb fuck." I shake my head and turn away, this time making it through the door.

"If you two have some smelling salts, you might want to use it on him so he can make his flight," I say to the guards and head back to the car that is still running and waiting for me outside.

"You finished?" Christian asks as I enter the backseat of the town car.

I nod.

"He still alive?"

"Yes."

"Pity," a frowning Lorenzo grunts.

"This fuck just likes seeing dead bodies. He's a little sick in the head if you ask me," Christian laughs. His laughter gives way to the fact that he might be a little twisted as well. But with a family business like theirs ...

"He might not make his flight," I say.

"He'll make it. Matteo has business in Boston with that fucker's father he needs to handle anyway."

I lift my brows, surprised to learn that bit of

information.

"The Genovese name goes further than you know," Christian claims.

"Apparently," I say. Not that I want to find out more about the family business.

"Where to next?"

"Home," I reply. I have more business to handle there.

Chapter Twenty-Four

Janine

Always trust your instincts, they won't ever steer you wrong. Emanuel's words echo in my head as I push my key into my lock, opening the door to my apartment. He told me those words on our first date back here in the States, as we salsa danced. They're giving me the same confidence now as they did months ago.

"Janet!" I call out as I place my keys on the kitchen counter and look around the space that is supposed to be mine. My mother's belongings are tossed haphazardly by my couch that doubles as her bed, and underneath the windowsill that was supposed to be my reading nook when I first moved in. I love how the windowsill extends enough that allows space for my body to fit, and how I can look down onto the street below to see the passersby and cars as they drive pass. But I haven't been able to do any of that since Janet's been here. That ends today.

"Janet!" I call again. I know she's here; I can hear her footsteps in the bathroom.

"What, girl? I was trying to take me a nice little bubble bath," she angrily answers coming up the hall wearing a long, pink, fuzzy bathrobe.

"Is that my robe?" I question.

"What? This?" Running her hand down the robe, as she

stares at it. "Yeah, I couldn't find mine. Hope you don't mind." She giggles as if she knows I do mind.

"I do mind." I press my hands against my hips, my anger growing. "You need to change and get out."

She frowns. "Get out? Oh, what, you and that boy across the hall made up? You need me to leave so you can have the place to yourself? I don't see why you can't just get it on at his place, but if that's what you want." She waves her hand in the air and turns to head down the hall, as if going to finish her bath.

"No. You need to *leave.* As in permanently, get out of my home."

She freezes.

I watch her back as I pull out the cell phone from my work bag. I place the phone on the counter.

She slowly turns her head. "What is this little tantrum about?"

"A tantrum was when I was five and I cried and fell out on the floor because my mother was once again leaving me with a babysitter I didn't know. A tantrum is when I was seven and I cried to my teacher all throughout recess so she wouldn't send me outside because the kids liked making fun of my dirty clothes and unkempt hair because my mother never had time to take care of either of those things. I was eight when I stopped having tantrums and learned to do my own laundry, braid my own hair, and babysit myself. *This,* right now, is not a tantrum. This is me kicking you out."

My mother's eyes close to slits as the anger rises on her face. "So, I wasn't the best mother in the world. *I'm sorry.* But I never kicked you out of my home. That's what you're doing now, Janine? Kicking your own mother out?"

I nod. "Hell yes. You never kicked me out because you never had the chance to. If it wasn't for me, after I turned thirteen, if I hadn't of worked and saved and begged our landlords, we wouldn't have had places to live. I left at eighteen and never looked back. Now, you show up on my doorstep and overstay your welcome and I'm supposed to feel guilty? I don't think so."

"I told you I'm just working some things out. Trying to get some things situated with a job I have waiting on me. I'll be gone then. Where am I supposed to live in the meantime?"

"Have you thought of giving Matthew a call?"

Her mouth flops open and shuts a few times before actual words come out. "Why would I call that boy?"

"I don't know. It's almost the same question I asked this afternoon when I saw his name appear on what I thought was my phone." I hold up the phone that I'd placed on the counter. "Turns out, you were right before. We do have the same cell phone. Case and everything. On my way to work this morning, I accidentally picked up your phone instead of mine. I discovered it as soon as I got to work but couldn't turn around so I figured I'd give it to you once I got home.

"Then this afternoon I see a missed call from a Matthew. Could've been a coincidence and not the same person *I* dated for years. But then I got to thinking about what he said when he confronted me last week in front of Angela's bar. That it was *you* who told him where I was going to be. Being the inquisitive person I am, I go to your text messages ... and low and behold, turns out it *is* the same Matthew. And I'm not the only woman in this family who knows about that funny shaped birthmark on the inside of this thigh."

I lift an eyebrow, folding my arms over my chest. My stomach begins to feel queasy just thinking of the woman who gave birth to me and my ex.

"Janine, listen, it was only one time, and—"

"I don't give a shit," I snap, holding my hand in the air. "As far as I'm concerned, Matthew is old news ... and so are you. You need to pack up and get out. Now."

"I-I can't. Wha—"

"Did you not hear me the first three times? Either you make the choice to pack up your belongings neatly and leave, or I'm tossing them out of the window and calling the police to have you escorted out."

"You wouldn't—"

"I would, and don't think I don't know about the

warrant for your arrest you've been hiding from. Which is the real reason you came to Williamsport, isn't it? You were in Boston but so is the warrant." I'd read that information in the text exchanges between her and Matthew as well. He was supposed to help her get the warrant erased or whatever.

"Get out."

"Janine—"

"I'm not saying it again." At this point, I wasn't even angry. I was just done. I'd always suspected Matthew had cheated on me throughout our relationship, but to know that it had been with my own mother? That was something she and I could never come back from. My feelings for Matthew had died a long time ago. I was completely and utterly in love with another man now ... and that was another story in and of itself. But I needed to tie up the loose ends with my mother. If she was willing to cross this line, who knew what other lines she would cross. I didn't need that in my life. I was no longer a child dependent upon her for survival or emotional stability.

I remain standing by the kitchen counter as she packs up her belongings, eyeing me every now and again, seemingly hoping that I will change my mind. By the time she changes into a pair of jeans, sweater, and her coat, I move to the door to hold it open for her as she carries her bags out.

"Here's your phone." I hand it to her. "Where's mine?"

"On the top of the refrigerator."

I don't even ask what the hell it was doing up there. Retrieving my phone, I enter the passcode to open it. That likely is the reason she placed it on the top of the fridge, once she realized she couldn't get into it.

"Next time you should try putting a passcode on your own phone when you have such private messages saved."

"Jani—"

I close the door in her face, not waiting for whatever she's about to say.

"You'll regret this!" she yells through the door. "I'm your mother."

I give the door one last glance before turning to head to my bedroom to pack a bag of my own.

"Hey," Angela's voice answers on the other end of the phone.

"Hey, can I still crash at your place tonight?"

"Janine, are you sure you want to stay at the top of the bar again? I mean, I'm sure your place would be more comfortable, and you and Em—"

"If it's not available I can stay at a hotel."

She sighs into the phone, obviously understanding that I'm not about to get into a back and forth discussion with her over this.

"Of course it is. I'll bring you the key to the back entrance once you arrive."

"Thanks."

After hanging up the phone, I pack a few of my things for the weekend. It's Friday and I've been staying off an on at Angela's bar in the apartment upstairs. I wanted to avoid Emanuel. I knew he'd stopped by my place more than once but I couldn't look at him just yet. The night before, I stayed at my own apartment since he worked an overnight shift. Luckily for me, I just so happened to have picked up my mother's phone on the way to work, otherwise I wouldn't have known the level of her deceit.

Now, since I know Emanuel is off this weekend, I need more time on my own to sort things out in my head about our relationship.

****

"Janine, are you sure about this?" Angela asks yet again.

We're sitting on the bed in the tiny apartment above her bar. The apartment is small but it's cute. She's decorated the bedroom in white and sky blue, with images of the beach in seashell frames that hang on the walls, giving the room a seaside feel.

"It's just one more night," I respond. Today is Saturday and I plan on going back home Sunday evening. "You think I'm being childish, don't you?"

"Yes," she says bluntly.

I sigh. "I'm not. You said it yourself how many times since I broke up with Matthew? That I lost myself to that relationship. I craved stability, marriage, a family of my own so much that I couldn't see the forest for the trees. He was never the one for me."

"And Emanuel? Is he not the one?"

Yes! my heart screams in response to her question, but I'd forgotten how to trust myself. Or maybe I never knew in the first place.

"I don't know."

"Yes, you do. You're just scared."

"Right. But you say that as if it's no big deal. Like I don't have a reason to be scared."

"You don't."

"I do!" I insist as I stand from the bed, pacing back and forth. "I told you about his family. How do I know whatever they're involved in won't affect our lives? How do I know that Emanuel and I won't settle down and start a family and then one day he drops a bomb on me and says he's going to work in the family business? What if he just ups and wants to move to Italy, of all places, to become closer with his family?"

"Or what if he remains a firefighter and runs into a building only to almost be crushed to death by a falling ceiling? Or what if you hear on the news that a firefighter had to scale a damn twenty something story building to save someone's life and you rush to find out if it was your guy up there? Or what if one day you're celebrating your thirty year anniversary with your husband and your plane crashes?"

I stop and stare at Angela who is now standing toe-to-toe with me. I avert my gaze because guilt begins to settle around me. I know everything she's just mentioned are things she's experienced in her life.

"And what if ..." she takes my hands into hers and places them against her belly, "one day you find out that you and the man you love are going to be parents? I promise that makes up for all of the bad stuff. All of the what ifs."

A small smile crests on my face as we both blink the tears away. "Really?"

Giggling, she nods.

"I knew it!" I yell, throwing my arms around her. "Congratulations! How long have you known?"

"Almost eight weeks."

I pull back. "Eight weeks?"

She smirks. "Eric and I wanted to wait until after the first trimester."

I understand.

"Wait, I'm the god-mommy, right?"

"Who else?"

Laughing, I wrap my arms around her again.

"But this baby is going to need a god-daddy. And my

husband is bound and determined to make the godfather a damn firefighter. It'd be so convenient if my best friend would get over her bullshit so she can marry the man she loves and we can ask them both to be the godparents."

I pull back, giving Angela an uncertain expression.

"Look, you have all of the reasons in the world to fear being with Emanuel. Yes, his family history or whatever could get in the way. And there's the flip side. He could never want to go into the family business but he *is* a firefighter and a member of Rescue Four at that. He works a dangerous job everyday. There are reasons to be scared. And that's still not enough to deny what you feel for him."

"Angela—" I shaking my head and pushing out a heavy breathe.

"Has he ever given you a reason not to trust him?"

"No."

"Has he ever made you feel unsure of who you are when you're with him?"

"No."

"Has he ever treated you like you didn't matter to him or that whatever was going on in his life was more important?" She questions with a lifted brow.

"No."

"Has he—"

"Okay, I get it."

"Do you?"

Forcing out a heavy breath, I pinch the bridge of my nose. "Pregnancy is making you pushy," I tease.

She grins. "That's 'cause this baby knows that his or her godparents need to be together."

I roll my eyes, knowing that Angela is right. No, Emanuel has never given me a reason not to trust him. He's been forthright about his family and his past. From the moment he told me about them he didn't try to hide what it is they did, and if he said that he had no interest in it, I had to believe him. Emanuel always made me feel like the most important thing in the world to him. Even now, during our separation, he continues to text me just to let me know he's thinking of me or that he loves me, or to wish me a good day at work.

"I'm such a fool," I groan.

"Yes, you are, but you're my fool." Angela hugs me. "Now that we've got that out of the way, why don't you call him?" She steps back and picks my phone up off the bed, handing it to me.

Slowly, I reach for it, taking it from her. I stare at the phone. "He's working."

"His shift ends in twenty-minutes."

Eric and Emanuel are working the same shift this evening.

"I'll give you some privacy to call. I hear my manager downstairs setting up for the night. I'll go help her."

I nod, having heard the downstairs door open and things being moved around by the manager. I watch Angela leave, and then hear the apartment door open and close before I turn my attention back to my phone.

Pulling up my most recent calls, I allow my thumb to hover over Emanuel's name for a few seconds. I'm trying to figure out how to accurately apologize for being so damn wishy-washy. Then I fear that he's over it and over me.

"Stop thinking," I tell myself and quickly press the screen to call his phone.

Unfortunately, it rings and rings until his voicemail clicks on. I hate using voicemail so I hang up and opt to send him a quick text message. Figuring he's likely on a call, I begin texting him to ask if we can talk once he's off work but to my surprise my phone immediately begins ringing.

"Emanuel," I answer.

"Hey, butterfly, I'm sorry I missed your call. Is everything all right?"

"Yes. I was jus—"

My response to Emanuel is cut off when I hear Angela's blood-curdling screams from downstairs.

"What the hell?" I shout as I run out of the bedroom.

"What's happening?" Emanuel barks from his line.

I'm too busy running to the door that Angela is now banging on to respond.

"Janine! Janine! Open the door! He's burning it down!"

"What?" I open the door, and Angela falls in. For a second, I glimpse a figure dressed in all black wearing a ski mask, with something shiny in his hand, trying to run up the stairs.

"Ahh!" I yell, dropping the phone and pulling Angela inside before slamming and locking the door shut behind her.

"H-He's setting the bar on fire!" Angela screams. "Call 911!"

My entire body begins shaking as I try to barricade the door with one of the lounge chairs from the living room.

"Emanuel, call the police! There's a man trying to set the bar on fire!" I pick up my phone and yell into it, hoping her hears me on the other end.

****

Emanuel

Pulling out my phone, I frown seeing I have one missed call. I hop off the truck and push out of my coveralls, hanging my jacket up on the hanger where it usually is when I'm on shift. We just got back from a call of a small warehouse fire, and on the way got sidetracked, helping out a man in a car accident.

I was happy to be winding down the end of my shift. I had plans to speak with Janine whether she wanted to or not. Eric had told me she was staying in the apartment above Charlie's for the weekend. Those plans were about to be interrupted.

So when I look down at the screen of my phone to see who the missed call is from and discover it's Janine, a little thrill passes through me. I don't give it much thought before I'm calling her back, and pressing the phone to my ear as I head up the stairs to my locker.

"Emanuel."

Her voice alone serves to calm whatever tension had been flowing through me since she walked out of my condo a week prior.

"Hey, butterfly, I'm sorry I missed your call. Is everything all right?"

"Yes, I was just—"

The abruptness of which she stops talking alarms me first.

"What the hell?"

That is the question that sends the hairs on the back of my neck standing on ends.

"What's wrong?" I demand as my hold on the phone tightens.

"I don't know."

I can tell by her breathlessness that she's running or moving quickly.

All I hear next is a loud noise, followed by screaming.

"Janine! Janine! What's happening?" I call into the phone, a sudden feeling of helplessness overcoming me.

"... he ... fire!" I hear on the other end of the phone but the voice isn't Janine's.

"Janine!" I yell into the phone.

By then I've turned around and am running down the stairs.

"Emanuel!" Janine shrills in the phone. "Call the police. He's trying to set the bar on fire!" Those are the last words I hear before the line goes dead.

"Eric!" I shout through the station, causing everyone to stare at me. "Something's wrong at the bar. Janine said to call the police. Someone's trying to set it on fire."

As soon as the words are out of my mouth, our entire team is throwing on their turnout gear, grabbing tanks, and jumping into the truck.

"Let's fucking go!" I shout from the back of the truck as Sean jumps into the driver's seat. Impatience is pouring out of every cell in my body. The only reason I haven't taken off and begun running to the damn bar myself is because I know it would take me longer to get there than the truck. But I hate waiting. All I can hear in my ears are the screams of Janine's and Angela's before the line went dead.

Captain Waverly finally jumps into the passenger seat next to Sean and we take off.

To the left of us, the second truck is also pulling out. I can make out Eric behind the wheel. He's just as anxious as I am to make it to the bar.

"Run them the hell over!" I growl from the back as Sean honks the horn to get slow moving vehicles to get out of our way. It feels like it's taking forever to make it to the damn bar. It's only about a ten minute drive from the station. But it's a weekend and there are more cars than usual on the road, due to events going on downtown.

"Make a right here!" I yell to Sean.

"The bar's in the opposite direction," he fires back.

"You can hook a left on the side street that's wide enough to take straight behind the bar."

"Fine."

I hang on to the window of the door as Sean makes a sharp right turn. I feel a small sense of relief when, just as I predicted, there aren't many cars on this side road and he is able to easily maneuver down the street. A few of the pedestrians and cyclists quickly make room, hopping up onto the sidewalk to allow us to pass without slowing down.

"Allende! Can you get in contact with them?" Captain Waverly calls from the front seat.

I try again on my cell phone, attempting to reach Janine. This time her phone is going straight to voicemail.

"Fuck!" I curse. "There's no answer."

Captain Waverly radios to Eric in the truck that is now behind us to see if he is able to get through to Angela.

"Nothing," comes Carter's reply who is in the passenger seat of the truck with Eric.

Six minutes later we are pulling up to the street where Charlie's is. My fucking heart drops to my knees when I see black smoke billowing out of one of the broken windows on the ground floor.

Hopping out of the truck, I look up to see if top windows are open or if there is any smoke coming out from the top. There's none.

"Angela!" Eric is yelling as he pounds on the front door. "It's jammed!" he says after trying his own key to open the door.

"The back entrance." I remember him telling me about the back entrance that is the quickest way to get up to the apartment without having to go through the bar itself.

I briefly glance over my shoulder to see Carter and Don setting up the hose while Sean is already running to the back. Eric and I follow behind him. We run through the alley that is folded in by the bar's building on one side and a chain link fence on the other.

"What the fuck?" Sean yells when we come to a mid-point at which we find the entrance of the backdoor to be barricaded by garbage cans and bags of trash. The three of us work in tandem to move the bags and trash cans out of the way, tossing what we can over the fence.

"What's the status back there?" Captain Waverly's voice questions into the radio.

"Working on it," I respond before quickly getting back to lifting the heavy trash cans. As Sean and I work together to push one of the bins over the fence, the lid comes open and a pile of bricks spills out. That is what's making the bins so damn heavy. Sean and I briefly make eye contact with one another before pushing the bins out of the way.

"Angela!" Eric shouts as he attempts to pull the back door open. It's locked. And again, his key isn't working to open it.

"We need the sledgehammer to break this lock."

The sentence is only halfway out of Sean's mouth before I'm running back to the front to the fire truck, pulling open the side door, and retrieving the sledgehammer.

"Move!" I yell as I run back around and stand far enough from the door to give myself room to adequately swing. The first hit to the doorknob bends it, but doesn't fully knock it off its hinges. It's the second swing that does the trick, instantly sending the doorknob to the ground.

The loud pang the steel doorknob makes as it hits the concrete barely registers as Sean, Eric, and I are barreling through the door. A thick blanket of smoke is there to welcome us.

I do my best not to think about what that smoke means.

Though my years on this job already informs me that smoke that dark and thick is not a good sign for people who may be trapped inside.

"Angela!" Eric and Sean yell.

"Janine!" I repeat her name over and over as we run up the back staircase to the closed door of the apartment. The fire hasn't made its way up the stairs just yet, but I can hear it pounding against the wood door, as smoke seeps into the space above and below the door.

I, along with Eric, shoulder our way through the locked door, nearly stumbling in.

"Status?" Captain Waverly demands through the radio.

"Made entry. Searching," Sean reports back.

"Janine!" I call out, looking around and feeling with my hands.

I get quiet trying to hear for any faint sounds or cries but there's nothing. I follow behind Eric, who knows his way around this place, and soon we're moving down a short hallway and coming to a closed door.

"Angela!"

"Janine!"

The three of us yell simultaneously while shouldering through the door. The door splinters and then flings open. As soon as it does, I make out two bodies on the floor.

"No, no, no!" I repeat as I move closer to Janine.

Stooping low, I don't wait to try and feel for a pulse. I scoop her up into my arms and carry her out the same way I came in. I don't pay attention to how limp she feels in my arms. I'm to busy silently begging and pleading that she be okay.

I carry Janine back out through the hallway, to the stairs, and back down the entrance we just came from, not taking a deep breath until we are outside again. Running as quickly as my legs will carry me, I take her around the front of the bar. Eric and Sean are on my heels with Angela.

I race around to the front of the building where there are already paramedics waiting. Placing Janine onto the gurney, I rip off my face mask. It's the first time I'm able to get a good look at her. My heart squeezes in my chest as I watch her labored breathing.

"Sir, you have to move back!" one of the female paramedics insists as she struggles to put an oxygen mask over Janine's face.

"Allende, let them help her," I hear Captain Waverly's voice say behind me as he attempts to pull me back.

"She can't breathe!" I say still watching her chest rise and fall uneasily.

"We need to check for injuries," another paramedic says.

This time, two pairs of hands are pulling me back, trying to put some distance between myself and the woman I love. I force myself to remember that these people are there to help her. To give her the medical treatment she needs. With that, I allow my body to be pulled away. However, I scrutinize every move the paramedics make.

"I'm going with her," I state as they begin loading Janine into the ambulance.

"You can't," Don says, holding me back.

"Get the hell off me." I push away from him and attempt to get into the back of the ambulance.

"Emanuel, there's no room. You can't fit, and the paramedics needs to do their job. Let them," Carter insists, holding me back. "There's an officer here who is going to take you and Eric to the hospital."

Angrily, I move back so the paramedics can shut the doors. I rip off the air tank that is strapped to my back and toss it angrily in the back of the fire truck.

"Let's go!" Eric yells, running to the patrol vehicle.

He climbs into the passenger seat and I get in the back. As soon as the door closes, the officer pulls off with sirens blaring, following closely behind the ambulance. All I can picture in my mind is Janine on that bedroom floor, unmoving. It feels like I'm living my worst nightmare come true.

Chapter Twenty-Five

Janine

I can feel the warmth of his hand in mine before I open my eyes. I have no idea where I am, but knowing Emanuel is here fills me with all of the comfort I need. Blinking my eyes open, I try to search for him but the bright overhead lighting is so glaring that I squeeze my eyes tightly again.

"Hey," he coos.

Shifting my head to the right, I again attempt to open my eyes. When I do I'm met with the most tender, loving expression. I try to smile but that's when I realize something is covering my mouth and nose. Reaching up with my free hand, I move it aside, realizing that it's an oxygen mask.

"You might still need that," he insists, trying to work the mask back over my face. "It's pure oxygen and your body was deprived of it for god knows how long."

Even though he's persistent I nudge it away, shaking my head. "Thank you," I strain to say. I let out a few coughs that hurt my chest but feel some relief once they've been released. "Thank you."

"Don't thank me. You scared the hell out of me." He clasps my hand into both of his and brings it to his lips.

"Am I okay?" I ask, realizing that I'm in the emergency room of Williamsport Central Hospital.

He nods. "Some smoke inhalation. No burns. Docs want

to monitor you overnight."

"Angela!" I say, suddenly remembering what happened before everything went black. "Is she okay?"

"She's doing well. Eric is with her right next door." His head juts toward the wall indicating my best friend and her husband are just beyond it.

Feeling slightly relieved, I relax against the pillow behind me. I want to ask what type of harm smoke inhalation can do to the baby but am not sure if Emanuel knows she's pregnant.

"They'll keep her overnight to make sure she and the baby are all right," he says as if reading my mind.

I smile up at him through blurred vision. "I love you."

Leaning down, he presses a kiss to my forehead.

"Hey, is this going to win you another one of those Thomas Webster Awards?"

He pulls back and gives me a funny look. "You're worried about a damn medal right now?"

"Yeah. I was thinking, if you get another one, we can hang it on our wall."

His eyebrows spike. "*Our* wall?"

I nod. "That's why I was calling you. I wanted to meet for dinner to apologize in person for not trusting in you ... for not trusting in us. If it's okay with you, I don't want space anymore. I just want you and me ... together."

At first, he doesn't respond, just staring at me as his nostrils flare. Then he says, "I wasn't letting you go in the first place, butterfly."

He pushes the oxygen mask fully over my head and leans down, fusing our lips together. At first, the kiss is soft, as if he's feeling me out, but soon enough, he's deepening the kiss and I lean into it, having missed this feeling over the past seven days.

"I love you, too," he says once he breaks the kiss.

I gasp as the memory of what actually happened before I woke up in the hospital fully comes back to me. "Did they find who did this?"

Emanuel's jaw tightens and his eyes darken. "Not yet. The police have been waiting outside to speak with you and Angela about what you saw."

"I need to tell them."

He nods. "I'll bring them in."

I watch as he walks to the curtain, stepping beyond it to call over the officers.

Once they enter, I relay the entire incident from my memory, up until the moment I came to in the ambulance. I save the memory of seeing Emanuel's face as soon as the ambulance doors opened, and the feel of his strong hand wrapped around mine as I was wheeled into the ER. I recall the worry in his voice as he questioned the doctors on whether or not I was okay.

When the officers leave, I squeeze his hand, which is already covering mine.

He turns to look at me with a wrinkle in his forehead. "Are you okay? Feeling pain? Need me to—"

"I want to spend the rest of my life with you," I say as a tear streams down my cheek.

Emanuel moves closer, wiping the tear away with his thumb. "That's already a foregone conclusion, babe." He presses a kiss to my lips. "We're in this for the long haul. I was just waiting on you to figure it out."

"Sorry, I'm a slow learner sometimes."

He captures my lips again. "As long as you always comes back to me, you can take as long as you need to."

Epilogue

"This shit is taking too long," I growl, feeling frustrated and pissed off.

Don, Eric, Carter, Sean, and I are standing at the back of the fire station in a huddle discussing what evidence Don has uncovered at the bar fire. It's been six weeks and the police have come up with jack shit.

"My woman could've died in that fucking fire."

"My fucking wife, too," Eric insists. "We need to figure out whoever the fuck is behind this and fast," he growls. Obviously, Eric is as pissed off as the rest of us but even more so due to the fact that Angela is about five months pregnant. He could've lost his wife and unborn child in that fire. It's bad enough his wife lost her business, at least for the time being.

"I know. And I'm getting nowhere with the police or the brass in the department. They keep saying it was likely just a random attack."

"That's fucking bullshit!"

"What the fuck?!"

"They're full of shit!"

Eric, Sean, Carter, and I all yell at the same time.

"Keep it down," Don insists, looking around.

We're off shift but stayed a few minutes late to have this

meeting.

"I know it's bullshit, which is why I'm still looking into it. And why I've brought someone else, from outside of the department to help us out."

"Who?" I question, crossing my arms over my chest.

"Someone who has just as much incentive as you to get this son of a bitch."

We all turn at the female voice coming from behind us.

Behind me, I hear Don sigh. "You were supposed to wait out front."

The woman frowns. "Did you really think I was going to sit silently as the men talked?"

"Of fucking course not," he grumbles.

I squint, studying the woman. She looks familiar, though I'm certain she and I haven't met.

"Jocelyn?" Carter says as she moves out of the shadows and into our little circle.

"Carter, nice to see you again." She smiles but there is a whole story behind that smile.

"Does your brother know you're here?" Sean questions.

The woman's face immediately pulls into a scowl. "Why? Do you think I need his permission?"

"He wouldn't give it anyway," Don confesses.

"Brother?"

The woman turns to me. "So you're the new guy, huh?"

"And you are?"

She sticks out her hand. "Jocelyn ... Stephens."

"Corey's little sister," Don adds.

Jocelyn's smile fades as she glares over her shoulder at Don.

"Younger by twenty minutes."

"Still younger."

Jocelyn waves him off, rolling her eyes.

But I don't miss how Don's eyes linger on her backside as she turns back to me.

"I'll be helping you out with this investigation seeing as how the police and the head of the department can't be bothered enough to figure out who the hell tried to kill my brother ... and your wife," she adds, turning to Eric and then looking to me. "... and your ..."

"Fiancée," I insert.

She nods.

"What are your credentials? Other than being Corey's sister."

She lifts a perfectly arched eyebrow. "Aside from my five years with the Williamsport Police Department working undercover, and three years working on my own as a private investigator ... Nothing."

"She's legit," Don says.

Again, I don't miss the protective tone in his voice and

the way his gaze seems pinned to her, even when she's not looking, *especially* when she's not looking.

"We'll get whoever's behind this."

"We fucking better," are the last words I say before slapping fives with the rest of my squad and heading to my car to head home. I have another important conversation brewing.

****

Pushing out a full breath when I hear her key in the lock, I give one final look around at the candles surrounding the living room and the soft music playing in the background. It's salsa music, because I want to recreate our first days together, as much as possible for this particular moment.

"Hi," Janine says as she enters the door, seeing me standing there.

A smile grows on my face and I move toward her, cupping her face in my hands and kissing her lips. "Hi."

I take her shoulder bag from her and place it on one of the stools by the kitchen bar.

"Welcome home." Taking her by the hand, I pull her fully into the condo.

Ever since the day of the fire, Janine has been staying with me. Two weeks ago, I finally convinced her to give up her lease and make it official, moving all of her belongings into my place. We've spent the last few weeks redecorating to fit both of our styles together.

"I thought you were working late tonight?" she questions.

"You were supposed to think that."

I stop at the center of our living room where I've turned the coffee table long ways and placed large pillows side by side to sit on as we eat, a dinner of homemade guacamole and chips, chile rellenos in a mole sauce, followed by flan for dessert.

"Do you remember this?"

She smiles. "You recreated our first dinner together in Mexico."

I nod. "I hope you're hungry."

"For you?"

Leaning over, I nip her earlobe. "That comes later. Sit."

"What's all of this for?"

"It's nearly our six month anniversary."

She lifts her eyebrows. "I never would've suspected you were the type to count or celebrate six month anniversaries."

"I'm not." I shake my head. "At least not before you."

She swoons, and I use the opportunity to kiss her lips again. I help her sit and serve up plates of delicious, homemade Mexican food.

"This is better than the first time around," she gushes after finishing. "Except for the fact that it's even better now because I get to do this freely." She moves in and licks my earlobe.

A shiver slithers down my spine and a groan moves up my

throat.

"You could've done that the first night, butterfly. I promise we'd still end up right where we are."

"Oh yeah, and where's that?"

I don't hesitate to pull the ring box out of my pocket, opening it up before setting it on the table.

Her jaw drops.

"With me asking you to be my wife." My voice is husky to my own ears.

"Emanuel," she whispers, eyes watering.

"I never pictured myself as the type who would voluntarily settle down ... or maybe I did but knew it just couldn't be with any woman. I needed someone who grounded me but wasn't afraid to take this crazy ride of life with me. I found that in you. And together, the both of us can build our own family. One where you get to raise our kids with the loving, kind spirit that you are, and I get to show them everything about being daring and fearless.

"Janine ... will you marry me?"

She looks to me, bottom lip quivering. It takes her a few seconds to vocalize but finally she says, "Yes, of course!" before tossing her arms around my shoulders.

Nothing in the world has ever made me feel this complete. Not serving in combat. Not becoming pinned out of the fire academy. Hell, not even pulling someone out of a burning building. But the moment she says yes with those tears streaming down her face, everything falls into place and I know I've found my permanent home.

The End

Looking for updates on future releases? I can be found around the web at the following locations:

Newsletter: Tiffany Patterson Writes Newsletter

FaceBook private group: Tiffany's Passions Between the Pages

Website: TiffanyPattersonWrites.com

FaceBook Page: Author Tiffany Patterson

Email: TiffanyPattersonWrites@gmail.com

More books by Tiffany Patterson

The Black Burles Series

Black Pearl

Black Dahlia

Black Butterfly

Forever Series

7 Degrees of Alpha (Collection)

Forever

Safe Space Series

Safe Space (Book 1)

Safe Space (Book 2)

Rescue Four Series

Eric's Inferno

Carter's Flame

Non-Series Titles

This is Where I Sleep

My Storm

Miles & Mistletoe (Holiday Novella)

Just Say the Word

The Townsend Brothers Series

Aaron's Patience

Mean to Be

For Keeps

Until My Last Breath

Made in the USA
Lexington, KY
26 August 2019